Matthe
Matthews, Owen
White fox : a novel

$28.00
on1371040324
First edition.

# WHITE
# FOX

## ALSO BY OWEN MATTHEWS

### Fiction

THE BLACK SUN TRILOGY
*Black Sun*
*Red Traitor*

### Nonfiction

*Overreach*
*Stalin's Children*
*Glorious Misadventures*
*An Impeccable Spy*

# WHITE FOX

A NOVEL

## OWEN MATTHEWS

DOUBLEDAY  NEW YORK

www.doubleday.com

DOUBLEDAY and the portrayal of an anchor with a dolphin are registered trademarks of Penguin Random House LLC.

Jacket photographs: (top) Michael Kittell/Getty Match/ Getty Images; (bottom) Thierry Esch/Paris Match/Getty Images; (inset) Michael Ochs Archives/Getty Images
Jacket design by Michael J. Windsor

Library of Congress Cataloging-in-Publication Data
Names: Matthews, Owen, author.
Title: White fox : a novel / Owen Matthews.
Description: First edition. | New York : Doubleday, [2023] |
Identifiers: LCCN 2022017842 (print) | LCCN 2022017843 (ebook) |
ISBN 9780385543446 (hardcover) | ISBN 9780385543453 (ebook)
Subjects: LCSH: Kennedy, John F. (John Fitzgerald), 1917–1963—Assassination— Fiction. | Soviet Union. Komitet gosudarstvennoĭ bezopasnosti—Fiction. | LCGFT: Historical fiction. | Thrillers (Fiction) | Novels.
Classification: LCC PR6113.A8914 W48 2023 (print) |
LCC PR6113.A8914 (ebook) | DDC 823/.92—dc23/eng/20220420
LC record available at https://lccn.loc.gov/2022017842
LC ebook record available at https://lccn.loc.gov/2022017843

MANUFACTURED IN THE UNITED STATES OF AMERICA

1 3 5 7 9 10 8 6 4 2

First Edition

*For Ksenia, Nikita, and Theodore*

# CONTENTS

# CONTENTS

# WHITE FOX

# JUNE–SEPTEMBER
# 1963

# 1

*VorkutLag 51 Strict Regime Penal Colony, Komi Autonomous*
*Soviet Socialist Republic, USSR, June 1963*

In the pale twilight of an Arctic summer night, three men ran for their lives through an endless sea of knee-high shrubs and scrub grass. Far behind them a huddle of prison buildings encircled in barbed wire stood like a lighted island in the surrounding gloom. A signal rocket soared into the sky and descended slowly, casting hard black shadows in the half-light.

High in a watchtower the penal colony's commander focused his binoculars on the fleeing figures, ignoring the mosquitoes which swarmed in clouds around him. By his side, his second-in-command shaded his eyes against the flare light and squinted at the retreating figures.

"Troika. Classic." The burly officer's voice was hoarse as rusty nails in a bucket. "Two old lags and a young kid. The cow."

The commandant lowered his field glasses and eyed his deputy with distaste.

"The *cow,* Major Chemizov?"

"If they don't find food within a couple of days, they smash the kid's head in and eat him. The cow."

"And where would they find food, out there in the tundra?"

Chemizov shrugged.

"Might find some native herders. Cut their throats, steal their food. Happened a couple of years back."

"Did they make it to freedom?"

"Freedom? The dead herders' relatives hunted them down, stripped 'em naked, and left them hog-tied in the tundra. Mosquitoes and crows ate them alive." Chemizov peered once more at the men's retreating figures as they shimmered and slurred into the twilight. "Range six . . . seven hundred meters, Comrade Colonel. We'll lose them in the undergrowth in a minute."

Wearily, the commander turned to a young soldier who had been keeping his sniper rifle beaded on the fleeing men as his superiors spoke.

"Very well," said Colonel Alexander Vasin. "Fire at will."

# 2

*Leningrad, USSR, September 1963*

A pool of lamplight illuminated a cluttered dressing table covered in scribbled notes. Andrei Fyodorov crushed out a cigarette on the upturned lid of a face powder tin and lit another. Inhaling deeply, he leaned forward and examined his own reflection in the glass of the grimy windowpane.

Christ, he thought. You look like shit. Even for a dead man.

Behind him a key fumbled in the door lock. Startled, Fyodorov hurriedly scooped his papers into a pile and turned them over, spilling ash and sending cosmetics rolling across the floor.

"Who is it?"

"*Andrei?* Is that you?"

Fyodorov picked up his chair, crossed the room, and wedged it under the door handle before opening the door a crack. A tall woman, gray-eyed and slim, stood alone in the brightly lit corridor. Ksenia.

Kicking the chair aside, Fyodorov opened the door and pulled the woman inside before relocking it. Ksenia reached for the light switch, but he seized her wrist. Her gaze traveled across Fyodorov's haggard face for a long moment before she pulled her hand free and embraced him.

"My God, Andrei! What are you doing here? How—"

Fyodorov silenced her with a lingering kiss before pushing her gently away.

"Were you followed?"

She shook her head but kept her eyes fixed on his.

"What happened? You're meant to be in America."

"I can't tell you."

"You said you'd be away for months. It's been three weeks."

"I was given new orders. Orders I could not follow."

"What do you mean? What did they want you to do?"

"All you need to know is that . . . I could not."

"Couldn't or wouldn't?"

In the shaded lamplight, Fyodorov smiled tightly in answer. Ksenia took two steps backward and sat heavily on a bed covered in scattered clothes. Her eyes glistened bright in the lamplight.

"You refused orders. From the KGB."

"Yes."

"How much time do we have?"

"I don't know, Ksenia. But I need you to hide some documents for me. I'll tell you where. Don't read them. Promise me. You can't read them."

"You're in danger." Ksenia's voice was hollow and flat. Her pale gaze, meeting his, was like a splash of cold water. Fyodorov turned to the window and ran his hands slowly through his hair.

"Correct. You won't see me for a while. But I have a plan."

Silently, Ksenia stood once more and embraced Fyodorov from behind, her face laid against his back. The sound of passing traffic rose from the street. From somewhere down the corridor came a muffled cacophony of martial music as one of Ksenia's neighbors turned on the radio.

"Andrei. Are they going to kill you?"

"They're going to try."

# PART ONE

# 22 NOVEMBER–
# 5 DECEMBER 1963

You are strong only as long as you don't deprive people of everything. For a person you've taken everything from is no longer in your power. He's free all over again.

—ALEKSANDR SOLZHENITSYN,
*The First Circle*

# 1

The news came over Soviet State Radio Mayak, blaring in the empty officers' mess as Vasin sat at a plain wooden table, eating alone.

"Comrade radio listeners. We have interrupted our broadcast because of a distressing report we have just received from New York."

Vasin looked up abruptly at the bulky speaker, as if at a television.

"It has been officially announced that US President John Kennedy has died in a hospital after having been the victim of an attack by, it is supposed, persons from extreme right-wing elements. US President John Kennedy and Texas Governor John Connally fell under the bullets of assassins while driving in an open car through the streets of Dallas. There were three shots. One of the bullets struck the President in the head . . ."

The report might have come from the moon, or some other distant planet of warmth and light. Somewhere, beyond hundreds of kilometers of tundra and boreal forest, there was a world where great events happened. Vasin understood the words of the news bulletin, but his mind could not put images to them, or meaning. He tried to turn his attention back to his cabbage soup but found his appetite had vanished.

For nearly a year, the VorkutLag 51 Strict Regime Penal Colony had been Vasin's kingdom—and his personal calvary. The American spy Oleg Morozov had been arrested and executed. Morozov's unwitting protector General Ivan Serov was removed from his post as the head of Soviet military intelligence and expelled from the Party. All thanks to KGB Lieutenant-Colonel Alexander Vasin.

But to accomplish his last mission Vasin had broken rules, burned bridges—even committed what some would call treason.

What his boss, General Orlov, head of the KGB's secretive Special Cases Department, *did* call treason.

As Vasin had always feared, Orlov's revenge had been particularly exquisite. He had sent his rebellious subordinate to VorkutLag, the Soviet Union's most notorious prison colony. Not as an inmate— General Orlov had at least spared him that—but as a camp commandant. The promotion was in reality a prison sentence. In this frozen world two hundred kilometers north of the tree line and four days by train from Moscow, Vasin felt more of a prisoner than the convicts under his charge.

In its heyday in the 1940s, VorkutLag had been a vast archipelago of coal mines and penal colonies that spread hundreds of kilometers across the swath of barren Arctic scrubland. Over the years of Stalin's rule some eighteen million Soviet citizens, most of them political prisoners, had passed through the gulag system—six hundred thousand of them in Vorkuta alone. At least a million and a half had perished. But on Stalin's death ten years before, the new Party boss, Nikita Khrushchev, had ordered the political prisoners freed. Now, VorkutLag was, for the most part, a wasteland of empty barracks crumbling into the swamps of the Pechora Basin. The coal mines around the city of Vorkuta itself remained open but were now manned by free laborers lured to the Arctic by the promise of high wages and long vacations in the south. Of the once sprawling camp complex that surrounded Vorkuta only Camp 51 and a handful like it remained, each housing some five hundred of the most violent criminals in the Soviet Union.

Vasin was the ghost-king of a ghost-camp, a vestige of a vanished prison empire clinging to the edge of the world. A place so remote that in winter the sun deigned to shine for only the briefest of spans before abandoning Vorkuta to its blue bowl of near-perpetual Arctic night.

Outside the officers' mess, a muffled klaxon wailed. A haggard woman in a gray smock and grimy apron approached Vasin— Tatiana, the commander's *bufetshitsa,* his personal cook and maid.

Moving carefully, she placed a china cup of steaming tea on the table and a saucer with two chocolates and a slice of lemon arranged on it. Vasin pushed away his chipped soup bowl and sipped the tea without looking up.

Shadows of black-clad prisoners flitted past the windows as they hurried to the evening roll call. Draining his tea, Vasin stood wearily. He joined a dozen officers in the vestibule as they chatted and laughed coarsely. To a man, they ignored their commandant as he tugged on his heavy sheepskin coat and buckled his pistol belt.

For all the attention his subordinates paid him, Colonel Vasin might have been made of cabbage steam and cigarette smoke.

# 2

The stumpy steam locomotive pulling a small train of prison wagons arrived from the Vorkuta railhead late. It plowed laboriously through the snowdrifts that obscured the branch line, the camp's only link to the outside world. The region had been battered for days by the scything winds of an Arctic ice storm that hurled freezing shards sharp as ground glass into Vasin's face while he tramped out into the rail yard to receive the convoy. The prisoners were unloaded one by one from the individual wire cages in the cars and led, heads down with their hands cuffed behind their backs, into the disinfection barrack.

Three men caught Vasin's attention as they clambered out of the rearmost car, reserved for the convoy's guards. Two of them were uniformed KGB officers, a captain and a senior sergeant. The third wore a padded black prison uniform but walked free, uncuffed. The senior KGB officer approached Vasin through the swirling snow.

"Urgent orders for the commander," the man shouted over the wind. "Concerning a special prisoner."

"I'm the commander."

The Captain, his pale face pinched with the cold, handed over a heavy attaché case secured by two wired lead seals. Vasin tugged off one mitten with his teeth and struggled with the fastenings. Bared to the wind, his hand went instantly numb. Inside the case was a slim and expensive leather document folder with a combination lock. Chalked on the cover were two words: NIKITA'S BIRTHDAY.

Nikita. The fourteen-year-old son Vasin had left behind in Moscow. Whatever was inside the file could only be a message from his old boss, General Orlov. Vasin struggled and failed to keep the anger out of his voice.

"Follow. Bring your prisoner with you."

# 3

In the welcome heat of his office, Vasin turned the dials on the lock to his son's birthday—17/08—and the mechanism snapped open. Inside was an envelope addressed to him, marked EYES ONLY in Orlov's looping handwriting. Vasin had to fight down a desire to throw the letter into the stove. Nonetheless, for perhaps the thousandth time since he arrived in VorkutLag, Vasin forced himself into obedience. He opened the note.

My dear Sasha. I hope you are keeping well in your new home. I am entrusting you with a delicate and most important mission. Keep this prisoner safe, comfortable, and alive at all costs. Secrecy is essential. Wait for my further orders—nobody else's. The two escorting soldiers must be eliminated immediately. You will find the discreet means to accomplish this inside this case. Your official report of the escorting officers' deaths will serve as acknowledgment that you have received and understood. Yu. O.

Vasin looked up at the Captain sharply. A flash of recognition: he'd seen this man before in Orlov's Special Cases offices on the ninth floor of KGB headquarters in Moscow. Vasin rummaged in the briefcase and his fingers closed around two small, cold metal cylinders taped to the bottom. The officer's pale blue eyes were on him.

"We were told to expect a written acknowledgment that the orders have been received, Comrade Colonel."

"Of course."

Vasin breathed deep. Orlov had ordered him to kill this man. Did Vasin dare defy him? Did the visitor from Moscow have orders to eliminate *him* if he refused to cooperate? Vasin knew his old boss all too well. If these men were not to be his executioners, someone else would be. And the message of the combination, Nikita's birthday, could not be clearer.

Vasin collected himself. "Captain, why don't you invite your comrade up here to have a drink. You've both had a long journey."

"Yes, Colonel."

"Cuff the convict to a radiator in the corridor, tell the duty sergeant to enter him on the books as a trusted prisoner, and find him a cot downstairs in the administration building."

Vasin waited a moment for the man to leave, then picked up the attaché case. Turning to the bookshelf behind his desk where he kept his private vodka supply, he slipped the two cold steel capsules into the palm of his left hand. Then he took down three grubby shot glasses and a bottle of Stolichnaya.

# 4

The camp doctor, a cadaverous drunk, lurched unsteadily in Vasin's office doorway. His lab coat was stained, and his eyes were bloodshot from a hangover that looked like it had been ongoing for years.

"Morning, Comrade Colonel. The two escort officers from Moscow are dead. Both suffered fatal cardiac infarction in the night."

Vasin pursed his lips in a struggle to keep emotion out of his face. "*Both* of them?"

After years in the gulag system, nothing seemed to surprise the doctor. He merely shrugged.

"Both. Shall I draw up the death certificates?"

"Do that, Comrade Doctor."

As the door closed, Vasin slumped back in his chair. He tried to picture the faces of the dead officers he'd drunk with only the previous night, but they were already indistinct in his memory. The men had blank, hard faces, like those of all Orlov's thugs from the ninth floor. Unlovable men, though wives and children as yet oblivious to their coming loss probably did love them. Vasin would never know. Two bodies now lay in the camp morgue, dead by his hand, on Orlov's orders. He felt nothing but a numbed revulsion. Vorkuta's biting frosts had turned him cold. Vasin had forgotten a language he had once known, the moral vocabulary of a distant, normal world that had faded from his memory.

Orlov had been right, as usual. The poison was discreet.

Vasin picked up the telephone handset on his desk and ordered the special prisoner be brought up from the cell where he had spent the night. As he waited, Vasin flipped through the man's file. Lazar Samuilovich Berezovsky, born in Rostov-on-Don in March 1910. Convicted in May 1963 for large-scale financial fraud, illegal commercial speculation, handling smuggled goods and black-market foreign currency, plus membership in a criminal organization. Sentence: fifteen years of hard labor.

A gangster, then. To be precise, evidently a gangster's *koshelek:* literally a purse, a crime gang's moneyman. But there was no clue in the file as to why Orlov would send him to Vorkuta. Or why this man merited such deadly precautions to protect the fact of his presence.

A knock on the door interrupted Vasin's reading. Without waiting for his commander's permission, the duty sergeant barged in leading the handcuffed prisoner.

"Com' Colonel, Convict S-8859."

Berezovsky was a tall, well-built man with a week-old beard and with his thinning hair neatly cut, not close shaven—which meant he hadn't come from inside the gulag system. He was fit and could not yet be forty, though the date of birth listed in the file put him as over fifty.

The man stood upright and impassive as he waited for his handcuffs to be removed, fixing Vasin with deep-set black eyes. Once the sergeant had left them Berezovsky rubbed his wrists and looked around Vasin's office with normal human curiosity. No sign of tattoos on his hands, no sullen hangdog subordination typical of a convict. He stared at Vasin with a frank directness no real con would ever dare. Definitely no jailbird, then. And maybe no gangster, either.

"You have something to tell me, prisoner? A message?"

Berezovsky narrowed his eyes.

"No message. Just a question. My escort?"

"Dead, both of them. Terrible accident."

The prisoner nodded slowly and relaxed, taking a seat without permission.

"Good," he said. "Good. You have an accounting department here, I presume?"

Vasin blinked in surprise, momentarily unsure of how to react to the man's confident authority.

"Because you are an accountant." Vasin gestured to the personnel file lying open on his desk. "Supposedly."

The prisoner returned his gaze but did not answer.

"How old are you, Prisoner Berezovsky?"

"Fifty-three years, eight months, and nine days old, Colonel."

"Very good. From Stavropol, correct?"

"Rostov-on-Don. Sir."

Vasin flipped the file shut. He closed his eyes for a long moment. *Orlov.* The boss and his fucking lethal games.

"You going to tell me what this is about, Berezovsky? Not that your name is Berezovsky, of course."

The prisoner did not break eye contact.

"Colonel, I understand you have some instructions from Moscow concerning how I am to be treated here? We will both be better off if you just follow them. *Continue* to follow them, I should say."

There was an edge of knowing complacency in the man's tone that caught on something deep inside Vasin. Do what you're told. Don't ask questions. The injunctions that had kindled fury in him from his early boyhood. Vasin stood, abruptly, savoring the sudden look of consternation in Berezovsky's face. Being manipulated by Orlov was bad enough. But to be told what to do by a damn convict was too much for what remained of Vasin's fractured ego. This place might be a shithole at the end of the earth. But this shithole was Vasin's kingdom. A little, miserable world where Orlov had allowed him a tiny measure of power. A power that he had been provoked into exercising, the feelings of Orlov's precious pet prisoner be damned.

"*Ladno, molchi dalshe, golubchik,*" grunted Vasin, slipping into the rough jargon spoken by prisoners and guards alike. "Fine, keep your silence, little pigeon."

He slammed his palm on a buzzer on his desk.

"Wait. Commander, I'm *kontora. Kontora,* you hear?" The *kontora:* literally, "the office." The KGB's jargon for itself.

Vasin felt his face tighten. Did this man imagine that he had any love left for the fucking *kontora*? The duty sergeant appeared at the door.

"You rang, respected Comrade Colonel?" A bad running joke among Vasin's staff, taking the piss out of their boss from Moscow by addressing him with exaggerated pre-Revolutionary formality.

"Yes. Punishment block for this man until I tell you to let him out."

Both commander and sergeant turned to the prisoner, who remained defiantly seated. The sergeant shot his boss an uncomprehending look.

"Fine, Vasin. Have it your way." Berezovsky raised a peremptory hand to wave the minion away. His familiar tone and sheer chutzpah stunned both officers. "Just don't say I didn't warn you."

Vasin hesitated for a second, utterly confounded. A word from the commander could cast this man into a nightmare world of violence, hunger, rape, and degradation. But Berezovsky remained utterly cool.

Are you one of them, Vasin? was the man's unspoken question. Or one of us?

"Leave us, Sergeant."

# 5

*Moscow, USSR*

KGB Major Gleb Kozlov peered out of the net curtains onto the arc-lit depths of a building site at the top of Metrostroyevskaya Street. A new overpass spanning Moscow's Garden Ring was under construction, and the din of cement mixers continued late into the night. Kozlov flicked back the curtain and sighed. The usual Soviet story. Work done in a mad rush just before the first hard frosts of winter after a summer dawdling around waiting for men, equipment, supplies that never arrived.

He stood in the once-grand upstairs hallway of a pre-Revolutionary mansion. The place was decorated with Soviet institutional pomposity—red carpets, polished pine flooring, ruched-up curtains. Only a large bust of Felix Dzerzhinsky, founder of the Bolsheviks' first secret police, betrayed the building's purpose as the personal preserve of the head of the First Chief Directorate of the Committee for State Security. The arm of the KGB charged with gathering foreign intelligence.

A bustle of doors opening and closing, followed by muttering, obsequious voices, rose up the stairs. Kozlov smoothed his hair and stiffened to attention as his boss lumbered upward. Boris Pashkov was a seriously obese man, his tiny frame inflated as though by an air pump. In private, his subordinates called him *pelmenchik,* the Siberian dumpling. Pashkov's face, as he narrowed his eyes to take in Kozlov, was pale and puffy as doughballs.

"Good evening, Comrade Deputy Director."

"Kozlov, come. Any luck tracking down our fugitive colleague's mysterious girlfriend?"

"None so far, sir. We know Fyodorov went to ground in Leningrad for a couple of days back in June. No leads on who he stayed with, though. We haven't been able to shake anything out of any of his known associates. Or his ex-wife. Or his daughter. He's covered his tracks pretty well."

"No matter. We have a lead on where our traitor might be."

The Dumpling waddled to the end of the hallway to his private study, where he fumbled with his locked briefcase and tossed a slim file onto the desk, gesturing Kozlov to read.

"That damn screwup when we tried to grab him in that sanatorium in Gagry. Two of our men wounded. A Special Cases bodyguard, too."

Kozlov glanced coldly up at his boss.

"I would have handled it better, sir."

"If *you'd* handled it we would have had three corpses on our hands, not three hospital patients. And hell to pay with the Director. The Comrade General Secretary would have asked uncomfortable questions. Maybe got wind of our . . . arrangements. It's bad enough as it is. Shoot-outs between State Security officers on a public street are messy. But what's done is done. The time has come for your special touch. I called you here because we have picked up a trail."

"From our little bird in General Orlov's office?"

"Perhaps. Comrade Orlov has seen fit to hide your treacherous former superior *in prison*. Want to take a guess where?"

"Kolyma?"

"Not yet. Right now, he's at Vladimir Central Prison. In transit. Read."

Kozlov furrowed his brow in concentration as he leafed through the report.

"Do we know which camp he's headed to?"

"No. Orlov's men forged their own transport orders, so there were no records in the Main Camp Administration's central registry. And the Special Cases officers sent to escort the man never returned. We suspect that Orlov had them silenced. His own people! But that means that Orlov must have sent our traitor to someone he trusts enough to kill on his orders. Find that man, and you've found the traitor Fyodorov."

Kozlov scanned the remaining papers, nodding. He spoke without taking his eyes off the last document in the file, a large photograph of Andrei Konstantinovich Fyodorov: former KGB station chief in Miami. Kozlov's onetime mentor and friend. And now a fugitive who carried a deadly secret.

"I am to bring him back alive?"

"You must, Kozlov. That is imperative."

"Because he may have spoken to someone?"

"You must clean up any loose ends. Which will require some very thorough questioning once we have him in custody. Your particular talents for persuasion will be needed. Now tell me who you need to take with you on your mission."

Kozlov shut the file, the pertinent details memorized, and tossed it on the desk.

"Comrade Deputy Director, I need Markov the Macedonian. Only the Macedonian."

# 6

*VorkutLag 51*

"Who the hell *are* you, Berezovsky?"

"A colleague, Comrade Colonel."

"*Kontora.* So you said."

"First Chief Directorate."

Vasin looked appraisingly at the prisoner sitting in front of him. Of course. The man's smooth self-possession. The officer-like pride in his bearing. A member of the KGB's elite foreign service. Vasin's mind had been blunted by a year in this godforsaken place of brutal stupidity or he would have clocked it sooner.

"What's your real name?"

"Now that you definitely *don't* want to know. But I can tell you that the real Lazar Samuilovich Berezovsky is alive and well and sitting in Vladimir Prison."

"Why are you here in Vorkuta? There are special camps for people like us who go bad."

The prisoner smiled thinly.

"And how about KGB officers who go *good*? Are you quite sure you wish to hear this?"

An impossible question. But whatever devilry Orlov had cooked up, Vasin wanted to hear it straight. He nodded impatiently.

"Very well. Back in '60 I was posted to Miami, Florida. America. My brief was to penetrate anti-Castro Cuban émigré groups. I ran some good agents. Then, last year, we picked up a crazy American, ex–US Marine Corps, hanging out with the émigrés. He'd been living in the USSR, if you can believe it. Minsk, to be precise, working at a radio factory. After a year or so, he'd found himself a Soviet wife and flown home to the US. He was strange. Intense. A little simple. When he made up his mind to leave he told the Minsk authorities that he missed *bowling*. The *kontora* didn't know what to make of him, either while he was in Minsk or once he'd had enough of the workers' paradise. They didn't even try to put him on the hook, not seriously. He was too unhinged for recruitment. Nonetheless, this guy showed up in Miami, so we kept an eye on him. He joined up with the anti-Castro hotheads on his own initiative. Told them he'd seen socialism close up and hated it. But it was all an act. When we finally made contact, he said he'd been waiting for the KGB to get in touch. Claimed he despised Kennedy for trying to 'strangle the glorious Cuban people's revolution.' He went to work for us immediately, informing on the Miami Cuban exiles. But he was always volatile. Working with him made me nervous."

"You approached him as Soviet intelligence officers?"

"Straight *kontora* recruitment pitch all the way. He was eager to help the great socialist cause and the brotherhood of nations. He didn't ask for any payment. For a few months we'd debrief him regularly on what the Cuban exile groups were cooking up. His information was chicken feed, but we stuck with it. Then in June I got an urgent summons to Moscow. Top secret. Full double cutout cover, via London and Helsinki, Finnish papers for the ferry crossing to Tallinn. Rendezvous at a KGB border station in Saarema, Estonia. Clearly, someone in the *kontora* wanted to keep my visit very quiet. Waiting for me at a Party dacha deep in the woods were my own boss from the First Chief Directorate, a few of his colleagues, plus five men I didn't know. Senior military and Party men, from the look of them, though we were all in civilian clothes. They asked if any one of my Miami agents was ready to head an assassination team on a high-profile target. I told them that I had one with US military training, a marksman. But he was nervous, unreliable, a crank. They'd have to eliminate him immediately. They liked that."

Berezovsky's voice trailed. He shot Vasin a sideways, almost pitying look.

"Don't play games with me, Berezovsky."

"My agent's name was Lee Harvey Oswald."

Vasin started back as though the words were scorching cinders bursting from a stove.

"Holy shit. The Oswald who . . ."

"Yes. Him. They gave me the pitch I should use with Oswald. Kennedy is a weak fool. A slave to the military-industrial complex. His death is necessary to avert a new attack on Cuba. Vital for international peace."

"What did you do?"

"I promised to follow orders and recruit Oswald for the hit. They wanted me on the first ferry back to Helsinki but I insisted that I had to see my daughter. My boss arranged for me to see my family in a *kontora* apartment. Not at home in Moscow, obviously. Too insecure. They got my ex-wife to bring her up to Leningrad for a couple of days. It had been a year since I had seen them. And then I came to a decision."

"You wouldn't do it."

"Correct. The men who gave me my instructions were too reckless to be acting officially. The plan was insane. They were raging about the Cuban missile crisis. You know the type—the outraged patriot. They were humiliated and wanted blood. Kennedy's."

"So you contacted the famous, omnipotent General Orlov in Special Cases. Thought that he would put a stop to it." Vasin smiled grimly. "Did he promise you protection? Assure you that he would handle it?"

Berezovsky nodded.

"And after you told Orlov everything, he did nothing?" Vasin continued. "Just filed his notes in his green steel safe?"

"You know Orlov well, Colonel. Indeed. But he did more than that. He got me to a *kontora* sanatorium in Gagry under an assumed name to cool my heels. With a bodyguard and a goon squad to watch me as I ate kebabs on the beach and flirted with bored officers' wives. And then Orlov killed me. Officially, that is. I crashed a stolen taxi into a wall in a Leningrad suburb. My body burned. A suicide note was left in my hotel room confessing to being tormented by guilt about a homosexual liaison back in Miami. Thanks to Comrade Orlov for that. But you are right in a sense—he did nothing about *Oswald*."

Vasin ran his hand over a badly shaved cheek. Orlov and his eternal game-playing. Just like him to mercilessly cut off Berezovsky, or whatever the man's name was, from his life and family and file his sensational information away for future use.

"And then, eight days ago . . ."

"Oswald shoots the President. And the next day Oswald is himself eliminated. Just like my old boss planned it. And at that moment my information, that men from the *kontora* ordered the murder of the President of the United States, became the most dangerous secret in the world. Dangerous to our homeland. Dangerous to the men who ordered it. And dangerous to Orlov."

"To Orlov?"

"He knew about the plot and did nothing. I could prove that."

A silence fell between them, interrupted only by the gurgling of the central heating pipes.

"Berezovsky, how are you still *alive?*"

The *kontora* man smiled grimly.

"Always leave an insurance policy before a potentially fatal mission. I wrote up a file of my own. Names of all the agents involved in contacting Oswald. Places and times of my team's meetings with him, all verifiable. An account of what happened at the Estonian meeting, with a list of names, at least the ones I knew. Plus an affidavit stating my intention to take it to the responsible authorities at Special Cases. To your General Orlov. And then I hid it."

"You *hid* it? And only you know where it is? What an excellent reason to kill you."

"I hid it where sooner or later it's going to be found, opened, read. Sometime in the next year or so, unless I'm around to take care of it."

"Where? An office? An archive? A library?"

Despite the strain in his voice, the man who called himself Berezovsky summoned a grimace that was almost a smile.

"Something like that."

"It's a time bomb."

"Just a trick I picked up from the American FBI."

"You ran an agent in the FBI?"

"Not exactly. I read it in an American true crime magazine. You should try reading them."

"So you're *blackmailing* Orlov with this file of yours? *That's* why you're still alive."

"This Vorkuta sojourn was Orlov's idea of keeping me safe. But hardly comfortable. Soon enough he would have sent you instructions to question me a little more closely."

"Why would Orlov punish you like this? It doesn't make sense."

"He's not punishing me. He's desperate. Somehow, my old bosses at the First Chief Directorate worked out that the burned body in the Leningrad taxi wasn't me. They probably have a spy in Special Cases, on your precious ninth floor. Because otherwise they wouldn't have sent an execution squad to my sanatorium in Gagry the very morning after Kennedy was hit. Inept bunch. Tried to arrest me on the street, dressed as police. My bodyguard engaged them. Shots were fired. No idea if anyone got hit, I was too busy high-tailing it through a park. Luckily, I never go anywhere without cash and my passport. Fake, in this case, provided by Special Cases. So I jumped in a taxi to Stavropol, got word to Orlov. He sent a couple of his trusted men to pick me up with the happy news of my new status and identity. As your humble servant, Prisoner Lazar Berezovsky."

The two officers Orlov ordered Vasin to murder.

"But why send you here to Vorkuta, of all places?"

"Good question. I assume my Berezovsky alias is flimsy. My escorts got me out of the transit jail in Vladimir so quickly it's likely that the real Lazar is still imprisoned there. As for why Vorkuta, that's simple. Because *you're* here."

"Me?"

"Orlov could trust you to eliminate my escort. And now you've heard my story, you understand why Orlov ordered you to do it. So you see, Colonel. We are hunted men."

"*We?*"

"That's the thing about secrets. Once you know them, you can't *un*know them. Just as you can't bring back to life those Soviet State Security officers you murdered. From now on, Comrade, we're in this together."

# 7

"Trouble, Comrade Colonel. From the prisoners who arrived in the latest transport."

Wearily, Vasin turned from watching columns of prisoners hurrying back to their barracks after morning roll call to face his deputy. Major Chemizov was a heavyset man with a boxer's broken-nosed face. The hard shadows thrown by the arc lights that illuminated the winter half-light made him look like a grease-painted actor from a silent movie.

"What kind of trouble, Major?"

"Fucking Chechens, boss. Mountain men. Hard. Disciplined. Twenty-three of 'em, all from the same gang, or clan, or whatever the hell they call it. Tossed other prisoners in barrack three out of the best bunks near the stove last night. Four men who tried to resist are in the infirmary."

"Weapons?"

"Naa. Chechens held the guys' faces down on the red-hot iron of the stove. Barrack stank of scorched flesh when my men opened up this morning."

"Let me guess—nobody saw anything. Don't trust anyone, don't ask for anything, don't fear anyone. And no snitching. Those are the rules around here, right?"

"Right, boss."

"We separate the Chechens. Two or three to a block. And keep them away from each other."

Chemizov worked his mouth before answering.

"The barrack bosses won't be happy with that. Sir."

"And why would they not be happy with it?"

"The Chechens will fight to stay together. Things could turn nasty. None of the bosses will want them in their huts."

"Do the convicts run this prison, Chemizov, or do we?"

Turning his stubby face away from Vasin's, Chemizov growled something under his breath.

"Didn't catch that."

"I said, 'Don't say I didn't warn you, Comrade Commandant.'"

Within days, informers in the barracks started to die. The prisoners who served as the eyes and ears of Vasin's officers were found by the morning patrol, drowned head down in the latrines. They had not died quickly.

Old Lyonka "the Beast" had once ruled the underworld of the notoriously criminal city of Voronezh. Now he ruled VorkutLag 51 as the camp's top convict boss. Vasin tracked him down in the prison bathhouse, holding forth to a gang of his cronies like a broken-down emperor in his court. Lyonka's once-powerful body had run to fat, distorting the prison tattoos that covered his arms and chest. Eight-pointed stars on his shoulders marked his rank as a senior made man, a "thief-in-law" in prison jargon. A sagging Madonna covered his left breast and a distended portrait of Stalin was tattooed over his heart. A gulag superstition from back in the old days: no Soviet executioner would ever dare fire a bullet into a portrait of the great leader. Supposedly. And on either side of the Beast's throat was an inked dagger, both tips dripping blood, a drop for every murder he'd committed.

Seeing the commandant at the open bathhouse door, Lyonka nodded his acolytes to their feet but did not rise himself.

"Comrade Colonel. My respectful greetings!" Lyonka's craggy face looked like a wedding cake left out in the rain. Vasin stood in furious silence, waiting for the old boss to get to his feet. With a theatrical sigh, the old man put a huge paw on the shoulder of the man who stood beside him and hauled himself upright.

"Everyone out!" Vasin tried to make his voice as commanding as he could. "Prisoner M-5572 stays."

The convicts glanced across at their boss for permission. Lyonka gestured a dismissal and the men filed through the low doorway, avoiding the commandant's eye.

"*Slushayu Vas, tovarishch kommadir.*" Lyonka's rasping bass voice betrayed a lifetime's vodka drinking. "I am listening, Comrade Commander."

"The Chechens need to get into line."

The Beast exhaled, the breath rattling in his chest like a growl.

"Bold boys."

"I thought your boys were meant to be the boldest around here, Lyonka."

"I thought so as well."

"So whip them into line. Extra rations for you to distribute when it's done. Soft work for your guys and a good word in your file. Or . . . the opposite. You choose."

Lyonka shook his huge, close-cropped head slowly.

"I don't know, boss. Might be best to give 'em their own barrack. Chechens create their own order. Let 'em get on with it, I say."

"Are you afraid of a bunch of kids?"

The old convict stiffened.

"I'm not afraid of any man alive."

"So get it done. I need their obedience. Any part you don't understand?"

Lyonka waited an insolent moment.

"I understand."

"Very well. Dismissed."

After the Beast had lumbered out, Vasin breathed deep. The steamy air of the bathhouse stank of rancid sweat, carbolic soap, and wet pinewood.

# 8

Two days later, Lyonka was found dead, electrocuted in the machine shop.

Vasin ordered the Chechens lined up on the parade ground, a troop of guards covering them with assault rifles. He kept them waiting two hours in the slicing wind as the guards rotated out every thirty minutes to the warmth of their mess. Vasin watched the miserable parade from his office window. The Chechen prisoners shivered uncontrollably, but not one of them fell, spoke, or flinched—much less broke or begged.

Vasin pulled on his heavy white sheepskin Arctic-issue uniform coat, felt boots, and fur hat and trudged out to face them.

"At ease, prisoners. Who's the senior man here?"

A strikingly handsome young man took a step forward with natural authority. He was maybe thirty years old with a film star's face, disfigured only by a thin scar that ran across his right cheek from chin to eyebrow.

"Prisoner Zh-7523. Ramzanov, Shamil Zelimkhanovich. Comrade Commandant."

There was something military in the young man's bearing, rigid and unbending even as his body was convulsed with shivers.

"Ramzanov. You're *not* going to screw up the order here. Touch another one of the bosses and I swear not one of you will leave this camp alive. Understood?"

"I don't know what you're talking about, sir."

Their eyes locked, and Vasin saw spreading whiteness on the edges of the man's nostrils. Frostbite. Vasin looked up and down the line. Not one of the other men had turned their eyes toward him. If he wished, Vasin could leave these convicts out on the parade ground until they froze to death. The doctor would sign them off as work accidents without a second thought.

Vasin shivered, both from the cold and from the loss of his own humanity. With a resigned sweep of the arm he dismissed the Chechens to the punishment barrack. As he trudged back to the commandant's office he flicked a gloved hand to his deputy.

"Separate them and work them over, Major Chemizov. See if you can't knock some of their pride out of them. Keep them all alive, mind."

A grin spread across the officer's face as he acknowledged the order. Cruelty grew on that man's heart like lard on a pig, Vasin recalled. The frozen god of this place had broken Chemizov so profoundly that inflicting violence was the only thing that seemed to give him any pleasure.

As he prepared for bed in the narrow cot in the commandant's log house, Vasin heard the sound of muffled, rhythmic curses and howls from the punishment block. Shouts not of fear and pain but of defiance, and furious anger.

# 9

—

"You *killed* him?"

Chemizov stood in front of Vasin's desk, his grimy uniform collar undone. There was a defiant grimace on the deputy commander's face.

"He fell. It's all in the reports."

Behind Chemizov stood two of his most notorious cronies, Lieutenants Vorontsov and Gostev, and two more junior guards who had themselves been former convicts. Every one of them was as hard and vicious as their leader.

Vasin leafed through the pile of handwritten witness statements, each one identically worded. The prisoner fell during interrogation, hit the back of his head. Vasin flung the testimonies onto the desk in frustration. The medic's report was similarly bland. Fracture of the neck vertebrae, no mention of the lethal beating these men had meted out.

"Ramzanov, Dzhohar Zelimkhanovich. Brother of the other Ramzanov, I guess?"

Chemizov pursed his mouth but said nothing.

"You know about Chechens and their blood feuds, don't you, Chemizov?"

"I should care about their savage ways?"

Chemizov was being frankly insolent. But both he and Vasin knew that all the system cared about was paperwork. His deputy's men feared and respected their pack leader more than they did the camp's commander. Vasin was no more than a yapping figurehead to these men. Rock the boat, disrespect their brutal rules, punish these officers, and Vasin, too, could meet with an accident. Such a misadventure would be by no means unprecedented. Vasin had heard the stories of camp bosses murdered by their subordinates. Or Chemizov could write an anonymous denunciation of his commander for embezzlement, or neglect of duty. Gulag commanders in reality commanded very little. Vasin was not ready to fight his way to the top of the guards' vicious hierarchy, which was an exact mirror of the prisoners' own. And that was a battle he could not win, nor ever wished to.

Vasin dismissed the guards with a weary shake of the head. As they filed out they took another shred of his failing authority with them.

# 10

Two nights later, just after the last of the surviving Chechens had been discharged from the prison infirmary, Vasin was woken just after midnight by a furious knocking on his bedroom door. One of the younger guards, a mop-haired Ukrainian lad, could barely stammer out the words.

"Revolt, sir. The camp's risen."

The man's sheepskin greatcoat was splashed with blood. Major Chemizov, wearing just his long underwear and a pair of boots, loomed behind the kid in the corridor.

"Boss, look lively! They've occupied all the barracks. The punishment blocks, workshops, kitchens. There's fighting in the guards' barracks. The Chechens have the guards surrounded. They're heading over here."

From the door of his cabin, Vasin saw the forms of men moving urgently about the camp as though electrified by freedom. The perimeter lights were out, though orange flames licking up from the roof of one of the cellblocks lit the night with a flickering glow. From the officers' quarters Vasin heard the sound of his subordinate officers' wives screaming in panic. Vasin sprinted the hundred meters to the door of the administration building, followed by Chemizov and the young guard. The steel outer door was locked. A group of shadowy figures appeared from behind the camp kitchens, milling uncertainly by the edge of the parade ground. Vasin pounded the door as more prisoners joined the group and began walking, then running, toward him. Bolts and heavy furniture scraped as the door opened. As Chemizov and the mop-haired guard scrambled clumsily over a pair of heavy desks that had been blocking the entrance, Vasin pulled his service pistol from its holster and pointed it at the approaching figures.

"Back!" he shouted, panic and anger rising, and he began firing into the air. Each muzzle flash revealed more prisoners closing on the building from all sides. An answering shot rang out from the crowd, followed by a rising cacophony of catcalls and insults. Vasin dived inside the door, kicking it shut as a terrified young sergeant slammed the bolts home.

Vasin's hands shook from the stinging kick of the Makarov pistol, but he forced his voice to sound steady.

"How many men do we have in here, Sergeant?"

"Including you, sir—twelve. Eight officers. Three prisoners. One woman."

"And the prisoner Berezovsky?"

"Here, sir."

Vasin fumbled in his pocket for his key chain.

"Open the armory. Let's get these ground-floor windows barricaded."

# 11

The Arctic night stretched interminably. From the upstairs windows of the administration block, the only two-story building in the camp, Vasin could see the whole complex, fitfully lit by the flames that leapt from the burning punishment block. Sparks from the fire ran down the wind. A body lay spread-eagled in front of the administration building, black against the snow. Shot by Vasin as he fired wildly to cover his comrades' retreat, or stabbed by fellow prisoners? There was no way to know.

Vasin wrestled open the triple-glazed window of his corner office and stuck his head out to listen to the freezing night. Muffled shouts and the smashing of glass. A thin, rhythmic, high-pitched wail of despair and pain. The stars were bright, pin sharp in the freezing cold. In the deep blackness of the Arctic sky, green wisps of the northern lights flickered like cosmic ghosts.

The telephone line was dead—probably cut. There was a radio transmitter in the main guards' barracks, but that was now in the hands of the prisoners. The tiny group of survivors were alone and surrounded, barricaded in a building at the limit of the world. Vasin crouched alone in the semidarkness, listening to fear seeping out of the icy air.

# 12

*Vladimir Central Prison, Vladimir, USSR*

Major Gleb Kozlov watched impassively as the man on the table bucked and writhed. His gasping screams were muffled by a wet floorcloth that covered his face. The prisoner's body was pinioned by a swarthy giant of a man in workers' overalls, his rolled-up sleeves exposing arms as hairy as a gorilla's. Kozlov sat backward on a chair, his arms folded across its back, looking into the terrified upside-down eyes of the man he was interrogating. The giant reached for a jar of water and poured more liquid onto the choking facecloth, sending the man into renewed spasms.

"Ready to speak, Igor?"

The man nodded and grunted his assent with hysterical emphasis. Kozlov casually lit a cigarette as the gorilla flipped their victim over and removed the wet cloth from his face, allowing the prisoner to take ragged, gasping breaths. Why did the *kontora* ever bother with the drawn-out, tortuous process of sleep deprivation, wondered Kozlov, when the French Army's method was so much better?

The water torture was extreme, direct, effective. Kozlov had read about it in a book by a French journalist who had somehow resisted it. But that was only because the journalist had been a European, and his interrogators must have taken pity. No Algerian prisoner had ever failed to talk. The gag reflex set off by water pouring up the nose triggered instinctual panic and extreme discomfort—which was somehow less bearable than pain. This was the Macedonian's first time doing it. But by God the brute was a quick study.

"The prisoner file that you stole. On the orders of this officer from Moscow."

The man, shivering in his prison undershirt, darted glances around the basement room as though checking that they were not overheard.

"Please. Nobody must know that I have told you . . ."

The hulking Macedonian flourished the dripping floorcloth menacingly, twisting it in his ham-like hands.

"Berezovsky. Their prisoner was transported under the name of one of the inmates here. Lazar Berezovsky. It was his file I stole."

"And where did they transport this man?"

"They took the train north. North with a party of prisoners heading to Kotlas. That is all I know."

"When? The exact date?"

"Ten days ago. No . . . eleven. Definitely eleven. Now, Comrades, I beg you . . ."

Kozlov stood, stiffly, and nodded to his companion. Flicking the cloth quickly around the prisoner's throat, the Macedonian crossed the ends at the back of his neck and began to wring it tight. The man's face turned red, then purple, his spasms squirting jets of dirty water as he died.

# PART TWO

# 6–7 DECEMBER 1963

If bones could freeze, then the brain could also be dulled and the soul could freeze over. And the soul shuddered and froze—perhaps to remain frozen forever.

—VARLAM SHALAMOV,
*Kolyma Tales*

# 1

It was well past eleven when the Arctic dawn finally came. In these last days before round-the-clock polar night settled on Vorkuta, there would be perhaps two hours of milky daylight, filtering through the frost-mist on the southern horizon.

A group of prisoners, undistinguishable in the murk in their identical black uniforms, appeared in front of the administration building. They carried a white flag.

Vasin surveyed his meager troops. Chemizov and his young sidekicks, Lieutenants Vorontsov and Gostev. Two sergeants, two privates. All weak, bad men—the first to abandon their comrades and run for safety when the revolt began. But Berezovsky was safe, at least. His quarters were in a cubbyhole next to the accounting office, not in the main prisoner blocks. He looked like a man who could handle a gun. Then there was Berezovsky's deputy in the accounts department, a skinny Estonian writer. The only real fighter among them was the prisoner Zeldin, a hulking man who had been hauling coal into the administration's bunker when the fleeing officers locked him and themselves in. But whose side was Zeldin on— the bosses', or his comrades'? And then there was Vasin's *bufetshitsa* Tatiana, a former convict no more than forty years old but with a sharp-angled face already as ravaged as a weather-eaten film poster. She'd been an Odessa whore who'd cut her pimp's throat, served her time, then chose to stay in Vorkuta as a so-called free worker. Maybe she was still capable of handling a blade. But again—whose throat would she choose to slit now?

Vasin rallied his men to cover the approaches to the building from the upper windows. The main armory in the guards' barracks was in the hands of the prisoners. The only weapons in the administration building's strong room were a pair of prewar Mosin-1897 model bolt-action rifles, six Kalashnikov assault rifles, and the same number of Makarov pistols. The weapons were all spotted with rust and badly oiled.

Ramzanov, flanked by two of his acolytes, led the procession. He had changed his ragged prison uniform for Army-issue winter breeches and an officer's tunic from which he had removed the insignia. In the gathering light, Vasin could see a shimmer of movement in the crowd of prisoners behind. A pair of heavy belt-fed DShK machine guns taken from the guard towers were brought up and trained on the facade of the administration building. The weapons were twenty years old, but well maintained and deadly. Their .50-caliber rounds could chew through a wall two bricks thick. The men handling them moved with the lumbering gait of old hands as they set up the tripod mounts with practiced movements while others set up a makeshift emplacement of coal sacks. Army veterans, doubtless. Vasin was heavily outnumbered and outgunned.

Ramzanov and Vasin stared at each other, officers from different armies.

"Comrade Commander." Ramzanov's voice was loud and steady as he called up. "The camp is now under the control of the Prisoners' Council. The guards have been disarmed. Some will answer to a workers' and peasants' tribunal for their violations of prisoners' rights. Surrender the murderer Chemizov to revolutionary justice, and you and the others will be allowed to leave this morning. You, Comrade Commandant, will lead your men to the railhead and take our demands to the Minister of the Interior . . ."

Ramzanov was interrupted by a high scream of pain coming from the guards' barracks. The Chechen's scarred face showed no emotion.

Vasin glanced across his office to the heavy bulk of Chemizov, squeezed into Vasin's own spare uniform greatcoat. God knows, if anyone deserved revolutionary justice, it was that pig. But Vasin fought the thought down.

"I will carry your demands to the authorities at Vorkuta," he shouted. "But you will allow *all* the state's officers to leave with me, including my deputy. And whichever prisoners wish to come with us."

"Why?" Ramzanov's voice was incredulous. "Give us one man, and the rest go free. One man, for all of yours."

"Prisoner, you know you're leading your comrades to their deaths. Tell them to stand down or this will end in blood. It's not too late. Release us, and you have a chance of pardon."

Behind him, Vasin heard the bolt of Chemizov's rifle snap quickly as he chambered a round. As he turned, the Major raised the weapon and put a bead on Ramzanov.

"Stop, you fool!"

Chemizov glanced at his commander with a contemptuous snarl, squinted once more down the sights, and squeezed the trigger. By the time Vasin dived across the room and wrestled him to the ground, Chemizov had gotten two more rounds off. The returning volley from the prisoners' two machine guns was deafening, shattering all the front windows and chewing the frames to splinters. Vasin and Chemizov huddled in a rain of plaster and flying glass as heavy-caliber bullets raked back and forth across the facade, smacking into the walls with deep thuds. A gurgling shout came from the office across the corridor as the gunners pitilessly ran through their entire 250-round belts. By the time the firing had died down, the area in front of the administration building was empty except for the machine gunners and their fellows huddled behind makeshift coal-sack emplacements. Gun smoke curled from the muzzles and steam rose from the hot barrels. But on the snow there was no blood and no bodies. Chemizov hadn't hit anyone.

"You fucking *idiot,* Chemizov."

By the time they reached the sergeant in the next room, the young Ukrainian had bled out onto the floor from a gaping neck wound. The plaster dust was clearing quickly as the warm inside air poured out from the shattered windows.

"Get these windows boarded up before we all freeze to death."

# 2

It was dark again by the time Vasin and his men rigged up make-shift screens from curtains and plasterboard cut from the office partitions. But the flimsy barriers were freezing cold to the touch, and their breath came steaming. Tatiana brought up tins of hot cabbage soup and tea as the soldiers worked. Downstairs most of the windows along the facade had also been smashed, and the desks and filing cabinets blocking them were shattered to splinters by gunfire. Cold, a more pitiless enemy even than the Chechens, relentlessly occupied the front rooms of the administration block like an invading army.

Vasin ordered the damaged rooms of the building abandoned to the winter and new barricades constructed in the corridors that ran down the center of each floor. The body of the dead soldier remained to freeze where it lay. A smaller perimeter to defend, two remaining rooms upstairs and two down, plus a small warren of storerooms, a boiler room, and a bathroom on the ground floor. There was plenty of coal for the furnace, at least. But food for just four days. Maybe a week, if they stretched it out.

And then there was the light . . . The moment Vasin had the thought, all the bulbs in the building went dark. From the yard came a slow creak as the pole carrying electricity to the administration building toppled into the snow, followed by the twang of snapping wires.

Vasin struck his cigarette lighter and looked around the survivors, blinking. As men disappeared into the kitchen to seek out paraffin lamps and candles, Vasin slumped against the wall. In the cruel privacy of darkness, tears of despair ran down his cheeks.

# 3

*Kotlas, Arkhangelsk Province, USSR*

Kozlov emerged from the Central Administration for Punishment Camps in Kotlas, resplendent in a brand-new Arctic-issue sheepskin uniform coat. The building was low and squat, its central colonnaded facade a provincial parody of a baroque palace. On the portico stood the Macedonian, smoking with his back turned to the wheeling wind. Kozlov slapped a handful of papers into his man's broad chest.

"Found 'em. They're north of Vorkuta. End of the line. Beyond it, in fact. Some dump called VorkutLag 51."

A gulag commanded by one Colonel Alexander Ilyich Vasin, late of Special Cases, Kozlov had noted as he leafed through the paperwork. But the Macedonian didn't have to know that. Kozlov and his assassin stood in silence for a few moments as the Macedonian finished his cigarette.

"Fucking awful assignment. If you don't mind me sayin', Comrade Major." For all his bulk, the Macedonian's voice was high and reedy as a girl's.

"I don't mind, Yanni. But tell me something. I've seen you kill. But could you keep someone *alive,* if you were ordered to?"

Yannis the Macedonian tensed his beefy jaw and shot his superior a quizzical look.

"First time for everything."

# 4

*VorkutLag 51*

Silence. Shadows shifted as a candle moved from room to room. From upstairs, a whispered, rapid-fire conversation. The soft grind of coal settling in the furnace. A rasping snore. Outside, the stillness had given way to a whirling snowstorm, gathering ferocity and burying the ground-floor windows in a giant snowdrift.

Two days into the siege, and time was already looping into a waking nightmare for Vasin. The main VorkutLag administration would have missed their daily telephoned reports. An armed rescue party should surely be on its way—just as soon as they could get the branch rail line to the camp cleared of snow.

A noise, as if from another world, broke into Vasin's consciousness. A ringing telephone, heard through the partition. His office phone. It rang on and on. Vasin grabbed a paraffin lamp, shrugged into his heavy sheepskin coat, and scrambled up the barricade that blocked the corridor. Two of the soldiers pulled rags and curtains from around a heavy upended desk and pushed it down with a heavy thud, letting in a blast of cold air. Vasin clambered through the gap and hurried into his freezing office, suddenly unfamiliar with its walls, shimmering with frost and icicles. He picked up the receiver. The plastic was deadly cold in his hand.

"Alexander Ilyich?" The voice was formal, and unmistakable. Vasin's body tensed.

"Ramzanov? You know that Vorkuta Central must know of this by now. They will be sending an armed force to relieve us. You cannot survive this."

A silence before Ramzanov answered.

"Maybe. Maybe not. You may wait to see if you were right, and starve as you wait. Or you could give us the man we need. Chemizov, for your lives. We both know that he is guilty."

"There is no escape from here. You know that, surely? You will all die here. Shot down like dogs. You hear me, prisoner?"

Vasin heard his own voice rising in fury. But the line had gone dead.

# 5

In the darkness, Vasin sensed a figure moving through the room where he slept with four of his men. Berezovsky's whispered voice, close to his face, hissed in the darkness.

"Boiler room. Quietly."

The prisoner spoke with such calm authority that after only a moment's hesitation Vasin rose from his makeshift bed of blankets and coats and followed the man downstairs.

The narrow, hot furnace room smelled strongly of coal dust. The iron door of the boiler threw off a dull red glow.

"There has been no rescue party, Comrade Vasin."

"The blizzard . . ."

"The radio."

"*What?*"

"We must assume the prisoners have commandeered the radio and made the daily report. They will have kept it simple: the phone lines are probably down. In any case, the captured guards will tell them exactly what to say. Vorkuta Command knows nothing of this revolt."

"How do you figure that?"

"If Command knew, they would be here by now, in force. But they are not. So we need to work out what the Chechens are planning. I spent four days in the convoy with them coming up here, remember? They're smart. Disciplined. Ruthless. They are not going to sit here and wait to be shot down. They aim to escape."

"There is no road out of here. Vorkuta is seventy kilometers away, down the branch line. Five hundred escaping prisoners somehow make their way along a snowbound railway, right to the headquarters of VorkutLag?"

"Not five hundred. Only the Chechens, and there are twenty-three of them. Twenty-two, now, after Ramzanov's brother's death. Maybe they'll take some foot soldiers along with them. That's thirty or thirty-five men."

"Thirty prisoners walk into Vorkuta?"

"No. Thirty guards."

"*Guards?*"

"Two things distinguish a prisoner from a guard: his uniform and his identity papers. That's it. How many of your guards were once prisoners themselves? There are eighty-seven guards here, or there were. I know—I did their pay slips, remember? That's plenty of uniforms and papers for Ramzanov and his men to use to get to Vorkuta and disappear."

"And how would they get there?"

"The weekly supply train is due in two days. Should be easy enough to ambush it with stolen uniforms and weapons. Then, if I were Ramzanov, I would stop the train short of the Vorkuta railhead and stage a derailment, or an escape. Create chaos and get my core of men off that train and into Vorkuta city. A man in an Interior Ministry uniform in that place is invisible. Then I would disperse. Get my men on trains heading south before anyone discovers what happened here."

"A brilliant strategy, Berezovsky. But these men are violent criminals. I know their world. It's every man for himself."

"You don't know these Chechens. They're tight as a troop of commandos, and they *know* the only way out is that supply train. The moment it arrives, the revolt will be discovered and they will all be shot. They have one option. Capture the supply train and ride it south."

"So we let them go and meet their death in Vorkuta instead of here. We have food and fuel and weapons. We wait here."

Berezovsky pursed his lips.

"You're forgetting something, Vasin."

# 6

The door of the boiler room burst open and the convict Zeldin lumbered in to stoke the furnace. From the corridor came the clump of boots and some low, grunting orders from Chemizov, who had taken effective command of the small group sheltering in the administration building. Chemizov glanced in at the door. His eyes narrowed at the sight of Vasin and Berezovsky alone together in the dark.

"All in order, Major?"

Chemizov nodded in reply and disappeared to supervise the measuring out of a dinner of boiled buckwheat and corned beef. Just as in the prisoners' own kitchen, Chemizov had instituted a hierarchy of who got the most. Full bowls for himself, Vasin, and his closest cronies, progressively less for the rest. Tatiana received no ration at all, on the presumption that she'd already furtively stolen enough spoonfuls as she cooked. Their remaining supplies were carefully arranged in a row on the kitchen counter. Four two-kilo Army-issue tins of beef and the same number of condensed milk. Half a ten-kilo bag of rice, maybe a quarter of a sack of buckwheat. A quantity of sweets taken from Vasin's secretary's office, and his cut-glass bowl containing sugar cubes.

Maybe three days' supplies for eleven people.

Outside, the relentless, madly whipping wind raged on, bombarding the upstairs windows with ice. The snowdrifts had risen almost halfway up the building.

# 7

*Vorkuta, Komi Autonomous Soviet Socialist Republic, USSR*

From the window of the slow-moving train, the city of Vorkuta appeared to be just like any Soviet provincial town. Rows of newly built apartment blocks receded in regular lines, giving way to a city center punctuated by grand municipal buildings. But at nearly ten on a winter's morning, the place remained deep in night, like a cursed city from a fairy tale. Kozlov shook the Macedonian out of his slumber and scooped his own clothing into a smart leather suitcase.

"We're here. End of the line."

The pair descended onto a platform swamped by crowds of fellow passengers, most in drab government-issue padded coats. The faces that surged in and out of the lamplight had the pinched look of convicts. Closed faces, hard as lumps of coal. Kozlov's lip curled in distaste. He knew that most of Vorkuta's population consisted of former prisoners who had stayed on to work the mines as notionally free men and women. An incongruous image of the tanned, broadly smiling migrant farmworkers of Florida he'd met just a few months before bubbled into his mind. They had been dirt-poor and abused. But at least they saw the sun in the sky every day. How desperate, how insane must a man be to volunteer to live and work *here*?

Kozlov motioned the Macedonian to follow as they crossed the station concourse to a taxi rank. A taxi hustler, the negotiator appointed to extract exorbitant fares from the few arriving civilians, retreated at the sight of the pair's green KGB officers' cap bands. The official rate dutifully ticking on the meter, Kozlov and the Macedonian trundled through the drifting snow past the State Puppet Theater, the October Cinema, the Universal Shop to the chief administration building of VorkutLag.

# 8

*VorkutLag 51*

"We have to run, Vasin."

Vasin narrowed his eyes at Berezovsky in the flickering lamplight.

"*Run?* The only place to run from here is into the tundra, and our own deaths."

"These Chechens won't leave before taking their revenge on Chemizov and his lieutenants. It's a matter of honor. They'll storm this place and take it. And when they do, what are the chances that they'll leave any of us alive?"

"I'd rather take my chances with Ramzanov than against the Artic, Berezovsky."

"Even if we survive Ramzanov and the Chechens, we'll not live through what comes after. Which would be the liberation of the camp by Soviet forces."

"Why the hell not?"

"Let's say we're very lucky and Ramzanov decides *not* to storm this building. Or he does storm it and leaves us alive and just crucifies Chemizov. Interior Ministry troops retake the camp and the revolt comes to nothing. Wonderful. I am taken into their custody for thorough questioning. You are, too, though doubtless more gently. How long will it take them to discover that I am not Berezovsky? And how long will it take for the *kontora* to hear about a prisoner-impostor in VorkutLag 51? And when the *kontora* knows, my hunters will know. And they will come for me. And for you, too, my friend. They need me alive. But you? That's why we have to run."

Vasin listened in tense silence to Berezovsky's urgent whisper. He felt the gears of his brain slipping, unable to get a purchase on the full horror of what this man was saying.

"The question is *how*," Berezovsky continued. "*We* can stop the supply train and ride it south to Vorkuta. I have a plan. We get as far down the track as we can and intercept the train before Ramzanov and the Chechens have a chance. We need to get out of here without being seen. If the train's delayed, we will have to wait in the tundra. We'll need the food. All of it. And the weapons. Uniforms. Identity papers. Travel orders."

"Is that all? We could be out there for days, Berezovsky. If we even make it out of the camp."

"Could be."

"It must be ten below, Berezovsky. Once the blizzard clears, it'll drop to minus thirty. We'd have to build snow shelters and keep fires burning. If the cold doesn't kill us, Ramzanov will, following the firelight. You can believe me, this is my second winter in this hellhole. There's no shelter out there. No real forest for two hundred kilometers. And we'll need half the surviving garrison just to carry supplies. And that won't happen unless we get that asshole Chemizov to let his men go."

"So we take Chemizov with us."

"You can't be serious."

"We need Chemizov to pick men who know how to survive out there in the tundra. And keep them in line."

"I know that man. He may be tough. And he knows the tundra. But he's no adventurer. Much less a hero. He's a sadist. And an untrustworthy asshole."

"This is no time for heroics. We tell him what we think Ramzanov is planning. We won't need to persuade him that the Chechens won't leave before taking their revenge on him. Those heavy machine guns could cut through the door in fifteen seconds. His only choice is to run with us. Chemizov could even get a commendation for saving the commander, a decoration or promotion maybe. Plus, I'll tell him that he will be privately rewarded for rescuing me, the banker of one of the USSR's biggest crime syndicates. Self-preservation; greed; promotion. Those are things your deputy will understand."

"Chemizov may be brutal, but he's not stupid."

"You're right about one thing. He won't hesitate to leave the rest of his men to the mercy of the Chechens."

"To save his own skin? In a heartbeat."

"But what if *I'm* not fine about abandoning my command? Abandoning *my* men to save my own skin?"

Vasin saw the whites of Berezovsky's eyes flash in the firelight.

"That's very proper of you, Vasin. Okay. You can stay behind. I'm sure the Interior Ministry will decorate you for gallantry. Posthumously."

Vasin closed his eyes. He felt himself adrift in a sea of fears, each one surging dark and menacing from a different direction. But most urgent of all, as Berezovsky straightened to leave, was the fear of abandonment. There was one man in this place who was in any way like Vasin himself in intellect, temperament, background, profession— and that was Berezovsky. Whatever else might divide them, they were both still members of the *kontora* tribe. And if the Chechens had taught Vasin anything, it was that tribes need to stick together.

"Wait." Vasin caught Berezovsky's sleeve. "I'm in. I'm coming with you."

# 9
—

"Good head on his shoulders, this prisoner." Chemizov jerked his head toward Berezovsky, addressing only Vasin as though Berezovsky were an inanimate object. The Major rubbed the back of his bull-like neck. "It could work. If you two soft ones are up to it."

"Berezovsky and I are your passports to a good report and a fortune, Major."

Chemizov snorted contemptuously.

"To enjoy our good fortune we'll have to survive first. Ever been on a three-day manhunt out in the tundra during polar night, Colonel? Made an ice dugout? Walked two days with shit in your breeches because it's too cold to bare your ass in the wind?"

Vasin began to answer, but Chemizov cocked his head, pointed a fat finger, and stepped closer to him.

"*I* am on those animals' death list. But why do *you* need to get out of here? A disgraced *kontora* colonel—shhhh, believe me, your reputation caught up with you pretty quickly, Comrade. And a mafia *koshelek*. What stops you from just sitting it out here and waiting for the Soviet cavalry to arrive? It makes no sense. Sounds like you're not telling me something. Some *kontora* trickery."

Vasin's patience finally snapped. His voice low and menacing, he slipped into the familiar form of address reserved for juniors and children.

"Chemizov, listen very carefully. You know why I didn't hand you over to Ramzanov, on that first day? Or put a pistol round in your thick head for insubordination after you started your shooting gallery idiocy? Because we are both, God help us, *Soviet officers*. You may have forgotten what that means, but I sure as hell haven't. We have rules, and honor, and goddamn *subordination*. The minute we get across those seventy kilometers of wilderness we will be back in the USSR. The *USSR,* you hear me? Far from this hellish barnyard of yours and its sordid rules. And I swear to you that if you behave like a decent officer from now until we get to Vorkuta I will forget everything that you have done to cause this rebellion. If not, the full report on your actions I locked in my safe yesterday awaits our liberators, whether I survive or not. The key is in the snowdrift outside the window. The truth will follow you, wherever you are, unless I am alive to contradict it. Your choice is simple, Comrade Major. *Get the both of us out of here,* or face court martial for your crimes."

Vasin was grateful for the deep gloom of the boiler room as he swallowed, masking his fear. But authority was something that his deputy understood with the deep, submissive instinct of a farm animal. Even a prize bull like Chemizov felt the gravitational pull of it. Vasin represented high state authority, mysterious as the seasons and unknowable as the logic of the slaughterhouse slicing knife.

"Okay, boss. But we leave tonight. 0200. Gives us nine hours before dawn. The three of us, plus two of my men."

"Only two? We'll have to take most of the rations."

Chemizov smiled grimly.

"Like you said—the rest'll be safer when I'm gone. Right now I need to get a raiding party together to scrounge what we'll need out there. We're going to have to get into the supply sheds to steal a sled. Tarpaulins. A can of diesel—"

"So get it done, Major."

As he rose from his convict-style crouch, Chemizov straightened into a salute. Which Vasin, after a moment's hesitation, returned.

# 10

Chemizov's voice, growling orders, came through the closed boiler room door. Berezovsky and Vasin were once again alone.

"Was it true about the report in your safe?"

Vasin looked at the man hard. The old gulag law—never show fear, never ask, never trust—had rubbed off on Vasin, and he merely scowled in answer.

"Because if you really chucked the key of your safe into a snow-drift, we have a problem." Berezovsky began counting off items on his fingers. "Half the payroll for the free workers is in there. Over two thousand rubles. And the official Interior Ministry stamps. And the blank travel orders. Your confidential internal telephone direc-tory, and pen and ink. And . . . and a damn inkpad for the stamps. So please tell me, Colonel, that key is in your pocket, because you need to get into your office the minute Chemizov leaves on his scrounging mission."

This man Berezovsky had *kontora* training, all right. First Chief Directorate training, the best the KGB had. Vasin patted his pocket and nodded.

With Berezovsky's brains and Chemizov's animal cunning, they just might make it to Vorkuta alive.

# 11

The foraging party slipped out of the first-floor windows three hours after dark, landing with soft crunches in the powdery snowdrift two meters under the window. Chemizov wore a capacious prison-issue black padded coat and cap he'd taken from Zeldin. Lieutenant Vorontsov, Chemizov's most loyal crony, wore Berezovsky's gulag uniform, while Junior Lieutenant Gostev made do with a ragged coat, full of burn holes, that had been used as a kneeler in front of the furnace door. All three had slung Kalashnikovs under their coats, and carried pistols in their pockets. The black figures were soon lost in the swirling snow that swallowed all movement and sound in the darkened camp.

In the gloomy silence that followed their departure, Vasin considered whether Chemizov might have double-crossed him and made a break for it on his own. Unlikely. The food stocks were still arrayed in the kitchen. And Chemizov needed his commander to save his own skin, or so Vasin forced himself to believe.

By the time Chemizov returned, Vasin and Berezovsky had slipped into the frozen office and packed a map case full of cash and papers. They also recovered Vasin's last two bottles of vodka, his second-best uniform overcoat, and a hiking rucksack he'd brought from Moscow. Vasin turned the sack's stiff, never-used canvas in his hands. Had he really once imagined he'd go on Sunday mushroom hunting hikes in the tundra?

Zeldin helped haul the three men over the windowsill as they scrambled up a makeshift rope made of torn curtains. All were trembling almost uncontrollably. Chemizov nodded nearly imperceptibly to Vasin before speaking loudly for the benefit of Zeldin and the two miserable privates who were also in the room.

"Nothing doing, Comrades. The sons of bitches have organized their own patrols. Pinned us down for a freezing goddamn hour behind the commandant's house. No chance of getting to the stores.

Nor the commandant's private food stash. Sounded like the cock-sucker Ramzanov himself was entertaining his cronies in the Colonel's house."

Chemizov gestured his men toward the warmth of the boiler room. He paused at the top of the stairs to whisper to Vasin.

"Took some diesel and stashed it by the stables. Oats. Sled. We're on."

# 12

Tatiana the cook had boiled a meager dinner of watery buckwheat. All the men except Berezovsky and Vasin ate their food prisoner-style, hunched in deadly serious silence over their tin bowls and chewing every mouthful. Vasin knew he would need all his strength but dared not suggest mixing one of the remaining precious tins of corned beef into the gruel to give himself additional sustenance. After dinner Chemizov ordered his buddies Vorontsov and Gostev to haul their bedding into the corner office, where Vasin slept alongside Berezovsky. Within minutes of putting their heads down, both of Chemizov's cronies were deep asleep.

Vasin, sleepless and savoring the delicious warmth of the radiator behind his pile of bedding, counted down the evening hours. Something like paralysis gripped him. How could he ever step out into the biting wind and danger of violent death outside, risking everything on the insane theories of the stranger Berezovsky?

Chemizov's hand closed on his shoulder. Vasin's watch read midnight.

"You get the food up to this room," hissed Chemizov. "I'll get the weapons."

Vasin took his empty rucksack and slipped downstairs. He needed a few moments alone to think, to make a final decision about this crazy escape plan. One sentry slumbered in a pool of lamplight by the window in the office opposite, surrounded by the snoring bodies of his comrades. Vasin crept down the ground-floor corridor and tried the door of the kitchen, where Tatiana slept alone, partly because she was the only woman in the building and partly because everyone tacitly trusted her to guard the stores.

Bolted. *Shit.* Vasin gave the door the firmest tap he dared.

"Tatiana? It's the commander. Open up."

Silence, then a muffled shuffling. The noise of a match striking, then the bolt drawing back. Tatiana opened the door a crack and darted a glance up and down the corridor.

"Comrade Colonel. I have been waiting for you. Wondering when you would come."

She scraped her hands through her thinning hair, twisting it into a ragged bun. Tatiana gave a brave smile, which she perhaps imagined was coquettish, and let him in. Stepping back toward her bedding, she began to unbutton her coat.

"Tatiana Georgiyevna—stop. I have come to tell you that rescue is arriving tomorrow with the supply train. You will all be safe just a few hours from now. But Major Chemizov and I must go and meet the train to warn them that the prisoners are planning to ambush it. We will use the telephone line to call for reinforcements, who will be with us within a couple of hours. And then I will come for you. That I promise."

"Ah." Tatiana shut her face, pulling her cheap civilian padded coat closed over her thin body and looking down. "I understand. Thank you, sir."

"The train may be delayed by the snowstorm. I must take all the remaining stores. For my party. Do you understand me, Tatiana Georgiyevna?"

Tatiana made no reply, standing mute and keeping her eyes to the floor. Vasin turned away and began gathering the tins of corned beef and condensed milk into his rucksack.

Behind him, the door creaked open. The prisoner Zeldin loomed in the doorway, his huge bulk filling it. He held one of the ancient Mosin rifles in his hands. Stepping back, Vasin drew his Makarov pistol.

"I knew it." Zeldin's voice was a hoarse, hostile growl. "Stealing our food. Leaving us to those Chechen animals."

Zeldin addressed Vasin in the familiar form, as though he was talking to a fellow convict, not the camp's commander.

"Stop right there, prisoner."

Vasin's glance darted to the rifle in Zeldin's hands. The prisoners had been entrusted only with the old bolt-action rifles, not the Kalashnikovs. Nonetheless, in Zeldin's hands it looked deadly enough. The safety was flicked left, off. Vasin's pistol didn't even have a round in the chamber. If the prisoner squeezed the trigger, Vasin would be dead. The room would fill with men. The devil take the escape plan—he would not leave this kitchen alive.

"Lower your weapon, Zeldin. *Now.* That's an order."

Vasin heard the urgent nervousness in his own voice. He knew that Zeldin would never obey. Instead, the man stepped toward Vasin. One pace. Two.

"Stealing our *food*. Cocksuckers."

The man's face exuded pure menace. An animal fear gripped Vasin's bowels, the fear of a powerless man about to die. The next words out of Vasin's mouth, he knew, would be a desperate plea for mercy.

Vasin barely noticed the sudden movement at the edge of his peripheral vision but registered a steely flash skimming across the bottom of Zeldin's face. A thin hand closed across the convict's forehead from behind, and the steel flashed again, slower and more deliberately this time. Zeldin sank slowly to his knees, black liquid spilling down his shirt, revealing Tatiana standing behind him. She supported the man's heavy, slumping body with something like tenderness. In her right hand she held a long kitchen knife.

Breath came into Vasin's body in short jolts. He realized that he had pressed himself so hard against the wall that all the muscles in his body were aching. His eyes met Tatiana's. She looked blank. And weary. Vasin opened his mouth but could find no words inside his throat.

"Go," Tatiana said in a low, hollow voice. "I believe in you, sir. Return for us soon. I will be waiting."

Vasin shouldered the heavy rucksack, stepped over Zeldin's body, and hurried back upstairs.

# 13

The drop from the first-floor window into the snowdrift was longer than Vasin had anticipated. The powdery snow had already been compressed by the raiding party into a hard-packed mass. He rolled helplessly down the slope to the ground, his rucksack and rifle bruising his sides. Lying winded, he waited for his men to help him to his feet. But of course, nobody came. He struggled upright alone.

The camp was quiet. Another crunch as Berezovsky leapt, then finally Vorontsov. The window they had jumped from remained gaping open. By the morning, another room would be lost to the frost. Chemizov, a dark shape crawling across the snow, hissed instructions. There was no doubt who commanded this operation.

The snowstorm continued to rage as the five men made their way crabwise around the corner of the commander's house. Striking across open ground would be safer, but the risk of getting disoriented in the swirling blizzard was too great. Beyond the commander's log cabin stood the cookhouse, also silent. Then the two-hundred-yard-wide parade ground. Chemizov waited until the group had gathered around him in the lee of the cookhouse's lean-to coal shed before gesturing for them all to hold each other's coats as he led the way. Visibility in the swirling darkness was less than a couple of meters. As he made the shuffling, desperate dash into the night, Vasin fought an almost hysterical desire to break ranks and run back to shelter and warmth. But a soft, rhythmic pumping noise ahead steadied him. The camp engine house.

The camp's main generator was powered by a coal-fired steam engine. It was old-fashioned but logical in a region where diesel had to be hauled a thousand kilometers but coal was everywhere. The machine, built in Birmingham, England, before the Revolution, was a trooper. Even generations of incompetent prisoner-mechanics hadn't been able to spoil the smooth running of its twin horizontal pistons and two-meter-wide flywheel. Day and night, the engine's boilers were kept stoked by a small team of prisoners privileged to spend their working days in the cozy warmth. Prisoners who had, judging by the steady puff and clank emanating from the engine shed, jealously held on to their duties.

Easy enough to steer clear and head past the shed to the nearby rail line, with its simple switchback junction. But the engine shed also housed the camp's stables, which sheltered half a dozen broken-down horses from the lethal cold. And they needed a horse to haul their heavy sledful of gear.

Chemizov gathered the group into another huddle by the hay-loft.

"Any man who fires a shot gets shot by me. *Get it?*"

Vasin found himself obediently nodding his acknowledgment.

The Major moved forward into the darkness but returned a minute later.

"Fuck. Stable's bolted from inside."

Natural enough. Everything in a camp not screwed down or accounted for disappeared instantly—and often enough even then. The stables were full of oats, horseshoes, shoe nails. Even free, prisoners still didn't trust their own. Maybe especially not now that they were free.

"We go through the engine shed."

Vasin moved over to Chemizov, hissing above the singing wind.

"How the hell do you propose to get in there?"

"How do you think? We knock on the damn door, Colonel. Better yet, *you* knock."

# 14

It took a loud ten minutes for Vasin to rouse a response from the stokers.

"*Che tam, na khui, takoe, a?*" came a gravelly voice from inside. "What the fuck's going on out there?"

"Prisoner, this is Commander Vasin. The revolt is over. Open up or we shoot the door down."

From a position in the darkest shadow by the door, Chemizov waved his hand: *That's enough.*

"*Ne pizdi*" came the voice. "Don't mess around."

Vasin recognized the growl of Semyonych, the oldest prisoner in the camp. A former mariner, engineer officer, veteran of the Arctic convoys during the war. He'd been sent to the gulag for receiving a thank-you present from the British sailors he'd helped limp into Murmansk after their ship had been strafed by German aircraft. The man was still in Vorkuta through the worst luck in the world. He had managed to accidentally drop a load of bricks from a hoist, breaking a guard's neck, just days before the general amnesty following Stalin's death. Now he was doing time for manslaughter and negligence.

"It really is me, Semyonych. Open up."

"*Bat'ka! Slava Bogu!*" the old sailor howled. "Little Father! Thanks be to God."

The bolt slid and the door opened. Before Vasin could speak, Chemizov grabbed the hand that held the door handle and twisted the old man around. He held a bayonet to Semyonych's neck as he pushed the man inside the shed.

"Everyone, hands on your heads!"

Chemizov's voice thundered over the throb of the steam engine as he barged inside, followed by Lieutenants Vorontsov and Gostev with their Kalashnikovs leveled. The engine shed was gloriously warm and smelled of good tobacco, hot machine oil, and coal dust.

The engine, half as long as a Moscow bus, clanked on rhythmically. Two white-haired prisoners who had been drinking tea by the boiler obediently stood and put their hands up.

Vasin, bringing up the rear, pulled the door shut behind him. Semyonych twisted toward him in Chemizov's grip.

"Sir, we had no choice! Them Chechens said any of us could join the guards, get tied up to the beds . . . and have our throats cut by them bastards. We're loyal, Commander! I swear—"

Without a word, Chemizov shifted his grip on the old sailor's coat and swung him bodily around once more, pitching him forward. Semyonych flailed in an attempt to catch a grip on the side of the engine's piston casing, missed it, and fell chest-first into one of the two whirring leather belts that connected the engine's driveshaft to the twin electric generators. The traction of the belt immediately flipped him half over, then dragged him fast toward the driving wheel. The belt slipped as the old man's head jammed against the smoothly spinning steel, crushing it after a second with a wet crunch. After a moment the jammed belt popped free, flapping blood across the room. The quiet that followed was filled only with the slowing whir of the now disengaged generator.

"Let's get moving."

Chemizov gestured toward his men, who pinioned the two remaining prisoner-stokers. In their shock, the old men offered no resistance. One after the other, with almost casual movements, the Major buried his bayonet in their chests.

"I said, get *moving*. Load the diesel and tarpaulins on the sled. Berezovsky, take that can of engine oil. And that hurricane lamp. Then get your ass up to the hayloft and fill a sack with oats and another with straw. On the fucking *double*."

Vasin stood paralyzed with horror at the explosion of violence he had just witnessed.

"Comrade Commander, can you harness a horse?"

Vasin shook his head, rooted. Chemizov looked at him for a contemptuous moment, then followed his men through the door to the stables.

"Then frisk the corpses for tobacco. And matches," Chemizov called over his shoulder. "And stoke up that boiler before anyone in the camp notices we're down to one generator!"

Meekly, Vasin obeyed.

# 15

The drifting snow had completely covered the rail tracks that led south out of the camp gates. A cage of barbed wire linked the inside and outside fences of the penal colony's double perimeter. To Vasin's relief both sets of gates stood wide open, also buried deep in snow. Of course nobody had escaped through them. There was zero chance of getting to Vorkuta on foot, precious little chance even by horse sled. Yet still he understood why the prisoners had left the gates open. The impossible, symbolic hope of freedom was better than no hope at all.

Chemizov led a horse, harnessed to a heavily loaded sleigh, while the other men struggled in his tracks. As they passed through the gates, Vasin glanced back. The only light visible was in the engine shed, now empty of life. The remaining horses lay trembling in their death agonies, bleeding out on the straw. Not exactly the discreet escape they had planned.

As they walked out of the camp, the dense swirl of the snow began to ease. Overhead in the whiteness Vasin saw a scrap of night sky among the scudding clouds. The sweat that had covered him in the engine shed began to set in a freezing chill against his skin. Behind them, they had left a swath of blood and death. And in front of them, maybe, a slower, lonelier death awaited.

But they were out. And they were running.

# PART THREE

# 8–9 DECEMBER 1963

Anyone who has once proclaimed violence as his method must inexorably choose the lie as his principle.

—ALEKSANDR SOLZHENITSYN,
*The Gulag Archipelago*

# 1

"Train to VorkutLag 51's delayed."

The Interior Ministry officer's voice was barely comprehensible through an ice-encrusted scarf he had wound around his face against the wind. His uniform coat was ragged and stained with engine grease. When Kozlov asked the officer to repeat himself, he snatched off his facecloth and revealed a cold-pinched, weather-hardened face.

"*Delayed*. You deaf or what?"

The Lieutenant spoke as though he was slurring drunk. Or maybe he was sober now but usually drunk, and just couldn't break the habit of mumbling.

"Comrade, we have orders to join this train, whenever it leaves." Kozlov flourished a sheaf of stamped movement orders, the magic talismans of this filthy world of gulag transports. The officer crumpled them in a grubby mitten, peering, then saluted.

"Lieutenant Andreyev ready for orders, sir."

"What is the holdup, Andreyev?"

"Seen the weather, Comrade Major Kozlov?"

The man gestured across the shadowy expanse of rail sidings and tracks that formed the northern hinterland of the Vorkuta railhead. The snow was settling in deep drifts in the lee of wagons, locomotives, engine sheds.

"We have to wait for an engine with a snowplow. Could be hours. Could be days. The phone line to the camp's down, which means we'll have to stop and fix it when we find the break. When the locomotive does come, we'll couple up and be right off. So best to stay here with us, boss."

Kozlov looked up and down the line of snowbound carriages bound for VorkutLag 51. A couple of prisoner transport wagons, a freight wagon evidently full of supplies, a van at the rear for the guards. All the windows were barred, and each carriage spurted smoke from its own coal stove. Each was a little self-contained prison on wheels, filled with human beings who were utterly indifferent to whether they moved or remained—just as long as there was hot tea and cabbage soup three times a day.

"Sling your stuff in here."

The Lieutenant led Kozlov and the Macedonian to the last wagon, built of rough timber planks slathered in heavy brown paint. As he opened the inner door to the living quarters, Kozlov blinked at the stench of urine, unwashed humanity, cigarette smoke, and spoiled food. Half a dozen prison guards, ragged pullovers atop their uniform undershirts, paused in their card game to eye the newcomers. If they hadn't all been in Army uniform breeches, Kozlov would have taken them for prisoners.

"Listen up, men," called Andreyev. "We've got visitors from Moscow. State Security big shots. Don't steal any of their fucking stuff! Hear that, Varegin?"

One of the men, low-browed with a boxer's face, turned and spat on the floor. Their commander indicated a rack of empty bunks, the mattresses brown with years of leaking filth.

"Bunk down here, mates. Nice and warm. Not too far from the stove." Andreyev lowered his voice confidingly and leaned into Kozlov. His breath stank of pickled garlic. "Word to the wise. Keep anything valuable close. Or sleep on it."

The Macedonian slung his rucksack onto the top bunk and unshouldered a long sheepskin gun case. He unzipped it and drew out a Dragunov rifle. The latest and most sophisticated Soviet sniper rifle, issued only to elite special forces, had a long barrel, a ten-round magazine, and an outsize set of sights. The Macedonian shrugged off his coat, snatched up the gun and a handful of rags, and strode through the carriage to take a place at the table that ran down its center. The men instinctively made room. Fixing his eyes only on his new toy, the Macedonian began to fieldstrip the gun as lovingly as if he was undressing a girlfriend. He seemed lost in the moment, steadfastly ignoring the awed stares from around the table.

Kozlov and the guards' commander exchanged a look.

"I think we'll be fine, Lieutenant."

# 2

*South of VortkutLag 51*

Dawn broke as a lightening grayness in the hazy southern sky. The snow-clouds had dispersed, and the tundra stretched flat and featureless to the horizon. An Arctic sun the color of steel crested the distant ridge that marked the limit of the Pechora Basin. Only a line of telegraph poles, strangely truncated by the deep snow, showed the path of the railway line. The five fugitives struggled through the new-fallen powder, leaving a wide and unmistakable track. The shaggy Siberian mare struggled, too, snorting through the snow that reached almost to her chest.

Chemizov raised a hand to mark a half-hourly rest. He bent double in exhaustion, his face nearly touching the snow that half swallowed his body. He straightened with difficulty and surveyed his companions. Vasin, the least fit of the party, had collapsed face forward. The two lieutenants, more experienced in Arctic treks, leaned their backs on the sides of the laden sled, panting with their eyes closed.

"Vasin! Get up. If your coat freezes we'll have to cut the damn thing off you."

Berezovsky crawled toward the commander and helped haul him to his feet. Seven hours into the trek and it was clear that the group had split in two: Chemizov's trio on the one hand and Vasin and Berezovsky on the other. Every part of Vasin's body screamed in pain as he forced himself to his feet, raising his face to the weak sunlight. Walking through powder snow was like wading through deep water. He could not feel his legs, or his face.

"Commander, break out the last of the sugar and sweets," panted Berezovsky. "We can't stop. They'll be after us by now."

Vasin wriggled out of his rucksack straps and handed the bag to Berezovsky. It contained only what was most valuable: the cash, the documents, the precious supplies of sugar. Vasin wolfed down a pair of Clumsy Bears candies and a partial handful of half-crushed sugar cubes in a single mouthful. Seeing the others scoop fresh powder snow into their mouths to chase down the sticky mess, Vasin did the same. The thought of continuing on this hellish hike was inconceivable.

"Chemizov. We need more rest. We stop right here."

Vasin had enough of his wits about him to notice a long, significant look exchanged between Chemizov and his two lieutenants. Leave him, or take him? Chemizov grimaced and turned to Vasin. He waved at the deep trench the sled had left in the fresh snow.

"If the fucking blizzard had held we'd have been able to hole up somewhere off the line. But now it's cleared up they can track us wherever we go. We have to get to that rise and set up a defensive position. Let 'em know that they won't take us without a fight."

*"Fight?"* Vasin replied weakly. "There are hundreds of them. They have heavy machine guns . . . Major, we're all going to die out here."

Chemizov snorted contemptuously.

"You truly thought they'd let us go without a bit of a chase, Colonel? They have no horses, so they'll have to haul the heavy guns by hand, if they're stupid enough to bring them. And you said yourself: it's a handful of Chechens running the show. They'll have to leave a garrison of their own behind to keep order. They'll send just a few men. And we'll kill them from the higher ground. No way to cross this open country without being shot to pieces. It's a couple of hours more to that ridge over there. Three, maybe four kilometers. Then we dig in. And wait."

The Major paused, screwing up his eyes against the daylight glare off the snow and scanning the horizon. Their own tracks scored the wind-hammered face of the landscape they had crossed like a scar. He turned to his lieutenants.

"Get the commander up onto the sled. We have to keep moving."

# 3

Vasin woke from a fitful sleep into full-blown panic. He was paralyzed, unable to move a single muscle except his head and neck. He heard his own voice, a gurgling scream. Vorontsov loomed in his vision, his face firelit.

"Hush, Colonel. You're just frozen in."

The burly young man hauled Vasin out of a cocoon of tarpaulins and sat him upright. His icebound overcoat cracked around his waist, and his stiff sleeves snapped at the shoulders. Now he could move.

The bivouac was simple but effective. A deep hole in the snow was covered partly by the upturned sled and surrounded by a wigwam of branches cut from the scrubby undergrowth that surrounded them, overlaid with tarpaulins. In the center, Berezovsky sat by a fire of brush and diesel that burned in a large upturned tin. The flames sawed in the wind, the embers paling and reddening like the breath of a living thing. Vasin moved stiffly to within a few centimeters of the fire and drank in the smoky warmth like oxygen. Berezovsky proffered a mess can of steaming buckwheat and corned beef.

"Eat, Colonel," he said. "Going to be a long night."

"Where are the others?" Vasin asked, breathlessly, after wolfing down his ration. Vorontsov answered for Berezovsky.

"On guard. You and me are up in . . . twenty minutes. Get warm while you can, Commander."

# 4

The night was clear and the stars were falling. The freezing air took Vasin's breath away as he crawled out through the tarpaulin flap of the bivouac. The horse stood motionless in the lee of the shelter, its head down, the wind stirring its shaggy coat. A low forest of stunted trees, no more than waist high, half disguised their camp.

Vorontsov advanced at a crouch, gesturing Vasin to follow. They moved awkwardly, wading through snow and pushing through the thorny branches until they reached a low ridge. What seemed to be a black rock groaned and rolled toward them. It was Chemizov, wriggling backward off a thick mat of branches he had made to insulate himself from the snow. He handed Vasin a Kalashnikov that he produced from inside his greatcoat, followed by four full clips of ammunition.

"Shoot anything that moves. You're on watch for an hour. Keep the rifle warm or the steel will take the skin off your hands. Watch the flanks. Keep your head down. Fall asleep and you're dead."

Vasin took the weapon and crawled forward to take Chemizov's place. The ridge overlooked a boundless snowfield punctuated by the retreating line of telegraph poles. Chemizov had chosen the position well. This rise was no more than twenty meters above the plain, but it commanded all approaches. The starlight reflected on the white snow was bright enough to see for miles. Vorontsov's soft footsteps receded into the distance somewhere to Vasin's right. But the scant warmth of the bivouac drained quickly from Vasin's body, and a steady freezing wind from the north made his eyes water, the tears freezing on his face.

# 5

At first Vasin thought the moving forms loping along the railway line were a herd of reindeer. They were white and fleecy and moved with long, sweeping strides, legs swinging sideways in a fast, crouched-forward shuffle. Squinting into the razor-pain of the wind, he saw that each form was cut with a single diagonal stripe, dark across the white. Not reindeer but men, all in white Army-issue sheepskin greatcoats and carrying rifles swung across their shoulders.

Vasin forced his arms to move, tugging his mittens off with his teeth. He struggled to make his fingers unbutton his coat to retrieve the Kalashnikov that had been cutting into his side. Vasin's hands felt like a pair of frozen clubs at the ends of his arms, completely numb. Eventually he succeeded in racking the cocking mechanism using the crook of his wrist and chambering a round.

The men were advancing in single file with alarming speed. In the faint starlight he could make out six . . . no, seven figures. Swearing constantly, Vasin fumbled with the heavy rifle to get a bead on the leading figure. Three hundred meters. Two hundred. Finally, the men's advance slowed as they waded through the deeper snowdrifts at the bottom of the long incline that led to Vasin's position.

A heavy rustling came from the bushes behind him. Chemizov dropped to his hands and knees and crawled alongside Vasin, peering through the thin brush.

"Let them pass. I'll get the others. Don't shoot till you hear gunfire."

Chemizov patted Vasin's leg in parting and scrambled back to the camp. The plan was obvious enough. Wait until their pursuers started to make their way up the gap in the ridge formed by the railway cutting and rake them with fire from the thick undergrowth of the higher ground. Vasin wriggled closer to the railway line, to the embankment cut in the ridge to ease the track's gradient. He followed a line of footprints that must have been Vorontsov's.

After two minutes of furious crawling he found the Lieutenant in a thicket of buckthorn.

"Keep fucking quiet."

Vorontsov's hiss was low and urgent. The file of men had paused halfway up the incline, just a hundred meters distant. With a sinking dread Vasin counted the men below them.

"Vorontsov! There were seven of them. Only five here. They're flanking us."

The lieutenant rolled over to give Vasin a hard look, then the other way to peer along the ridgeline. "We'll deal with the others later, Colonel. You take the rear pair. Just drop them the second we open fire."

Vorontsov leveled his rifle, and Vasin followed suit. The freezing steel seemed to burn Vasin's bare hand, but he kept his weapon aimed steadily at his targets. In the shallow gulley, the column's leader pulled down a white cloth wrapped around his nose and mouth, raised his head, and inhaled deeply. The wind had died down, and the smell of the smoky diesel fire wafted in the air. The leader unshouldered his rifle and hissed something to his companions, who did the same. They advanced more slowly, falling out to the far edges of the embankment for cover, disappearing from Vasin's sight.

Silence. A very faint crunching of the snow. Were they creeping straight up the side of the embankment, or continuing along the tracks? Vasin exhaled in relief as the men reappeared in the middle of the cutting, barely thirty meters away and now to his left. The moment the figures came into view Vorontsov opened fire. Vasin pressed his own trigger, raking the two rearmost men with a full clip. At his side, Vorontsov had risen to one knee and expertly dropped one man after another with quick bursts of fire.

The stabbing muzzle flashes had blinded Vasin. He tried to blink away the bright fire in the center of his vision as Vorontsov jumped forward and rolled down the embankment. While Vasin scrambled down after him he heard three short bursts of automatic fire, then silence. Four figures lay in the snow, their blood spreading black. A fifth figure plunged awkwardly down the slope, running lopsided.

Chemizov came alongside Vasin, raised his rifle, and fired three single shots. The retreating figure slumped lifeless into a thicket.

"It's the fucking Siberians, sir." Vorontsov knelt by one of the corpses. Chemizov lumbered over, followed by Vasin. The broad, flat face was unmistakable, one of the camp's native Siberians, a Buryat from beyond Lake Baikal. "And Vasin said he saw two more than we got here. They're out there, somewhere."

"Shit." Chemizov's head darted left and right. "Hunters. Those fuckers could shoot a wild mink through the eye so as not to spoil the pelt. Smell bear shit a kilometer away. We need to get out of here. Now. Just give me a hand with this damn coat."

Chemizov tugged the heavy, bloodstained sheepskin coat from the largest of the fallen men. The convict groaned in pain as the coat was yanked from his bullet-shattered arm. Chemizov ignored the man's whispered words as he shrugged off Vasin's wool greatcoat, pulled on the warmer garment, and set off behind Berezovsky, Vorontsov, and Gostev.

Vasin crouched down by the dying man. "How many are there of you? Are more coming?"

The Buryat's face crumpled in pain as he peered into the commandant's, but he said nothing.

Vasin stood and turned to trudge after the others, leaving the wounded man to freeze to death.

The bivouac was now just a scattering of dark forms in the whiteness, the fire doused and buried deep in the snow. The horse stood passively as Chemizov and Vorontsov fumbled with its harness. Berezovsky and Gostev loaded up the sled. Vasin stumbled in the dark, scooping up tarpaulins and hauling cans of kerosene. After endless blundering minutes they finally got on their way. Chemizov led the horse by its bridle while the rest walked point, one facing each side and two covering the ground behind them, training their weapons on the featureless, patchy landscape of bushes and snowfields. Nothing stirred.

A darting panic sent Vasin stumbling backward into a buckthorn bush, then again, and again. He could feel the strength draining from his legs. His whole body shook with fatigue. The cold gripped his face and hands like a vise. Only urgent fear kept Vasin marching on. And when, after what seemed like a thousand hours, the adrenaline of flight faded into numbness, he continued to march because to halt would mean that he would die.

Somewhere out there in the night, the two surviving Siberians would be watching the party struggling on. Slowing. Stumbling. Then, soon, inevitably, they would have to stop.

# 6

*Vorkuta Station*

Kozlov and the rest of the troopers in the guards' wagon were woken by a thundering jolt that sent bottles skittering from the table onto the cockroach-infested floor. A sergeant turned up the wick on the hurricane lamp that swung over the main table as the men swore, struggled out of their bunks, and began to pull on their uniforms.

"What's going on?" Kozlov shouted to one of the guards as he hurried forward, jamming a fur hat onto his head.

"Locomotive's being coupled up, Comrade Major. Final headcount of the prisoners, then we're off."

On the floodlit platform, Kozlov looked up at the starry sky. The blizzard had passed, the clouds chased away by a stiff northerly breeze. And with the wind came a crushing cold. Even in his sheepskin coat and winter thermals, the air stung Kozlov's lungs as he inhaled. At the head of the train a powerful locomotive loomed black in the darkness. The cold intensified the steam that poured from the engine's smokestack and cylinders into gigantic, boiling clouds of white vapor. Kozlov joined a huddle of officers standing close to the heat radiating off the massive belly of the locomotive's boiler. He counted five driving wheels on each side of the engine, each a meter and a half high and painted deep scarlet. And bolted to the front of the locomotive was an arching steel snowplow, like the inverted prow of a ship and as high as a house.

"Quite a machine," Kozlov called to Andreyev over the noise of escaping steam.

"*Nemets*, we call this bastard. The German. Class-52 Kriegs-loko-motiven." Andreyev pronounced the learned word with care, then smiled at Kozlov, showing a mouth full of steel teeth. "Kriegs-Loks for short. Means 'war locomotive.' Nazi made. One hundred and two tons of first-rate trophy ironwork you see there. We took hundreds of 'em off the Krauts after the war. If anything could get through the drifts on this line, this Kraut fella can."

"How long will it take for this monster to get us up to Vorkut-Lag 51?"

"At full speed, it should just plow through the deepest drifts. But if we get buried, we got to reverse and take it again, see—"

"Spare me the details. How soon can we get there?"

"If there's no trees or telegraph poles blocking the line? Two hours. Maybe three."

# 7

*VorkutLag 48*

Ahead in the starlit wilderness, dark streaks of shadow seemed to solidify into long, block-like forms. Regular black patches material-ized against the whiteness, low and half-buried in the snow.

"Snegeri Camp," breathed Chemizov, his voice husky and ragged. "VorkutLag 48. Abandoned since 'fifty-three."

The five men struggled on, a little faster now as they hurried toward some kind of shelter. No sniper bullets had cracked through the night. There had been no movement in the brush around them during their ever-more-frequent rest stops. Vasin, his brain swimming in a delirium of pain and cold, dared to dismiss the phantom hunters as a trick of the mind, lost in the swirling mists of time. Could it really have been just a day since they had escaped from Vorkut-Lag 51? It felt to Vasin as though eons had passed.

The abandoned camp seemed to have sunk into the earth, the buildings sagging into the tundra like the wrecks of waterlogged ships. An outer perimeter of tall wooden posts was bare of wire—carefully rolled up for future use, doubtless, by the thrifty administration when the camp was shut down. The railway line ran on an elevated embankment through the low-lying place, flanked on both sides by the tumbledown camp buildings. A low concrete train platform stood proud in the surrounding landscape, rusty signals crookedly posted at each end. The horse, its head low and panting heavily, came to an unbidden standstill at the wrought-iron camp gates.

All five men stood doubled over, catching their breath.

"Gostev?" gasped Chemizov, his words coming in choppy bursts. "Get up on that embankment. Take a look. We need a building. Defensible."

The Lieutenant unshouldered his Kalashnikov and used the butt as a walking stick to help him struggle through the drifts up to the main line. As his blood and breath slowed, Vasin experienced a chill so profoundly shocking and painful that it felt like approaching death.

"Sir!" Gostev's voice from the top of the embankment was half snatched away by the wind.

The man made a chopping movement in the direction of a maze of abandoned buildings. But in midmovement he jolted, as though he had touched a power line, and his head jerked to one side. For a split second Vasin did not understand what had happened, until the crack of a sniper rifle fired from somewhere in front of them snapped out. Gostev's body twisted in an almost balletic fall, his arms flung outward, and his body tumbled down the embankment, skidding to a halt at Vasin's feet. Berezovsky, Vasin, Chemizov, and Vorontsov all watched as black blood spread from Gostev's upside-down corpse.

"Take cover!" Chemizov shouted as he began to run for the nearest building, dragging the exhausted horse behind him. Vasin and Berezovsky dived for a pile of railway sleepers half-buried in a snowdrift. Vorontsov pushed the heavily laden sled from behind, slipping in the snow as he shoved the thing onward.

Another shot cracked out, and Chemizov fell flat. But he scrambled back to his feet, unhurt, and barked a command to Vorontsov. The Lieutenant jerked out the corners of the tarpaulin and began tossing gasoline cans off the sled into the snow. Chemizov hopped onto the front of the sledge and flogged the horse into a trot, then a plunging canter. Vorontsov jumped on the sled from behind, fell, sprinted, jumped again, and wriggled his way to a firm hold. The suddenly lightened sledge, slewing wildly as the terrified horse struggled through the powder snow, careened south toward Vorkuta.

Vasin and Berezovsky watched in disbelief at the retreating sled. Berezovsky, after a paralyzed moment, stood, racked the slide of his Kalashnikov, and leveled it at the fast-disappearing figures. But before he could fire the horse plunged headfirst into a drift, tumbling shoulder over head as though diving into a deep hole. A split second later came the hard snap of a rifle shot. The sledge tipped over, spilling its remaining baggage and passengers in a spray of snow. A figure staggered up from the wreckage and began to run, madly, back toward the relative shelter of the railway embankment, but was immediately dropped by another shot.

A steady fire began, slow and deliberate. One round after another snapped out, hitting the prone body, then the horse, the sled, and its load with a series of thuds. Then silence.

Vasin and Berezovsky had their weapons trained on the tumbled pile of tarpaulins and bodies, and the impenetrable wall of night behind it. Vasin's heart was pounding so hard that he could barely keep his rifle steady.

Then, a movement. Slowly, very slowly, one of the tarpaulins that covered the wagon slid to the ground, edged forward a yard, and froze. It moved again, more urgently, before pausing once more. As the creeping tarpaulin approached Vasin and Berezovsky's position, they could hear the low, painful grunting of the man beneath it.

"Chemizov? Vorontsov?" hissed Vasin, as loudly as he dared. "Are you hit?"

"Shut the fuck up." Chemizov's voice came as a high-pitched wheeze. "Stay under cover."

The tarpaulin slumped flat and motionless. Berezovsky and Vasin exchanged glances. Berezovsky gestured toward the embankment that overlooked them.

"They'll try to come up along the other side of that, shoot us from above."

Berezovsky half rolled, half crawled behind the pile of railway sleepers which had given them some protection. Rising to a crouch, he grabbed the end of one of the heavy wooden beams and with a heave tumbled it off the pile. Vasin joined him, and together they slewed off another five timbers, forming a low, solid wall in front of the stack of sleepers. A bunker, of sorts, protecting them now from two sides. Vasin and Berezovsky squeezed themselves into the narrow space, shoveling snow on top to give themselves better cover. Still no movement from Chemizov's tarpaulin. And no sound but the rising howl of the wind.

Vasin peered south toward the scattered wreckage of their sled, the food and diesel. Both hunted and hunters, crouching or creeping through the bitter cold among the ruins of VorkutLag 48, knew that without those supplies none of them would leave this place alive.

The makeshift bunker gave a little respite from the keening wind. Vasin and Berezovsky huddled together for warmth. The cold spread through their bodies like deadly rising water, reaching into their sheepskins like a cold, fatal hand. Vasin began to shudder uncontrollably. Above, on the ridge of the embankment, he saw a dark form creeping slowly along, deep black against the starry sky.

"Fuck this," Vasin said.

And struggled slowly to his feet.

# 8

*North of Vorkuta*

The Kriegs-Loks thundered up the track, a gigantic plume of powder snow shooting up from the steel plow as it bit through the deep snowbanks. The wave of snow spray mingled with the furious jet of smoke and steam pouring from the engine's funnel. Ten enormous driving wheels churned and slipped on the icy steel of the rails. The train gained a rise and gathered speed in the thinner snow of the high ground. His head wrapped in layers of sackcloth, the driver leaned out of the cabin to peer into the darkness ahead. He saw almost nothing through the sheet of whiteness kicked up by the plow. He felt the gradient dip and the engine's speed increase. The snow would be thickest at the bottom of the incline.

The driver's hand hesitated for a moment, then reached for the lever that fed already superheated steam back through the boiler to double its pressure.

"Hold tight, Vasya," he shouted over the tremendous noise of the engine. "Giving her more juice." The fireman slammed the furnace door shut, dropped his stoking shovel on the steel floor, and braced himself against the rear wall of the cabin.

In the rearmost wagon, Kozlov, the Macedonian, and the prison guards clung to the wooden uprights of the bunks to avoid being pitched across the cabin by the wild, jerking acceleration and deceleration of the train. Kozlov relaxed his grip for a moment as the train seemed to gain an even keel and felt a welcome, steady gathering of speed.

"Wait for it." Lieutenant Andreyev jammed a leg against one bunk post and embraced the one behind his head with both hands. "Lads: Brace!"

The train was going close to sixty kilometers an hour now, the steel of its snowplow slicing smooth and clean as the prow of a speedboat through the half-meter-deep snow. The downward incline leveled out and the pistons began to labor as the snow deepened. The driver, leaning once again out his window, watched as the sheared-through drifts rose to a meter, a meter and a half as they churned past. Two meters, and the snow was almost level with the cabin. The locomotive was still making over forty kilometers an hour, driving a plume of thrown snow so enormous that the driver could hear it thudding down on the roofs of the wagons behind like a monstrous hailstorm.

Suddenly the blanket of powder descended to engulf the driver's vision. The drift came level with his window, snow spilling through like water pouring into the wheelhouse of a sinking ship. The locomotive came to a grinding halt that threw the driver hard against the scalding mass of tubing. The driving wheels ground on for a moment until they had chewed through a layer of ice, bit on the steel of the track, then stalled. An instant later, the pressure in the boiler spiked. The safety valve on top of the engine blew open, exploding in a mad banshee shriek.

"Mother*fucker*." The driver punched a scalded arm into the wall of ice that now entirely blocked his window to ease the throbbing, familiar pain. "Vasya, move your ass."

The fireman struggled to his feet and hauled the long brass throttle lever to zero, releasing a gigantic exhalation of steam from the top of the engine and from the pistons. Reaching across his wounded boss, he threw the lever of the servo mechanism, putting the machine into reverse. He edged the throttle up once more, and the pistons began to move slowly backward. The screaming of the safety valve abruptly halted as the overpressure eased, and the Kriegs-Loks crept backward through a tunnel of snow whose roof collapsed onto the track in gentle thuds as it reversed.

Back in the guards' carriage, Lieutenant Andreyev grinned crookedly as Kozlov and the Macedonian, stunned, nursed bruised temples and arms.

"Comrade Officers, ready for a bit of exercise? Reckon we've got enough shovels for all of us guards and the prisoners. And a couple spare for you fine gentlemen."

# 9

*VorkutLag 48*

Vasin straightened unsteadily, stretching his arms against the frozen stiffness of his coat. The moving figure on the railway embankment stopped, then disappeared.

"Prisoner! I am Commander Vasin, here with Prisoner Berezovsky, from the accounting department. We have no quarrel with you."

Over the whine of the wind, Vasin thought he heard urgent, low voices. Then a shout.

"Show yourselves!"

The voice was thickly accented. Vasin turned to order Berezovsky to stand, but the man was already by his side, his hands linked behind his head in surrender. Unbidden, he dropped to his knees, head down, in the regulation pose of convicts during escape emergencies. Less chance of a sudden attack from a man on his knees. Vasin did the same.

"Where is the third man?" called the voice from the embankment. Vasin hesitated.

"No idea."

More whispering from the embankment. Vasin stole a glance at his companion. Why would the Siberians not simply shoot them down where they knelt? Vasin raised his voice.

"Help me, and you will not be punished. I will tell the authorities that you assisted us in our escape. I swear this to you." Vasin's voice swelled hoarsely. "Shoot us, and you are dead men."

Slowly, the outline of a man rose to his feet, his silhouette a deeper black than the night sky behind him. He slid down the embankment holding a Mosin rifle in his right hand, pointed steadily at Vasin and Berezovsky all the way down. The man was squat, and his sheepskin coat trailed in the snow as he approached. With a jerk of the rifle he indicated that they should raise their faces to the starlight.

"Colonel?"

"Yes."

"Safety? Pardon?" The man's Russian was rudimentary, and he mangled the last word: *pomily,* instead of *pomilovanniye.* Pardoned.

"Help us, and you both live. 'Pardon.'" Vasin pronounced it the same way the convict had. "You have my word. Now lower your weapon, prisoner."

The man made no move. Vasin summoned his most commanding voice, though his lips were numb with frost burn from eating snow.

"I said, *lower your weapon,* prisoner. And fucking help me up."

Vasin's obscenity jolted the man into action, and he shouldered his rifle and put out an arm to help Vasin stagger to his feet.

"Snow! Brush it down!"

The Buryat reflexively began to dust the commander's coat as Berezovsky struggled up. The second prisoner loomed on the embankment and began to descend the slope. In the periphery of his vision, Vasin noticed a movement from Chemizov's tarpaulin. A corner of the snow-covered oilcloth rose, propped by the distinctive front sight of a Kalashnikov.

*"Down!"* Vasin grabbed the startled prisoner around the shoulders and tackled him into the snowdrift. A flash of automatic fire shattered the darkness. The second Siberian, halfway down the embankment, managed to raise his rifle and fire from the hip. There was a sharp metallic ping and clack as the man chambered another round, still sliding, and got off another shot. Then a third. A black stain spread across the tarpaulin. The chamber clacked once more as the Siberian took careful aim, from the shoulder this time. The fourth bullet hit flesh with an unmistakable thump.

Vasin stood shakily and faced the man whose life he had just saved.

"Names. Your names?"

The man reflexively drew himself to attention as he addressed the commandant.

"Bulat. Bulat and Talat, Comrade Colonel."

"Very good. Let's get these supplies inside. Find somewhere to light a fire before we fucking freeze to death."

# 10

*North of Vorkuta*

The snowplow had driven a deep, solid wedge of tight-packed snow before it. A good ten meters of hard, compacted ice blocked the line ahead as surely as a thousand tons of bricks. Every man on the train was mobilized to hack through the ice wall—prisoners working nonstop, the guards taking turns to warm up inside the train. Relays of prisoners carried buckets of scalding water drawn from the engine to splash and dribble on the ice face as they chopped and shoveled. The Macedonian did more than his fair share, using the edge of his shovel like an ax to hack at the hard white mass. Prisoner and guard alike understood that winter, their common enemy, had made them desperate equals. The heavy locomotive, moving forward, could cut through drifts at least as high as itself. But try to reverse down the line, and the light guards' wagon at the rear of the train would derail in minutes. The only way was forward to the next siding, where the steaming Kriegs-Loks could reverse its direction for the homeward journey.

Weaker prisoners were assigned to ferry canisters of hot tea to the rest of the men as they worked. After two hard hours the men had broken through the ice wall into soft powder. Lieutenant Andreyev called a halt, and the exhausted work party trudged back to the train, guards and prisoners once more in their separate worlds. As the prisoners were counted back into their wagons, Kozlov and the Macedonian mounted the steps of the rear carriage. Inside, they were greeted by the overpoweringly welcome scent of hot sour cabbage soup.

The driver reversed nearly half a kilometer down the line before he and the fireman shoveled as much coal into the firebox as it would hold. As they waited for the boiler to rise to full pressure, the fireman tipped two cans of sardines onto a wiped-clean stoking spade. He arranged them with a greasy finger before shoving them into the furious heat of the furnace for fifteen seconds. Kicking the firebox door shut with a practiced movement, he offered the steaming meal to his comrade. Both men picked at the burning-hot roasted fish in contented silence.

With the steam pressure gauge edging up to its red zone at fifteen atmospheres, the driver was finally satisfied. He pushed the throttle lever up and the engine began to move forward once more, gathering speed as it rumbled toward the deep cut in the snowdrift. Instead of powder, the snowplow flung the pieces of compacted ice that littered the track skyward to rain down on the carriage roofs like projectiles. But this time the engine powered through the other side of the drift, gaining speed across to the flatter ground that ran on to VorkutLag 48.

# 11

*VorkutLag 48*

The abandoned camp's cast-iron stoves had all been stolen long ago. But there was a good brick-built cooking stove still intact in the kitchen of the two-story infirmary. Half the building's roof had collapsed, but the upper story's timbers remained solid enough. The place even had doors that closed, and, miracle of miracles, the remains of a store of split birch logs, desiccated by many freezing winters to tinder-like dryness. As Vasin stoked the stove, his eyes watering from the thick smoke of the diesel-soaked rags he'd used to start the fire, his body drank in the heat. He left the stove's steel door open as the logs caught and spluttered, unwilling to lose a single second of warmth and light. His three companions huddled about, four pairs of pale pink-and-white hands stretching toward the life-giving warmth. The fact that just half an hour earlier they'd stood ready to kill each other on the railway embankment seemed like a memory from a distant, fireless epoch.

The heat came like oxygen, unspeakably wonderful as it spread through Vasin's arms and chest, but even as the front of his body thawed, his back and legs felt the intense cold bite like a steel claw. Talat and Bulat turned their backs to the fire, flapping their coattails to draw heat up their backs, then rebuttoned their coats and turned to Vasin.

"We bring in supplies. You stoke fire."

Unexpectedly, Berezovsky wrapped himself up, too, and made to follow the Buryat prisoners out into the cold night.

"W-where are you going?" Vasin's trembling jaw could barely get the words out.

"Bodies gonna freeze, too," said Berezovsky, and without further explanation slammed shut the kitchen door, leaving Vasin alone.

The three returned lugging hemp sacks—one containing food, the rest with kerosene, lamps, tarpaulins, and a cooking pot. Wordlessly, Talat handed Vasin the pot, already full of fresh snow, followed by a bag of rice and corned beef. Vasin hauled the pot onto one of the cast-iron cooking circles set into the top of the stove. Berezovsky had returned carrying what looked like a bundle of rags. Shrugging off his coat, he began to strip off his prisoner's padded jerkin, breeches, and the footcloths that Soviet soldiers wore in place of socks. In their place, he pulled on a pair of uniform breeches, followed by an Interior Ministry officer's tunic, then rewrapped his feet and calves in grimy footcloths and tugged on a pair of officer's boots.

Vasin glanced from the Buryats, who watched the fire, apparently oblivious to Berezovsky. The *kontora* man held Vasin's eye as he buttoned up the uniform and fumbled to adjust the leather belt and shoulder strap. His steady gaze said: Stay quiet. The stars on the epaulets were a lieutenant's. The uniform had been stripped off Vorontsov. Only a black stain on the collar and neck betrayed signs of its former owner's death wound. A clean head shot, evidently. "Shoot a wild mink through the eye," as Chemizov had found out. Berezovsky shrugged on the dead man's sheepskin coat and rejoined the trio around the now-roaring fire. Vorontsov's uniform was a little baggy in the chest and knees, but at least in the flickering firelight, Berezovsky looked every inch a Soviet Interior Ministry officer.

Talat poured rice into the boiling water, stirring it with a dusty stick. A two-kilo tin of beef followed it. As the blessed warmth began to spread through the bricks of the stove and into the room, the four men wolfed down their first hot meal since they had left the rebel camp. Once the pot had been scraped clean and refilled with snow to make tea, Vasin passed around his last Orbitas. They all smoked, their faces red from the heat and shining with grease.

"Shhh!"

Talat, his ears sharper than the Russians', raised a hand for silence. Vasin strained to hear. A strange, low hiss, like leaking steam, came from the direction of the main line.

"The train!"

# 12

Vasin pulled on his hat, grabbed his Kalashnikov, and ran out into the aching cold. The sky was lightening now, and Vasin could see clearly the path their footsteps had trodden through the snow. In the distance, maybe half a kilometer south of the camp, a high and steady plume of snow exploded from the ground. It looked as though some giant creature was furiously forcing its way out of the earth, tossing snow high as it surfaced.

Vasin broke into a run. It would be impossible for the train driver to see anything on the track ahead through the flying white wall kicked up by the snowplow. As the boiling snow-cloud approached with alarming speed he racked the slide of his Kalashnikov, snapped the safety bar to full automatic, and began firing bursts into the air.

He was engulfed in a deluge of white powder. He fired blind now, wildly, until the clip was empty. But the train gave no sign of slowing.

"Stop, you bastards! Fucking *stop!*"

From behind Vasin came the crisp report of a single rifle shot, then another. An answering metallic clang came from somewhere above the rushing wagons. In the settling whirl of snow he could see that Talat was taking careful aim at each carriage as it passed, shooting at the protruding stove chimneys, neatly hitting each one. A screaming squeal came from the steam brakes on the train's wheels. Vasin saw the bogies of the last, retreating carriage lock and skid, spilling sparks from the steel brake pads. Steam spilled in a gigantic cloud from the locomotive and the plume of snow spray collapsed onto itself.

"*That* got their attention!" Vasin shouted to Talat.

Vasin scrambled up the slope and began to run toward the slowing train. Once he gained the top of the embankment, he shouted to the others over his shoulder.

"Stay close, unless you want to get shot down by our own rescue party!"

Up on the freshly cleared railway line, Vasin sprinted along the sleepers, racing for the red lanterns of the last wagon. As the train slowed to a walking pace he caught up, making a leap for the coupling. He began to bang hard on the wagon's wooden wall.

"*Svoyi! Svoyi,*" he shouted. "Our people! Ours! Don't shoot."

Armed guards poured out of the open doors of the rear wagon, leaping down onto the track even as the train kept moving. Vasin, still clinging to the coupling, passed the first of them, shouting and waving.

"I'm Colonel Vasin! The commander! *Svoi!*"

A feeble electric flashlight pierced the half-light, then another. Vasin stood in the wavering beams, hands above his head. Lieutenant Andreyev, the train's commander, peered warily through the dawn murk, then lowered his pistol.

"Colonel! What are you doing here? Who opened fire on us?"

"We did. Only way to get you to stop. The camp has risen. VorkutLag 51 is in the hands of the prisoners. A group of us officers escaped to raise the alarm. We have to return for reinforcements from the city. Immediately."

Kozlov clambered down the steps of the guards' wagon and approached. The Macedonian loomed behind him, clutching his Dragunov rifle.

"Colonel Alexander Ilyich Vasin?"

Vasin eyed the two men blearily. The relief of safe haven was washing over him, overwhelming and exhausting as steam heat. But there was something in the tone of this man, in his brand-new Arctic uniform and polished pistol belt, that froze Vasin's melting consciousness.

"That's me. And who the hell are you?"

Kozlov flipped open a familiar scarlet identification card. Vasin stooped to read, but the words made no sense. Perhaps he was hallucinating? First Chief Directorate of the Committee for State Security. The familiar shield-and-sword emblem of the *kontora*. The formal photograph of the man who stood in front of him, in a suave suit and knitted tie. A visitor from another world.

"I don't understand . . ." Vasin felt the cogs of his mind skidding like a dog's claws on ice. There could be only one reason this foreign-service KGB man was up here in the Arctic wilderness.

"How many survivors, Colonel?" Kozlov's nasal voice was peremptory.

Vasin turned to look down the track where the two Buryats knelt in the snow some fifty meters behind the train, their rifles lying discarded. Soldiers surrounded them, covering the men with their Kalashnikovs. Berezovsky, in his lieutenant's uniform, was walking down the line toward the train. Vasin's exhausted mind flicked through ways he could warn the man about Kozlov, but nothing came. He hesitated for a moment before replying.

"Two officers. Two prisoners. We lost three more . . ."

"Where is the prisoner Berezovsky?"

So it was true. This Kozlov was here for Berezovsky. Or maybe, for the both of them.

Vasin suppressed an instinct to glance back at Berezovsky once more and cleared his throat, steadying himself. The daylight was strengthening now, milky white and translucent as steam from the engine drifted on the northerly wind. Kozlov's eyes narrowed, and his gaze seemed to pierce Vasin.

"*Berezovsky,* you say?" Vasin replied weakly. Did this Kozlov know Berezovsky's face? Should he try to bluff, and damn himself, or throw the man to the dogs? In a few steps Berezovsky's crunching footsteps would be right behind him.

Kozlov's eyes focused somewhere over Vasin's left shoulder. The *kontora* man's face hardened into a taut smile of hatred.

"Andrei! How many summers, how many winters?"

With a liquid-smooth movement the Macedonian's rifle was raised to his shoulder and a round racked into the chamber. He trained the gun steadily on Berezovsky.

Berezovsky's eyes blazed.

"*Kozlov?*"

"Hi, boss. Been a while."

"How the hell did you find me?"

"By being better at hunting than you are at running."

"Is there nothing you wouldn't do, Kozlov, for the sake of your precious career? You're scum, you know that?"

"Coming from a traitor to the Motherland, I consider that a compliment."

Tension cracked between the two men like arcing electricity.

"Are you happy with what you did, Kozlov? Did that work out well for the Motherland? Made the world a safer place, did you, you dumb son of a bitch?"

Kozlov stepped forward, pushing Vasin aside. He slapped Berezovsky's face, the blow savage and sharp. Then he kneed him hard in the groin, sending Berezovsky crumpling to the ground.

"Interior Ministry lieutenant is it, now, Andrei?" hissed Kozlov into the kneeling man's ear. He tugged the epaulet on the shoulder of Berezovsky's sheepskin coat hard enough to yank out the threads of the button that held it.

"Guards!" Kozlov called. Another yank, and the epaulet was off. "Guards! This man is an escaped prisoner!"

"Stop! I can explain," stammered Vasin. "This man saved my life."

But Vasin's voice was hoarse and lacked the conviction of Kozlov's triumphant bellow. The Macedonian was behind Berezovsky now, jabbing the muzzle of his rifle into his cheek as soldiers crowded around. Powerful hands twisted his unresisting arms behind his back. A corporal hurried from the train with a clanking pair of cuffs. Berezovsky was frog-marched to the prison wagon, head bowed.

Vasin began to speak, but Kozlov talked over him.

"*Two* officers escaped, did you say, Colonel? And *two* prisoners?"

Kozlov didn't wait for Vasin's answer. He turned on his heel and followed Berezovsky and the Macedonian onto the train, leaving Vasin alone in the bleak, pale dawn. The two Buryats were also handcuffed and led past him. They yelled something imploring at Vasin, but he did not respond. Instead, he sank into a crouch, then rocked back to sit on the cold steel rail, his frozen mittens pressed into his eyes.

Vasin would so love not to care. Above all, God, let this not be my problem. Damn Berezovsky. Let his own people take him back. Do what they will with him. Damn Orlov to hell, for bringing this man into my godforsaken life.

He'd told Kozlov two officers had escaped. One was Vasin himself. The other was an impostor. A prisoner posing as an officer. An escaping prisoner, in a stolen uniform, vouched for by his commander. For reasons that this man Kozlov would soon be demanding to know.

Vasin lowered his gloved hands from his face. The Arctic light was slanting and golden. He'd become almost used to the cold. If only he could just sit here, very still, perhaps the world could forget him. All that he needed to do to die here, where he sat, was just to remain still. The deadly whiteness would gather him into its deadly, numbing embrace soon enough.

But then anger swelled, seeping through Vasin's exhaustion like blood through a bandage. Vasin didn't like Kozlov's face. His type. Didn't want the little shit to win. And while he didn't exactly like Berezovsky, the man didn't deserve whatever fate his former First Department bosses had in mind for him.

*We're on the same side.*

The sentence rose unbidden into Vasin's brain. What side that might be, Vasin couldn't right now figure out. But it was time to save Berezovsky's skin. And he'd been sent to Vasin by Orlov. Let Orlov save both their skins.

Painfully, as though his knees were suddenly a hundred years old, Vasin struggled to his feet. He breathed the cold air. In. Out. Enough for a good bellow.

"Sergeant!"

"Sir?"

"What's your commander's name again?"

"Lieutenant Andreyev, sir."

"Get Andreyev out here. Now."

Soldiers scurried, calling for their commander. Vasin stretched his back straight. It felt good to be in command of someone again, even if it was a pimply bunch of Interior Ministry conscript soldiers. The officer appeared before him. Vasin glowered until the man summoned a salute.

"I assume you've got a working telephone apparatus on board, Andreyev?" said Vasin in his best commanding bark. "Get someone up that telegraph pole right now and get us hooked up to these phone lines."

Andreyev remained frozen for a moment, then obeyed, shouting orders. Vasin walked, frozen stiff as a wooden doll, to the train. At the steps to the guards' van he stood aside for a pair of soldiers unspooling a heavy reel of telephone line out the door. Another soldier was preparing to shimmy up the telegraph pole and hook steel connectors over the paired wires. In no more than fifteen minutes, Vasin guessed, the train and everyone on it would be once again connected to the world. But that was a problem for another, future, time. As Vasin mounted into the blessedly warm fug of the carriage all other thoughts were crowded out by an overwhelming, physical rush of relief.

He was alive. He had survived.

# PART FOUR

# 9–10 DECEMBER 1963

Human beings are born with different capacities. If they are free, they are not equal. And if they are equal, they are not free.

—ALEKSANDR SOLZHENITSYN

# 1

Soldiers, stiff with cold, filed into the guards' van. One carried a large kettle full of snow and hauled it onto the top of the stove. Others began to unwrap their footcloths and draped the dirty rags over the hot stovepipe. Chatter rose. The antiquated phone attached to the wall of the carriage gave a tinny ring. The noise startled the men, though they must have spent weeks at a time in this stinking wagon. It was evidently not often that this apparatus received a call.

Lieutenant Andreyev poked his head around the door.

"Got a decent phone connection to Vorkuta patched through for you, sir. Central Administration on the line."

Vasin struggled to his feet as painfully as a cripple. The world was calling. Over a crackling line, he made a halting verbal summary of the revolt. Number of rebel prisoners. Arms captured. Survivors from the guards and administration. Vasin hurriedly wound up the report. He had another, much more important, call to make before Kozlov reappeared.

Lieutenant-General Yury Orlov's private communications system worked through the web of phone lines, some of them pre-Revolutionary, that linked every railroad station, locomotive yard, and signal box in the USSR. It was independent of the civilian phone network and unmonitored by the *kontora*. This branch line was the property of the sprawling empire of roads, railways, prison camps, and towns that made up the Main Camp Administration of the USSR, GULag for short. But it connected to the rest of the country's rail system via the railhead at Vorkuta. Which meant,

Vasin hoped, that this phone line also connected to the railway's main phone system. To Moscow. And to Orlov.

Vasin picked up the receiver and cranked the antiquated dynamo handle to send an electric pulse down the line to the switchboard.

The Vorkuta station operator, her voice a rasping crackle, came on the line.

"I hear you, Prisoner Convoy 411."

"It's the commander speaking. I need you to connect me to the All-Soviet Railway Network number," Vasin ordered. With an effort he remembered the code words and the numbers that Orlov had given him when he had been dispatched to Arzamas two years before. It seemed like two lifetimes. "Moscow Ring Line 334. Most urgent. Priority code 999." He had to repeat the information three times before the operator got it right.

"Stand by, caller."

A cacophony of female voices, each more distant than the last, repeated a jumble of switchboard names. "Vorkuta: connecting!" "Ukhta: connecting you!" "Kirov Central: go ahead, caller!" "Moscow-Yaroslavsky Central, line connected for you."

Finally, Vasin heard the familiar voice of Orlov's secretary, followed a minute later by the General himself. Orlov's deep voice, faint and hissing as though speaking through a wind-whipped forest, came on the line.

"Comrade Colonel, I've been waiting for your call. How is the prisoner?"

Despite everything that he had done to Vasin, the sound of General Orlov's voice was almost comforting. But something was off. The boss's usual booming baritone sounded strained, like a cracked bell.

"There was a prisoner revolt. But we escaped. Your valued comrade is alive. We are safe."

A pause.

"Thank the Lord and all his angels. Sasha, my boy, I *knew* I could rely on you. Where is he now?"

The relief in Orlov's voice made an old memory rise in Vasin's mind. The days when all he ever wanted was to please and impress this old man.

"Thanks to the heroic vigilance of one Comrade Major Kozlov, he is now in custody." Vasin glanced at his audience of soldiers, who made no effort to hide their curiosity. He plunged on. "Kozlov. K-O-Z-L-O-V. Of the First Chief Directorate. We are now at Vor-kutLag 48. In a few hours we will return to Vorkuta Central."

At that moment the carriage door opened, banging into Vasin as he hunched over the telephone apparatus. Kozlov, accompanied by a blast of cold air from the vestibule at the end of the carriage, loomed over him.

With an effort, Vasin kept his voice calm. "End of report, Comrade General. Awaiting orders."

Orlov was saying something, but the line cut out. Vasin replaced the receiver and made eye contact with Kozlov.

The two had barely spoken, but Vasin already had something of Kozlov's measure. A smooth, urban face like Vasin's own, not ruddy and weather-beaten. Clean fingernails, the lingering traces of a tan. Quick, intelligent eyes, unafraid to stare a man down. A *kontora* field officer to his fingertips, and like Berezovsky, Kozlov was no desk jockey. A First Directorate man, a professional spy. Or spy runner. Yet he was a mere major. A midranking piece on the board. Not a pawn, but no queen either. Here and now, in this wagon on this train, Vasin outranked him. Kozlov had no authority over the guards. Vasin was a gulag commander, one of their own, and he controlled their only communication with the outside world. And the keys to Berezovsky's wagon, his cell door, and the handcuffs on his wrists were in the hands of Vasin's men, not Kozlov's. The window of advantage would be brief. But for the moment, it was Vasin who had the upper hand.

"Where's your man, Major?"

"The prisoner is secure, Comrade Colonel."

"I meant your gorilla."

Kozlov stiffened in indignation at Vasin's peremptory tone.

"He's watching the prisoner. We have special orders to—"

"I have special orders of my own, Major. Inside this train, everyone is under the authority of the senior Interior Ministry officer present."

Both men knew this was a public conversation. A game, to establish authority. And Vasin knew that Kozlov was aware of exactly what he was doing, and why. Protecting Berezovsky. Kozlov stepped closer and lowered his voice confidentially.

"But, Colonel, this prisoner . . ."

". . . is my responsibility. Your subordinate stays in this wagon until we get back to Vorkuta. Understood, Major?"

Kozlov waited an insolent beat before replying.

"Understood, sir."

"Sergeant, go order that man to come back here at once," Vasin called out to the soldiers at the stove. "Take four extra men to guard the escapees."

As the men bustled to dress and arm themselves, Vasin and Kozlov retreated to opposite sides of the carriage, like boxers between rounds, to make room for them to pass.

Kozlov's meek bowing to Vasin's orders seemed to confirm Berezovsky's story. Kozlov was a KGB officer—a foreign-service officer, to boot—operating deep in alien Interior Ministry territory with only one enforcer. Until he could reach his own bosses in Moscow, Kozlov and his goon were on their own. And under Vasin's orders.

Would Orlov be able to pull off his best loved and favorite trick—calling thunder from the heavens, making lesser bureaucrats quake at the power of the KGB's Special Cases Department? They would find out as soon as the train pulled into Vorkuta Station.

# 2

The phone gave its tinny ring once more as the soldiers filed out to take up their posts. Orders from Central VorkutLag Administration: Colonel Vasin to come back down the line to Vorkuta and report in full, immediately. Leave as strong a garrison as could be spared at VorkutLag 48 to intercept any escaping prisoners. Forces to retake camp VorkutLag 51 were being assembled.

Lieutenant Andreyev busied himself unloading arms and supplies and organizing his men. The engine drivers uncoupled the locomotive and prepared to reverse it up the switchback to the rear of the train for the return journey. Vasin, Kozlov, and the Macedonian were left alone huddled around the guards' car stove. Kozlov stared, mute, at the steaming coffeepot. The Macedonian glowered unwaveringly, hostile as a guard dog, at Vasin.

The locomotive, now turned around for its return journey, hit the rear buffers of the train with a juddering bump. A clank as the couplings were fixed in place. Andreyev came in to make his final report, and to offload the telephone apparatus. Four soldiers, plus the locomotive crew, would remain with Vasin on board to escort the prisoners back to Vorkuta. The rest of the men would stay to guard the line, under Andreyev's command. Salutes were exchanged. The train got under way with a jolt, and Vasin followed Andreyev out to the van's vestibule. Reluctantly, the Lieutenant jumped off the moving steel steps into the snow as the train gathered pace. This wasn't how Andreyev had planned this routine prisoner-escort detail to end up.

Vasin ducked quickly back into the guards' carriage to warn Kozlov and his man to stay put. In an afterthought, he shouldered the rucksack filled with the payroll cash from the VorkutLag 51 safe and took it with him.

The prisoner transport wagons consisted of a series of narrow cages constructed of steel grilles with a walkway running along one side. Each cage was twice the width of a narrow plank bed, and each was equipped with a stinking latrine bucket. From the open guards' space at the head of the compartment Vasin could see every prisoner as they lay or sat on their cots. All were anonymous in their identical, filthy black prison coats except for one—Berezovsky, still in his incriminating field-green lieutenant's uniform. As he approached, Vasin saw that Berezovsky was also the only prisoner who remained handcuffed.

Vasin unlocked the outer of the two steel gates that closed off each cage and crouched close to Berezovsky.

"Listen," Vasin said in a quiet enough voice not to be heard over the clanking of the wheels. "I've alerted my boss in Moscow. He's going to get you out of here. You're safe. For now."

Berezovsky's answer came as a whisper, forcing Vasin to lean closer still.

"*Orlov?* No chance I'm trusting that man again."

"Do you have a better idea? You told me that you had him by the balls. So, let him get us out of this."

Berezovsky chewed his lip.

"Kozlov and his killer still on the train?"

Vasin nodded.

"Any way to keep them out of the way? The killer, especially."

"As long as they're on this train, they're under my orders."

"Good. How many men do you have?"

"Just four. The rest are staying to guard the railway."

Berezovsky nodded and lowered his head onto his cuffed, clasped hands, deep in thought.

"Okay. Here's what we're going to do. You're going to stop the train close enough to the city for me to get there on foot without dying of frostbite. Say five kilometers out. Then you're going to stage an execution. Of all three of us: me and the two Buryats. Tell your men you have special orders. Post one soldier to guard Kozlov and keep him out of the way. Two more to escort us out into the snow, one by one. Leave one man in here to guard the rest. You shoot the two Buryats first, then pretend to shoot me. Leave me in the bloody snow. I get myself to Vorkuta. We meet up. You give me the travel papers and cash I need to get out of there. Got it?"

Vasin glanced across to the cages where Bulat and Talat sat hunched and motionless.

"Why the hell should I kill the Buryats? I promised them their lives."

"Because they've seen my face. Because we need them dead to make my execution look convincing."

"You want me to shoot two good men in cold blood, to cover your escape." Vasin's voice had gone very hollow.

"You believe that General Orlov is going to save us?" Berezovsky's glare was rinsed with rage. "You think the *kontora* has never ordered anyone shot without trial? This is all Orlov's doing. Let *him* take the blame."

"You're crazy, Berezovsky."

"And you're a sentimental fool, Vasin."

Vasin straightened from his crouch and looked up and down the carriage at the penned prisoners. He'd rather have Berezovsky in here, under lock and key, until Vorkuta. Because he knew that Berezovsky was not just trying to get away from Kozlov. He was trying to escape from Vasin, too.

He tried to concentrate. Vasin needed to keep Berezovsky both close and alive. He returned to his crouching position, inches from the prisoner's face.

"You are blackmailing Orlov. You told me that if you die, he's screwed. But if Kozlov and his guys get you onto their home turf, he's done for too. So Orlov *has* to save our asses. Or did you think you could escape from Vorkuta on your own? Escape from the USSR? Your chances are zero, I promise you that. You and I are in this together, Berezovsky. Stick with me, and you might survive, or go it alone and die."

Berezovsky, his eyes hooded with exhaustion but still as blearily malevolent as those of a fighter on the ropes, scanned Vasin.

"I come along meekly, so you can deliver me trussed like a chicken to Orlov?"

"No, Berezovsky. I'm not going to deliver you to Orlov. We'll get you and your dossier to someone high up in the *kontora*. Someone who could roll up your Kennedy plotters and punish Orlov. Don't you see, that's the only way we both live? Otherwise both of us will spend the rest of our short lives running. And we'll die tired."

"The noble whistleblower? I tried that, once. It didn't work out so well."

"You went to Orlov. The wrong man. We find someone else."

"And you know an honest man in the *kontora*?"

Panic and exhaustion hadn't quite extinguished Berezovsky's

sharp mind. This was the question Vasin himself had been turning over in his head for hours.

"What I know for sure is that Vorkuta isn't the USSR. It's a separate empire, the Interior Ministry's empire. Kozlov and his thug have no personal authority here. We have enough time to get you out. Trust me."

"Your plan is to use Orlov to get us out of this fix, then fuck him and help me instead. Do I have it right? And if I don't choose to trust either of you?"

Vasin stood once more and pulled the turnkey's large jangling ring of keys from his pocket.

"For the moment, Comrade, you have no choice."

He slammed and locked the outer grille of Berezovsky's cage.

# 3

Kozlov sprawled on the edge of the cushioned bench, his stocking feet propped casually on the central table of the guards' carriage. Watching Vasin as he entered, Kozlov sipped delicately from a battered tin mug as though it were full of fine cognac.

"All well with the prisoner, Colonel?"

Vasin made no answer but approached the stove. Rocked off balance by the lurching of the train, he sat heavily on the bench opposite Kozlov.

"May we have a private word?" Kozlov said, nodding in the direction of the soldier who had been guarding him and the Macedonian. Vasin knew this old interrogator's trick. Ask, or order, a man to do something he was about to do anyway. Sit down. Stand up. Read this.

"Sure. As long as we *are* in private."

Without waiting for his boss's word the Macedonian stood and clumped out of the compartment, followed by the scruffy Interior Ministry private. Kozlov placed his cup on the floor, straightened up on the bench, and glanced around him as though checking for unseen listeners.

"What do you know about Prisoner Berezovsky?" Kozlov began, flatly.

"He's a crime gang *koshelek*. Some big wheel in Tambov, they say." Had Vasin waited a fatal second too long before launching into his bluff? He blundered on. "The kind of man whose friends would be grateful to see him alive. Grateful and *generous*."

Kozlov nodded slightly, as though acknowledging a decent chess move.

"You assisted the escape of Prisoner Berezovsky in the hope of receiving money from his associates. Do I have it right?"

"These friends could be good to you, too. You and your comrade."

Kozlov spread the fingers of his right hand from where it rested on his knee in a gesture that said: I got your play.

"You surprise me, Alexander Ilyich. Your actions don't sound at all like those of the man described in the *kontora* personnel file. Idealistic and intelligent, it said. Independent-minded, well, that could fit. But above all, it describes a Special Cases man. What could Berezovsky possibly offer you that our esteemed colleague General Orlov could not? What use is *money* to you, up here in VorkutLag?"

"Damn you, Kozlov. You know nothing about me." Vasin failed to keep the anger out of his voice. His lie hadn't worked. But it was the only story he had, and he had no choice but to stick to it.

"So you *were* still working for Orlov." Kozlov leaned forward so his face was within an inch of Vasin's. "Tell me something, Comrade Colonel. What does 'Dallas' mean to you?"

Vasin did not answer immediately. But his mouth thinned into a tight smile as he sat back, holding Kozlov's gaze.

"It means nothing at all to me, Comrade Major. And never will."

# 4

The platform at Vorkuta Station was floodlit, illuminating columns of soldiers forming up to meet the train. A group of grim-faced, heavyset men in snow-dusted winter uniform coats waited by the buffers. Vasin made sure that Kozlov and the Macedonian preceded him down the steps, then descended from the train himself. The local brass surrounded him, firing questions about the uprising or demanding news of their comrades stuck up at VorkutLag 51. "Is Krivorukov alive? Shein? Venyediktov?"

Major-General Vsevolod Semashko, commander of what remained of the VorkutLag empire, shouldered his way through the crowd. He was short and thickset, his Astrakhan uniform fur hat perching pompously on his round head like a bucket on top of a snowman. The General's usually pasty face was flushed.

"*Chto za karaul ty nam ustroil?* What's this mess you made for us?" he said, seizing Vasin's upper arms and turning him left and right as though inspecting a cracked vase. Semashko's tone was more gruffly friendly than his words. "Let's get you debriefed right now. The relief force commanders are waiting for you at HQ. Plans all pinned up. Come."

"At once, sir. But we'll take the prisoners who escaped with me to the debriefing. They've proved their loyalty. Let's hear what happened from their own mouths."

Semashko frowned and paused. In the world of the gulag, where he'd spent his entire career, prisoners were human livestock to be processed and kept alive, rather than to be listened to and trusted.

"I insist, General. Two Buryats, Bulat and Talat. And a prisoner called Lazar Berezovsky, he's wearing the uniform of a dead lieutenant on my orders."

On Semashko's nod, the three named prisoners, all handcuffed, were led out of the prison wagon and through the crowd. Among the milling faces on the platform Vasin spotted the looming head of the Macedonian, then a moment later Kozlov himself, watching helplessly as his quarry was led away under heavy escort to Vorkut-Lag HQ.

# 5

Under the fierce electric lights of General Semashko's office, Vasin felt like a fish grilling on a barbecue grill. The grim, pale faces of his bosses glared at him from all sides of the General's long conference table.

"Without regard for our personal safety, Comrades, we were determined to get word to Vorkuta and bring the criminals swiftly to justice," intoned Vasin, his chin suitably upturned in an attitude of duty. "Thus, Comrade Chemizov redeemed his errors by saving his commander, even at the cost of his own life."

Semashko's scowling face actually broke into a surprisingly child-ish smile, as Vasin had calculated. The dream of every bureaucrat on the hook for a fuckup: a chance to turn disaster into a stirring story of Soviet heroism.

"I have a radiogram from the Deputy Interior Minister here." Raising a pair of folded glasses up to one eye, Semashko squinted at the paper through a single lens. "Prisoner Lazar Samuilovich Berezovsky is to be accorded 'special status' and 'special security.' Marked 'urgent' and 'secret.' Any idea what they're talking about?"

Silently, Vasin blessed Orlov and the alchemic power at his command to shoot rockets up the backsides of Soviet ministers.

"Berezovsky must be protected for reasons that may in time be shared with some of you by the competent authorities of State Secu-rity." Vasin's voice turned grave and confiding. "All I am authorized to say is that he is *one of ours*." He paused as though considering what he could add, then lowered his voice. "A dedicated servant of the Motherland. Under deep cover."

The phrase was nicely turned. One of *ours*. Most of the men around the table knew something of Vasin's story as a fallen *kontora* hotshot exiled to the Arctic. And though it had been nearly a decade since Khrushchev emptied the gulags of most of their political prisoners and turned their administration over from the KGB to the humbler Interior Ministry, most of these commanders had risen through the ranks as *kontora* men. Vasin was a relative newcomer to the gulag world, but he had delicately complimented his superiors by pretending they were still in the charmed circle of State Security rather than mere thuggish jailers.

Semashko, at the head of the table, swelled up like a toad.

"Yes, yes! A matter of state security," he bleated pompously. "Exactly as I had assumed."

By the time Berezovsky was summoned from the holding cells in the headquarters basement, he looked more human. He'd been allowed to shave and had been given a clean, though worn, black prison uniform. As he was led in, handcuffed, every officer at the conference table turned to examine him. Once the cuffs were off and the prisoner's escort had left the room, Semashko greeted him warmly.

"Comrade colleague!"

"Comrade *Major*," Vasin corrected, from down the table. Berezovsky, meeting his eyes, blinked in grateful acknowledgment. Vasin knew he was smart enough to guess what was going on and play his part.

"Comrade Major, indeed!" Semashko gestured Berezovsky to an empty seat. "Come. Your assistance is needed."

# 6

For a long afternoon Vasin and Berezovsky pored over camp ground plans with the commanders of the relief expedition, going through lists of prisoners' names, singling out the known and the likely troublemakers and crossing off the names of the dead. Through the strange magic of *telefonnoe pravo*—the power of the telephone call from above—Vasin found himself treated not like a disgraced incompetent who had lost control of his own camp but as a man with powerful friends. It was not an unfamiliar feeling for Vasin. Many times during his career as a Special Cases officer, General Orlov had summoned fire from the heavens down on the heads of local bigwigs who obstructed his agents' investigations. Orlov was still, at least, good for that.

Beyond the triple-glazed windows of the VorkutLag headquarters, snow swirled once more in the cold darkness. As plans of the camp were rolled and new ones pinned up, Vasin's gaze wandered to the hostile world outside. Somewhere out there Kozlov and his killer were doubtless making their own moves, sending their own coded telegrams. Blocking out the drone of military plans, Vasin turned over in his mind what the hell they might be up to.

"And what shall we do with, er, 'Prisoner Berezovsky' here, Colonel?"

An expectant silence brought Vasin back from his reverie. Before Vasin could collect his thoughts, Berezovsky answered for him.

"With respect, Comrades, may I request that I be allowed to make urgent contact with my superiors in Moscow? My usefulness at VorkutLag 51 is at an end, and the *kontora* will confirm the formalities of my discharge. Or should I say, of Lazar Berezovsky's *temporary* discharge. May I suggest being sent to hospital, or for special interrogation, to avoid the complications of a formal prisoner release? Because of course the real Lazar Berezovsky has done nothing to merit early release and remains under strong guard in Vladimir Prison."

He was off script. Vasin's first instinct was to take control; he'd be happier with the man safely under guard until he could speak to Orlov and work out their next move. But Vasin could not contradict Berezovsky now without risking raising suspicion. Damn the man. His few weeks as a prisoner had taught him a keen sense of the rules of the gulag bureaucracy. Officially releasing a convicted prisoner would involve a complex judicial procedure. But a change of status or location of imprisonment was easily in the purview of the men in this room.

"Colonel Vasin, do you agree?"

Vasin, containing his irritation, nodded his approval as Berezovsky cracked a smile.

"Very good," Semashko continued. "We will reclassify Prisoner Lazar Berezovsky an inmate trusty, first class. With permission to be at liberty in the confines of Vorkuta city. And release him to the personal custody of Colonel Vasin. Paperwork could be done in a couple of hours."

Berezovsky nodded curtly and saluted.

"Thank you, Comrade General. Your leadership and zeal in this matter will not go unremarked. We need more men like you in Moscow."

Semashko shook Berezovsky's hand, beaming at the prospect of his promotion.

# 7

It was ten at night before Vasin finally settled into a deep, hot bath at Vorkuta's Red Star Hotel. His filthy and soiled uniform lay crumpled on the floor on top of his soot-stained rucksack. His frost-raw hands, feet, and face smarted at the touch of the water.

He was woken by a quiet but insistent knocking on the bathroom door. Berezovsky poked his head into the steamy room. His face was haggard, but the eyes had not yet lost their hungry, dangerous intensity.

"Time's up."

"Okay, okay. One second."

Vasin struggled up, drained the bath as he shaved, then considerately rinsed the black ring of grime from the tub. The suite that the two men had been given to share was, by local standards, luxurious:

a whole private bathroom just for themselves. As Berezovsky lowered himself into the refilling bath, Vasin snapped a freshly laundered shirt free from its military creases and pulled on a brand-new uniform from a crisp pile left in the sitting room. He combed his hair in the wardrobe mirror. He was still gaunt, his cheeks spotted here and there with blood vessels burst by the cold, but he felt nearly human. Vasin brewed a cup of tea using the hotel's newfangled electric coil heater, which dangled into the mug on its own little hook.

Berezovsky emerged from his bath equally transformed and tugged on his own fresh Army uniform. Both tunics, straight from the stores, were as yet without insignia. Vasin's year in the prison system had ingrained the psychological barrier between officer and inmate so deeply that it was a shock to see Berezovsky dressed no longer as a prisoner. He was a man once more.

Both men slurped down tea and biscuits in a silence that was almost companionable. Berezovsky struggled to his feet from the deep armchair, switched on the wall-mounted radio, and turned up the volume. The Mayak late-night news bulletin was just coming to an end with information on the latest meat production records.

"When do you speak to Orlov?"

"First thing in the morning."

Berezovsky scanned the room with wary professionalism, twitching the curtain. Third-floor window, no balcony. One exit, through the door into the corridor. He snatched up a sturdy chair and wedged it against the handle.

"Settle down, man. Have some more tea."

Berezovsky completed his circuit of the suite and sat down heavily opposite Vasin.

"One telegram generated by your boss got me sprung from jail. You think that Kozlov's bosses can't send telegrams? I promise you they can. And they will. But they probably won't make a move till tomorrow."

"What can they do?"

Berezovsky shrugged.

"Vorkuta is a company town, deep Interior Ministry territory, so nothing like a messy kidnapping. I expect something administrative, an urgent State Security arrest warrant. We don't have much time—much as I am grateful to you, Vasin, for helping me. And for these charming quarters."

His tone was more bantering than bitter. The two men had been through too much over the last three days for rancor.

"I need to know what you want, Berezovsky. Not that your name is Berezovsky. Don't I deserve to know your name, at least?"

The man considered, half smiled, then shook his head.

"Knowing my name won't help you live to old age, Vasin. I need free passage to a neutral country. An official Soviet exit visa. A new identity. Just one will do. A promise to leave me alone."

"And you'll tell Orlov where to find your file, but only once you're safely abroad?"

"That's the deal."

"You know Orlov doesn't trust anyone, right?"

"Neither do I."

"Not even me?"

"I think you want to use my story to sink your old boss. To take revenge on Orlov for whatever it was that got you sent up here to this shithole. And you need Kozlov and his friends neutralized, because the Kennedy story is bad for your health as long as they are at liberty. And you can't do that without me. I trust you, Vasin, because I have linked your fate to mine."

"Thanks for that."

"You might even have some moral compass, my dear Colonel. I think if *you* had a choice you'd rather not see an innocent man punished for trying to do the right thing. You'd prefer guilty men punished for doing the wrong thing."

"Patronizing asshole."

"You're welcome. But I mean it."

"Berezovsky. You'll fucking say anything you need to keep yourself alive."

Neither man had the strength to speak any more. With a titanic effort, Vasin hauled himself across the room and fell into the bed, leaving his companion slumped in his chair. Over their snores, the radio played on.

# 8

Vasin was woken by loud knocking on the door. It was still dark outside, but the flimsy curtains were illuminated by a wash of yellow streetlights. The heavy iron radiators generated a volcanic heat. In the sitting room Vasin heard Berezovsky stirring in his chair.

The knocking continued.

Berezovsky was on his feet before Vasin. He took up a position behind the suite's door, gesturing Vasin to approach.

"Who is it?"

"Reception clerk, Comrade Colonel. Urgent telegram for your attention."

Instinctively, Vasin looked to Berezovsky for approval. The man nodded, and Vasin inched away the chair from the door handle and accepted the clerk's proffered paper.

It was from Orlov.

ARRIVING THIS AFTERNOON. KEEP VALUED COMRADE SECURE.

Vasin sighed.

"Orlov's on his way."

"Coming *here*? To Vorkuta?"

"We need a plan."

"You must meet your boss alone. Tell him what I need."

"And you just walk out of here with Kozlov on your trail?"

"Kozlov knows exactly where I am, and no guard that you could post is going to refuse a KGB officer with an official arrest warrant. So yes. You are going to let me walk out of here."

As usual, Berezovsky was right. At the hotel he was a sitting duck. And frankly he was right not to risk a meeting with Orlov, too. Vasin could not allow Berezovsky to be caught, yet he had nowhere to hide him. He had no choice but to let the man look after himself.

"Fine. Where do we meet?"

"Where does anyone meet in a Soviet city they've never been to? The theater. And every theater lobby in the country is full of people in the half hour before curtain at seven o'clock. So see you there. Six thirty tonight. Come alone."

Vasin nodded and checked his watch. He was due at Semashko's office in half an hour.

Vasin walked to the wardrobe, where he'd stashed his filthy rucksack. He pulled out a twenty-five-ruble note, not much the worse for being soaked and frozen.

"Here. Might need this to get yourself a coffee. Take care of yourself, Berezovsky-not-Berezovsky."

In the lobby of the Red Star Hotel one of Semashko's adjutants waited impatiently to hurry Vasin to brief the commanders of the VorkutLag 51 relief force. He gestured for the man to wait and turned to the reception desk.

"Need to send an urgent telegram. Reply to this one."

Vasin proffered Orlov's early-morning message and his battered ID card. Was he about to do something stupid? He hardly knew. There was only one person in the *kontora* he could—almost—trust. The clerk passed over the stamped and addressed telegraph form. Vasin's pencil hovered over the paper, then wrote in block capitals: ATTENTION: LT. GEN. YU. A. ORLOV. URGENT AND PERSONAL . . .

# 9

—

Vorkuta's airfield was veiled in snow that billowed in across the flat, featureless tundra. The pinpricks of red on the wings of the little An-24 plane yawed and pitched as the pilot lined up for his final approach. Two bunny hops and the plane was down and braking in a macho squeal of rubber.

Orlov emerged first, resplendent in the uniform of a KGB lieutenant-general. He had a young aide-de-camp in tow whom Vasin didn't recognize. But among the dozen men dressed as civilian apparatchiks he spotted several familiar faces: Special Cases troopers in plain clothes. Orlov was evidently taking no chances. In the shelter of the terminal building's lee, Orlov greeted Vasin with an unexpected bear hug.

"Son of a gun, Vasin," the General hissed in his ear. "Can't keep a good man down, eh? Now where the hell is our fugitive?"

"Safe, sir. I'm seeing him tonight."

Orlov abruptly broke the hug, holding Vasin by the shoulders instead and gazing furiously into his face.

"He's not in custody?"

"No, boss."

Once, in different times when they were both different men, Orlov might have exploded into fury. Now, he merely looked deflated. Luggage was unloaded; local officials fussed and directed the VIP party to a line of waiting cars and a military van. The last man to emerge from the plane was bundled in a heavy tweed overcoat and expensive fur hat. Vadim Kuznetsov hesitated at the plane's door as though having second thoughts about stepping out into the threshing wind. When he caught sight of Vasin, Kuznetsov's expression of distaste changed to a hard, furious glare.

"Good to see you, Vadim!" called Vasin.

Kuznetsov worked his mouth as through biting back something very rude.

"What the hell am I doing here?"

"It's a long story. I'll tell you later. Glad to see you."

"Well I'm *not* glad to see you." Kuznetsov took an incredulous look at the swirling snow and the enveloping darkness. "Sasha, your choice of assignments is getting worse and worse."

# 10

Closeted in the bathroom of Orlov's suite at the Red Star Hotel, all taps running, Vasin briefed his boss on what had happened at VorkutLag 51. For once he had the advantage over Orlov. Only Vasin knew where to find Berezovsky.

And, privately, Vasin had another advantage, albeit a dangerous one. The deadly knowledge that could sink Orlov.

"General, Berezovsky will deal with me, nobody else. He was very insistent." Which was at least a tiny bit true. "Please don't tell me why he is being so secretive. I *really* don't want to know."

Orlov's suspicious stare was as penetrating and dangerous as a snake's.

"You've cooked something up with this man. I can smell it."

"All I know is that he's afraid of you, and afraid of some of his old colleagues, who are here right now hunting him."

Orlov's eyes narrowed.

"He never told you *why* he was afraid of all these people? You never asked?"

"Of course I asked. 'It's more than your life's worth to know. First Chief Directorate business.'"

The General's chin sank into his flabby neck while he pondered, his eyes intense as a chess player's as he studied a point in space between them.

"What about your telegram? Why insist on bringing Kuznetsov, unless you've got a plan worked out?"

"I wanted Kuznetsov because he is solid. Smart. Because *you* trust him." Did Vasin dare try to push his deception one step further? "And to request letting Kuznetsov handle Berezovsky. I would introduce them. Berezovsky will trust him. Kuznetsov's a good man. Because I want no more part of this. If you will allow me."

"You want *out* of this? Not your battle? Unwilling to risk your neck for a chief who's punished you so grievously? That it, Vasin?"

As usual Orlov touched the heart of the matter with a needle. The General spoke with his customary precision, but all the pent-up anger of former days was gone.

"I am always ready to do my duty for the USSR, sir." The hollowness in Vasin's reply was his true answer, and both men knew it. And both knew that they needed each other—though for very different reasons. Another long silence elapsed as Orlov's devious mind turned over. Vasin felt that his own loyalty, his own credulity and vulnerabilities were being weighed in the balance. But this time

Vasin held hidden cards that Orlov could not know or see. And in this round of their long game Vasin no longer had anything to lose. What more could Orlov take from him that he had not already taken? His old life, even his son, Nikita, had become little more than amputated memories. Finally, Orlov spoke.

"You saved his life, getting him out of that prison revolt. This damn Berezovsky, as you call him, trusts you. So no, Vasin: you may not quit."

"I am at your orders, sir, if you need me."

Orlov's face tightened. Was this young pup daring to mock him? Because yes, damn it, he *did* need Vasin.

"I still want Kuznetsov to work with me, sir," Vasin continued while he held a momentary advantage. "I can't bring Berezovsky in on my own. And I need to know what to tell him, concerning his demands."

"Offer him anything he wants, of course. I can arrange a passage out of the country. Money, passport, whatever it takes." Vasin knew that Orlov's answer had come too quickly to be credible. The General was back on familiar ground now, in charge, listing his powers. "I brought your precious Kuznetsov. I brought you men. Reliable men. Get Berezovsky to Moscow by any means necessary. When you do, I make you this promise: the past will be forgotten. You will remain in the capital with me, at my right hand."

Vasin stood to attention and saluted.

"*Slushayus, tovarishch general.* I obey, Comrade General."

"At ease, Colonel. Dismissed."

The formality of the exchange seemed to have rebalanced the order of Orlov's world. Vasin was ready to be his obedient little fly once more.

"One more thing about tonight, General. Berezovsky is *kontora*-trained. If he spots surveillance . . ."

"Understood, Sasha. This is your show now."

By which Orlov meant, if you screw up, it's your head.

# 11

Vasin found Kuznetsov moping in the corridor.

"Again, Vasin, you pull me out of my quiet life into some crazy top-secret adventure of yours. *Again?* Let me tell you, the joke's wearing thin."

Vasin could not risk letting his old comrade in on the truth until they had time alone, away from the brooding presence of Orlov and his legion of informers. And Vasin needed to be sure that Kuznetsov wasn't one of them.

Bringing Kuznetsov in had been a gamble. Could an appeal to basic decency overcome the man's deep cynicism and basic survival instincts? Could Vasin turn the man who had been, variously, his handler, his protector, his agent, and his pawn into an ally? A friend, even?

Vasin had no choice but to try. His own fate was in the hands of the man he called Berezovsky. He had told Orlov one absolute truth: Vasin could not handle a man as slippery and desperate as Berezovsky on his own.

"I promise you this will be worth the trouble, Kuznetsov."

"Just tell me, who are we saving this time? The USSR? The world? Preventing World War Three, once more?"

Vasin grinned wearily and put a hand on his old comrade's shoulder.

"This time? Maybe just me."

# 12

As far as Vasin could tell, he was free of Orlov's eyes as he approached the Vorkuta Miners' House of Culture. For two hours he'd ridden buses from one grim end of the city and its suburbs to the other, dry-cleaned himself through the miserable Univermag department store and the city's smelly produce market.

The theater had been built a decade earlier in the most pompous Stalinist style. A pillared portico three stories high dominated a wide square planted with young, spindly trees. An empty plinth in the center of the square marked the former site of a statue of a former man—maybe Stalin himself, maybe some henchman of his who built this impossible Soviet city in the high Arctic on the backs of a hundred thousand convict slaves. The stateless space was a sign of the times, common to all Soviet towns—the old heroes had fallen but no new ones had yet replaced them.

Vasin scanned the snow-dusted marble steps and the neatly shoveled snowbanks on the sides of the paths and pavements. The show tonight was the ballet *Giselle,* a tour by the Sverdlovsk State ballet troupe. What crimes had the unfortunate ballerinas committed to land a gig in this freezing hellhole? Vasin wondered. Groups of women and children hurried from the bus stops into the building. A few young men, some clutching boxes of chocolates in lieu of unobtainable fresh flowers, waited in the chilly portico for their dates. A memory from his ancient policing days flashed into Vasin's mind. He'd once mentioned to his detective colleagues that he was taking his wife, Vera, to the ballet, causing general amusement. *"Ballet?"* they had scoffed. "You've already got her into bed, fool!"

One by one the dates arrived, their hair permed and carefully wrapped in bright woolen scarves. The pretheater crowd thinned. Vasin went inside, scanning the people queuing for the coat checks. No sign of Orlov's men—now Vasin's men—nor of Kozlov or his dangerous associate.

And no sign of Berezovsky either.

The third bell rang, summoning stragglers into a trot as they hurried into the auditorium. Vasin stood alone in the lobby under the unsympathetic eyes of a line of elderly coat-check ladies. To them, he was another middle-aged man stood up by his mistress. Instead of sympathy, his predicament seemed to trigger only mocking glances.

—

Back in the lobby of the Red Star Hotel, as Vasin had feared and half expected, the Macedonian sat slumped in an armchair. He glowered with undisguised hostility as Vasin hurried past him to the lifts.

The suite was empty. Vasin ran to the wardrobe and shook out his rucksack on the floor. The cash, close to two thousand rubles, was gone, along with the blank movement orders and the official stamps.

Vasin realized with a sensation like a punch in the gut that he'd been played.

Berezovsky was gone.

# PART FIVE

# 10–14 DECEMBER 1963

If you live among wolves, you have to act like a wolf.

—NIKITA KHRUSHCHEV

# 1

*Vorkuta*

Vasin stormed into the hotel restaurant. Six Special Cases men, plus Kuznetsov, sat at a long table morosely slurping the Red Star's pale beetroot soup. At least they were drinking nothing stronger than Borjomi mineral water.

"Where's Orlov?"

Kuznetsov, a spoon in his right hand, made an upward flapping gesture with his left. A couple of the older men continued to eat, ignoring Vasin. The others dutifully laid down their spoons to look at him in sullen obedience.

Vasin's hellish year in Vorkuta had given him a hard edge. And it had taught him that tolerating insolence was fatal to any commander.

"What does *that* mean, Comrade Major?" Vasin growled, mocking Kuznetsov's flapping gesture. All seven men had stopped eating now. Kuznetsov took a long moment to wipe his mouth on a napkin before answering.

"General Orlov has had to fly back to Moscow, Comrade Colonel." Kuznetsov's voice was flat.

"Good. It's just us, then. Berezovsky has run. We're going into action. Your names?"

The men answered with their names and ranks, up and down the table: two junior sergeants, two senior, and two senior lieutenants. Kuznetsov merely crossed his arms and fixed Vasin with a resentful stare.

"You." Vasin pointed to the smartest looking of the bunch. "Go to the lobby, get on the phone, and find out what planes left Vorkuta airport today. Scheduled and unscheduled. Wait at reception till I call you. And you." Vasin selected the youngest man, a ruggedly handsome village bully with a mop of blond hair who looked handy with his fists. "You, Sergeant Bodrov, have a special mission. There's a man in the lobby, and you are going to make sure he knows he's being watched. If he tries to leave, you're going to fight him. Make sure he throws the first punch. My advice—don't try to box him. Get him to the ground for as long as it takes for the hotel security to come. Insist on filing a police complaint. He must be detained until the cops come. Do not let him out of your sight. Got it?"

"Comrade Colonel, you want me to—" stammered Bodrov.

"Tell me which part you didn't understand, Sergeant."

The man looked desperately around at his comrades, who suppressed smirks. Vasin pointed to a second young officer.

"Good. You stay as well, give the Sergeant here moral support. The rest of you, get on a bus to the train station. Leave quietly through the service door. And as for you, Major . . ." Vasin turned to Kuznetsov and lowered his voice. "*We* travel by taxi, old man."

# 2

Kuznetsov hunched into the upturned lapels of his coat as a snow flurry whipped across the pavement in front of the taxi rank.

"Vadim. Old Comrade, you need to know four things," said Vasin, his voice raised over the wind. "One, we have to find a man who fled this hotel sometime after eight this morning. Two, he has a couple of thousand rubles in his pocket, a fistful of blank movement orders, and an Interior Ministry uniform. Three, he's a trained First Chief Directorate officer. And finally, there's a team from his old department on his trail, too."

Kuznetsov said nothing. Vasin tried to make his voice as ingratiating as possible.

"I'm sorry to get you into this. Really. Now, let's get moving."

"As you say, Commander." Kuznetsov's answer was a deliberate parody of a gruff taxi driver's drawl. The tiny spark of humor drew the first smile to cross Vasin's face in days. He opened the door of the taxi at the head of the rank and bundled Kuznetsov inside for the short ride to the station.

After a few minutes contemplating the sagging wooden barracks of the city's outskirts, Kuznetsov turned to Vasin.

"You're sure your friend didn't take a car out of Vorkuta? A bus? A truck?"

Their driver answered for Vasin, twisting backward to address his ignorant passenger.

"Car? You must be joking. Vorkuta is an *island*. You didn't know that? No roads out. No roads to the rest of Russia before Ukhta. Seven hundred kilometers south of here. We just got the railway."

"Only way out is plane or train," said Vasin, finishing the driver's part.

"Plane, train, or *grave*." The man grunted, hauling the wheel of his Volga-21 to steer the heavy sedan into the station's forecourt. "*Grave's* most common way outta this fuckin' place. Eighty-eight kopecks. Call it a round ruble."

As Vasin hunted for change the driver eyed them in the rearview mirror.

"No trains out tonight. You know that, right? If you comrades are looking for some company this evening, my wife's sister's in town. Just divorced, lovely girl, lonely . . ." His voice trailed off as Vasin handed over the exact fare. "Fine. Suit yourselves."

# 3

Two trains had left that day down the single-track line that was Vorkuta's only connection to the rest of the world. One, bound for Leningrad, had left at 09:32. The other, to Adler on the Black Sea coast, at 11:45. Vasin did a quick calculation. He had last seen

Berezovsky at the hotel just before 08:30. The man had cash—the payroll cash—but to get on a train Berezovsky would need ID. No Soviet citizen could buy a train ticket without a passport or military identity card. There was not enough time for him to steal papers and make the 09:32. A call to the Special Cases man at the Red Star Hotel confirmed that only one scheduled flight left that day, for Perm, at 07:20. Too early. Two other flights, including Orlov's KGB An-24, bound for Moscow, were private military planes. The Adler train was the fugitive's only option.

It was now past eight p.m., with no trains due for eleven hours, when the express from Leningrad was scheduled to arrive at this, the deadest of the All-Union Soviet Railways dead ends. But this was the USSR, so a full night shift of staff was just clocking in despite not having a damn thing to do until morning.

Vasin rapped on the ticket window, summoning the duty manager. The passenger records for the Adler train needed to be crosschecked with documents reported missing. On cue, the municipal bus arrived with Orlov's three officers inside. Vasin dispatched one of them to the station's police office, the first port of call for any travelers missing their passports, and another by taxi to Vorkuta's central police station.

With so many professionals rifling through the railway office's records and questioning the cops, it took less than an hour to find Berezovsky's new identity. Captain Nikolai Mikhailovich Mironov had reported his passport and Army ID stolen while at breakfast at the Cafe Tsentralny in Vorkuta that very morning. And a little later, one Captain Mironov had bought a soft-class ticket an hour before the 11:45 train departed. Carriage 6, berth number 14. His ticket's destination? All the way through to the end of the line, the tropical Black Sea coast, four and a half days' journey to the south.

Got the bastard.

The man that Vasin had deputized as backup at the Red Star Hotel appeared, flustered and sporting a black eye. Sergeant Bodrov had done as ordered: started a fight as soon as the Macedonian realized that Orlov's party had quit the hotel. And now Bodrov was in the hospital with a cracked jaw and bruised ribs. Vasin was too distracted to spare much sympathy.

"And what about the giant?"

"He's being held in the police precinct, sir. Overnight."

"Excellent. Carry on."

The battered officer nodded respectfully. Belatedly, Vasin realized that he should say something encouraging, but he checked himself. Orlov was right about another thing: being an asshole did get you respect in this god-awful world.

# 4

Vasin and Kuznetsov conferred in the station's empty waiting room. In front of them was an enormous plate-glass covered railway map of the USSR. Crossing it, in a vertical north-south meander, was the line that wound from Vorkuta down to where the foothills of the Caucasus rose from the Black Sea coast.

"In twenty minutes they're due at Mikun," said Vasin, tracing the train's progress against the timetable and the waiting room clock. It was now 22:13. "A thirty-two-minute stop, must be a coaling station. Or a place they switch locomotives. We'll call on the railway's internal phone system and have him taken into police custody."

Kuznetsov grunted noncommittally, his eyes still on the map.

"If I were traveling on a stolen passport on a long-distance train, sitting in a seat in a compartment which had been logged back where I bought my ticket . . . well. I'd be pretty keen to get off. Think about it, Vasin. Especially if the *kontora* was on my trail." Kuznetsov tapped the map with a finger. "The first stop with a road connection to the rest of Russia is here. Ukhta. Mikun is here, way south. So, by all means put a call through. Get the attendant for carriage six on the phone and order the passenger in berth fourteen detained. But a million rubles says he's long gone."

Vasin checked the timetable again. Berezovsky would have reached Ukhta at 18:32, the exact time of their appointed meeting at the Vorkuta theater.

"Damn."

It took fifteen minutes to connect a call to Mikun Station and fifteen more for the stammering, youthful-sounding attendant's voice to come on the crackling line and prove Kuznetsov right. Passenger Mironov had left his compartment at Sosnogorsk, a stop eleven kilometers short of Ukhta. The attendant had thought he'd gone to the restaurant carriage, but the man never came back.

# 5

Vasin and Kuznetsov stood in a glassed-in atrium outside the station entrance. Vasin sucked down his Orbita cigarette, panic flickering in his chest like a kindling fire.

"We've lost him. What do we do now?"

"*Do?* We put ourselves into your man's head, Vasin. Step by step. Berezovsky's priority will be to get rid of his Mironov ID and steal a new one. To do that he needs a crowded public place. We know he hopped off the train just short of Ukhta at some remote rail junction. That was smart. He was afraid we'd pick up his trail sooner and arrange a welcome party. Sosnogorsk is, what, eleven kilometers from Ukhta. Probably thumbed a lift into town. And that's where he is, right now, lying low in Ukhta."

"Pure guesswork. But we should check the hotels."

"Vasin, catch up. He's way ahead of you. Obviously, he's ditched the Mironov papers. I'd bet they're still on the train, in the ashes of the compartment's stove. He'll need new papers to register in a hotel. Risky. No, I reckon he's holed up somewhere private. With two thousand rubles in his pocket, he could easily find a taxi driver who'd take him to a whore."

Prostitution was illegal in the USSR, of course. But as every adult

Soviet citizen knew, the country was full of part-time semiprofessional women ready to turn a trick to earn a bit of housekeeping money.

"Okay, let's say he's in Ukhta. He knows we're on his trail, so he can't risk staying. The next train through isn't till tomorrow, but we'll be watching. He can't risk the train either."

"Right. Your brain's in gear, finally, Vasin. He'll head south by road, first thing in the morning. Hire a private car, or more likely catch a lift on a long-distance truck. Let's take another look at that railway map."

The lonely branch line that led north to Vorkuta joined the USSR's main railway network at Kirov. Kuznetsov tapped a finger on the glass.

"There. From Kirov he could take the Trans-Siberian, east or west. Connections to Moscow and Leningrad, here. Connections to Adler and the south this way."

"I don't know, Vadim. Why wouldn't he steal a car? Stick with riding trucks? Get on a plane?"

"Riding trucks all the way across the Soviet Union would take weeks. Steal a car and any local traffic cop could stop him and radio in the number. As for a plane: it's a possibility. But up here in the north, in these shitty little towns? There are maybe a couple of dozen passengers on each flight. He knows we would get his description to all likely airports. No. Trains are much safer. Hundreds of passengers. Just a cursory document check to buy a ticket. Easier to melt into the crowd. I think he'll take his time creeping into Kirov by bus or truck, then make a break for it on an express train. Except we don't know in which direction."

Berezovsky had told Vasin his family lived in Moscow, but he'd chosen to meet them in Leningrad. He'd spent a few days there before deciding to approach Orlov. Which meant he had friends there. And Leningrad was just half a day's drive from the Finnish border.

"He's going to Leningrad."

"Are you sure?"

"Leningrad. He has people there." Vasin peered closely at the map. "If we wait for him at Kirov Station, we could spook him. So we stake out this place, right here. Kotelnich. One hour, forty-eight minutes west of Kirov. Every train going west from Kirov has to go through it. If we check them all, we'll find him."

Kuznetsov grimaced thoughtfully at the map for a few moments before nodding.

"Good a plan as any. Now are you going to finally tell me what this is all about?"

Vasin was grateful for Kuznetsov's dry professionalism and his basic intelligence. It made the urgency of knowing that Berezovsky was moving, inexorably, away from them somehow easier to bear. Kuznetsov needed to be told about the secret Kennedy file Vasin hoped to find in Leningrad. But not before Kuznetsov agreed to Vasin's terms.

"I will, Vadim, I promise. First, we have to get out of Vorkuta. The stunt we pulled at the hotel got that gorilla out of our hair for a night. But Kozlov will have sprung him from jail first thing in the morning. They'll know that Berezovsky has fled and he'll be waiting for us to lead them to their man."

"You want to get an eight-man team from Vorkuta to Kirov, invisibly, and preferably before morning. Do I have it right, Sasha?"

"Not the whole team, Kuznetsov. Just you and me."

# 6

Vasin and Kuznetsov pulled up outside Vorkuta's humble aerodrome shortly before four in the morning. The building was unlit except for a single night watchman's lamp. Just one flight was scheduled to leave that day, the 06:30 to Perm, eleven hundred kilometers due south. From there it was only four hundred kilometers west to Kirov. By Siberian standards, just a short hop.

Most likely, there would be no tickets and they'd have to pull rank and kick off a couple of civilian passengers. Vasin would leave the talking to Kuznetsov, not only because of his natural talents as a blustering asshole but also because he had an all-powerful KGB ID. Vasin was merely Interior Ministry. They waited in the taxi, the meter ticking, until an early bus brought in the bleary-eyed staff.

Passengers began to arrive. An elderly pair of brothers attempted, halfheartedly, to argue against being bumped from the flight with some story about a dying relative. But their protests were doomed. The stony-faced flight manager's choice was final. State security trumped family medical emergencies. As the Arctic wind moaned past the waiting room windows, Vasin nervously munched a dry bun he'd managed to scrounge from the hotel kitchen, scoping the forecourt for signs of pursuit.

The plane landed half an hour late. A flurry of activity began as the An-24 trundled up to the terminal, its engines spluttering and coughing alarmingly. There was a rush to refuel before the airframe started to ice up, a scramble of passengers clambering up the steel steps to take their places in the fifty-seat plane. The stairs were stowed and the door pulled shut. The engines spooled up; the generator and fuel trucks backed off, and Vasin dared to relax. They were finally getting away from this hellish place.

But no. Instead of revving up to taxi, the engines slowed back down to an idle. The stewardess unbolted and reopened the door. A pair of men hurried across the floodlit patch of ice in front of the terminal, accompanied by the tubby Aeroflot flight manager.

"Passengers Lykov, A., and Lykova, V. Your seats have been requisitioned."

Silence. The unfortunate Lykovs maybe imagined that if they kept silent they could stay on board. Finally, a young couple sitting right next to Vasin and Kuznetsov slowly rose, pulled their hand luggage off the rack, and left the aircraft without protest. In their place, two figures in military greatcoats and fur hats boarded the plane.

Major Kozlov paused to scan the passengers, his eyes settling on Vasin. Behind him, his hulking subordinate carried his precious rifle in its sheepskin case. His bruised face smoldered with violence.

"Welcome to Aeroflot Flight SU-225, Vorkuta to Perm," announced the purser on the intercom as the stewardess resealed the door. "Your seatbelts must be fastened for takeoff and landing. Please note that smoking is permitted only in rows nine to thirteen and only after the NO SMOKING signs have been switched off."

Kozlov and his man took their places, right across the aisle.

"Good morning, Comrades," said Vasin, fighting to keep his voice even. "Have you met my colleague, Major Kuznetsov?"

"Morning, Colonel," replied Kozlov. He suppressed a triumphant smirk. "You'll remember Sergeant Markov."

The Macedonian glowered at Vasin with eyes as black as gun bores. If the dirty look had been a punch it would have knocked Vasin clean through the window.

"He certainly remembers you."

# 7

The aircraft followed the route of the railway and then the main road from town to town, airfield to airfield, rather than risk a beeline over the endless Siberian forest. Dawn was still hours away, and Vasin peered out over settlements glowing like islands of light in a vast sea of black woodland, his fists clenched on the armrests as the little plane lurched and plunged southward.

He couldn't do this anymore. Vasin's reserves of strength, and his nerves, were tapped out. Kozlov had tracked them down easily enough; it would hardly take a genius to check that day's flight out of Vorkuta once the desk clerk or some unknown watcher tipped him off that Vasin and Kuznetsov had left the hotel.

Beside him, in the window seat, Kuznetsov sat hunched and thoughtful. After half an hour of brooding he turned to speak into Vasin's ear.

The roar of the engines made discreet conversation possible, even a couple of yards from their adversaries. Vasin shook his head. He could not summon the will to keep running. He was almost ready to just tell Kozlov their guesses about where his man was and accept the consequences.

Vasin took a moment to ride out a particularly sickening lurch and breathed deep.

"Yes, Kuznetsov."

"Our friend Comrade Berezovsky had a pretty good system going, this hopping on and off trains before the terminus. We'll do the same. At Perm aerodrome we get a taxi. Our two friends will get the next one, follow us into town. We ride around till we lose them. Then hit the gas and head to the first station between Perm and Kirov and get on the first train."

"We *lose* them. Just like that."

"Thought you'd been a cop yourself, Vasin. Have you ever tried following a car in moving traffic, with no backup? In a taxi, with a good, wily driver—we'll lose them in half an hour. Tops."

"What makes you think they won't have backup?"

"Their department of the *kontora*"—Kuznetsov raised a single finger to suggest the First Chief Directorate—"is focused on enemies abroad. They have no business in Perm, no contacts or resources there. You saw how they sprinted for the plane? I bet they had no time to call or telegraph ahead for help. But they will, if we give them time—so we keep them moving. Forgo the delights of lovely Perm and get on the first train to Kirov. It's a seven-and-a-half-hour journey. We'll be there by dinner, while our friends run up their taxi bill, circling around Perm looking for us."

# 8

Train 001E pulled into the tiny station of Vereshchagino on the dot of 11:44. The locomotive was a powerful, high-wheeled engine with a huge red star emblazoned on the front of its boiler. The train it hauled was unusually long. Each of the first set of carriages that clattered past Vasin and Kuznetsov bore the same stenciled destination plate: 001E: VLADIVOSTOK–MOSCOW. The daily Trans-Siberian Express. Lacy curtains decorated the windows of first class, cotton ones for second, roll-down leatherette blinds for *platzkart,* third class. No faces peered out of the windows. The passengers on this part of the train had already been aboard for five days of their seven-day, nine-thousand-kilometer journey. They'd evidently tired of views of snowbound forests.

A gaggle of miscellaneous carriages had been coupled behind the Trans-Siberian cars. Like hitchhikers, they would be uncoupled farther down the line and hooked on to different trains to different destinations. 091: NOVOKUZNETSK–LENINGRAD, read the plaque on one of the carriages that rolled past Vasin and Kuznetsov. 063: TOBOLSK–VOLOGDA was the next. The final two-carriage section was the humblest, due to part company from the express first: 145: SVERDLOVSK–KIROV.

With a prolonged squeal of brakes, the train slid to a halt. No doors opened. Vereshchagino was an engine depot where the locomotives were swapped out for the next leg of the journey. It was barely a village, just a few sagging houses apparently sinking into the earth like listing ships, a line of telegraph poles, a pair of thin cows. Vasin could just see the gray form of their taxi bouncing down the potholed road into the distance, back toward the main Perm–Moscow highway forty kilometers to the south. The driver, a grinning rogue with steel teeth, had fifty of Kuznetsov's rubles in his pocket and instructions to go straight home and speak to nobody about his passengers. The wily old man had indeed lost their pursuers in under twenty minutes, faster than Kuznetsov had predicted, executing a neat dash over a changing traffic light followed by a swerving progress through the courtyards of downtown Perm. Kuznetsov, sitting up front, grinned contentedly all the way to Vereshchagino.

Vasin banged on the door of the last carriage, which a haggard conductress opened after a long pause.

"Two tickets to Kirov."

She frowned disapprovingly at being made to do her job, fished out a book of tickets and a pen from her apron.

"Six rubles forty. Each."

Kuznetsov's grin widened. Long-distance tickets could be bought only at mainline stations, the passengers' details logged in booking-office ledgers. But local trains, like buses, could be boarded anywhere, and the passengers' names were recorded nowhere at all.

The carriage was of prewar manufacture, furnished with sturdy wooden benches. There were some twenty passengers on board, mostly farmers and workers. Their belongings were stuffed onto the overhead racks in sacks, bundles, and the occasional leaking leather suitcase. The carriage was pervaded by a distinct farmyard smell, rotting straw and wet dog, stagnant socks, chicken grease, spilled beer. Two Soviet apparatchiks—Vasin in an officer's greatcoat and Kuznetsov in a conspicuously luxurious woolen overcoat—attracted stares. Kuznetsov wrinkled his nose at the powerful odor. Without putting down his smart leather grip bag, he turned on his heel and pushed past the conductress.

"Anyone wants to see our tickets, we'll be in the restaurant car."

# 9

Kuznetsov ripped the steel cap off the cognac bottle, tossed it under the table, and poured two large glasses. The tablecloth was fresh; there were just two of them sitting at the table. No *kontora* ID card had been needed to get this VIP treatment. Kuznetsov had the demeanor, the clothes, the cheery I'm-a-big-tipper look that waiters understood instinctively. A young couple had been hastily evicted from their places midmeal and squeezed in somewhere else; table linen had been quickly dug out and snapped straight personally by the restaurant carriage manager.

"To the friendship of peoples," intoned Kuznetsov, knocking

back half the glass and reaching for a plate of pickled mushrooms from the cook's private stock. Vasin puffed out his mouth as the fiery Armenian brandy went down. It had been a while since he last drank. With a shudder, he remembered the fate of his previous drinking companions.

"Apparently, Vasin, I'm the only person in the world able to save your sorry backside. This is the part where you finally tell me what the hell this goose chase is all about."

Vasin smiled crookedly. They might not be exactly friends, but he was absurdly glad to have his old colleague by his side. Kuznetsov was the only person to whom Vasin could turn to get himself off the hook, and Orlov onto it.

"Vadim, this is a big game. The biggest of your life. It's going to be dangerous."

Kuznetsov poured two more glasses. Plates of pungent borscht soup, the thickest stuff, scooped up from the bottom of the pot, were served by a middle-aged waitress. She'd done her makeup while the soup was warming.

"It's not like you to be melodramatic, Vasin. I thought your hard ass would become even harder up in that Arctic shithole. Enough with the coyness. This isn't a Communist Youth dance, and I'm not trying to get your bra undone. Orlov pulled me off assignment in Moscow at an hour's notice and told me you needed my help. That was an order, so here I am. Now: talk to me."

"This is about sinking Orlov. For good."

Kuznetsov leaned back in his seat and ran a hand down his face.

"Knowing you as well as I, unfortunately, do, I did have my suspicions. This is a private Vasin vendetta that you have dragged me into."

"No, Vadim. It's not a private vendetta." Vasin reached across the table and grabbed Kuznetsov's wrist. The fire of the booze and his friend's contemptuous tone had sparked something angry and desperate in Vasin. He badly needed a friend, an ally. "I promise you I wanted no part in this. I didn't ask Orlov to send this man Berezovsky up to Vorkuta. I didn't want to murder two Special Cases officers on Orlov's fucking orders. I didn't ask to be told that some *kontora* madmen organized the murder of the President of the fucking USA."

Kuznetsov's face went very pale. He looked around at the chattering, oblivious diners in the car and turned back to lock his gaze once more with Vasin's. The sarcastic sneer had gone from Kuznetsov's mouth, along with the usual mocking humor in his eyes.

"Mother of God. *Kennedy?* Start from the beginning."

# 10

Heavy snow-clouds dragged black tendrils across the sky like ink drops spreading in a beaker. The restaurant car kitchen had closed after a prolonged clatter of pots, pans, and splashing water, but Vasin and Kuznetsov sat on. The bright electric light from the train windows illuminated endless, flitting stands of pine and birch woods. The cognac bottle was nearly drained.

"Let me get this right. We need to find some bigwig who can muzzle Kozlov and his First Department crew. *And* take out Orlov. Plus keep the Kennedy secret safe. And us alive. That's the riddle, correct?" Kuznetsov was hunched forward, his fingers poised on his temples. "And before we do that, we have to find the man Berezovsky and persuade him to give us his file. Which is also his life insurance policy. That about the shape of it?"

"Pretty much." The booze that at first had fired Vasin's anger was now leading him on a steep descent into brooding melancholy. "Any ideas?"

Kuznetsov poured the last drops into their glasses.

"Here is what I can do for you. I can get off this train at Kirov, fly to Moscow. Tell Orlov that you have gone crazy and our mission has failed. Get back to my life. Leave you to yours. But then . . ." Kuznetsov knocked back the last of the cognac. "That would make me the same as all the other assholes at the *kontora* who turn a blind eye. Before you get any ideas, I'm not converted to the Vasin doctrine of constantly trying to save the world. A couple of months ago, I *would* have got on the next plane, and advised you to do the same. Throw yourself on Orlov's mercy. Hope Kozlov and his gang never find you."

"What's changed your mind?"

"There is a rumor from Semichastny's office." Vladimir Semichastny was the KGB's veteran director. Politburo big beast. As formidable a survivor as Orlov himself. "After the fiasco with our missiles in Cuba last year, Khrushchev's looking like a spent force. People are talking about a change at the top. Very quietly. Leonid Brezhnev is making moves. Don't you ever read *Pravda*? Brezhnev is head of the Presidium of the Central Committee. Semichastny's on the fence for the moment. He wants to come out on the right side of this, and he needs ammunition if he's to move against his rivals in the *kontora*. This could be just what he's looking for. Big enough to justify a quick, ruthless purge, when the time comes."

"Orlov's got secret files on everybody at the top of the Party and the KGB. The Director needs him as an ally. Why would Semichastny want to move against Orlov?"

"The Director needs Orlov's *files*. The secrets are the power. Orlov just happens to be their custodian. That's the trouble when you get as powerful as Orlov, so gorged with compromising materials on so many powerful men. Those self-same powerful men hate you as much as they fear you. And they want you gone. It was the same with Beria, back in 'fifty-three. The all-powerful head of State Security held the entire Politburo's lives in his hand. Right up until the Politburo had him kidnapped right out of the Kremlin. And shot him."

"I know the story. But who knows who Berezovsky names in his file? It might implicate the wrong people. And it may be useless to Semichastny."

"Vasin, you were at the *kontora*, what, five years? All they need is a serious crime as the foundation. They make up the rest, put whoever needs to be guilty in the frame. And in this case, the conspiracy is so dangerous that it has to remain a top state secret forever."

"Where does that leave us?" It pleased Vasin to finally use that word. At long last, there was an "us."

"On the winning side, hopefully. Change of leadership means the old guard gets kicked out. New guard comes rolling in. Look at what happened after Comrade Stalin's death. New men arrived, like Orlov. Like Semichastny. Now, *they're* the old guard. It's time for new blood."

"Never suspected you of ambition, old man. *General* Vadim Kuznetsov?"

"Has a ring to it, no? It sounds better than Major Kuznetsov."

"If you like that kind of thing."

"That's your problem isn't it, Vasin? No politics or guile in you. No ruthlessness."

"You want to take this to Semichastny."

"No. We take this direct to *Brezhnev*."

"How? Are you now connected enough to call his office and make an appointment?"

Kuznetsov cracked a knowing smile.

"No, Vasin. You are. You will go through Katya."

Kuznetsov's arch tone and straight look could mean only one thing—he was talking about Katya Orlova. The boss's wife. And Vasin's former mistress. He'd had no idea that Kuznetsov knew.

"I was friendly with Katya, once. And?"

"She never mentioned her friend Galya?"

"I remember Galya."

"Galya is Galina Leonidovna *Brezhneva*. Brezhnev's daughter."

Vasin looked at Kuznetsov quizzically.

"You're very well informed."

"You know: live with wolves, howl like a wolf."

"Right. Except right now we're dividing up the skin of a wolf we haven't caught yet. And even if we do find Berezovsky, we still have to persuade him to tell us where the damn file is."

"Leave that part to me, Vasin. I can be *very* persuasive."

# 11

After three days, Vasin was starting to hate Kirillovka as intensely as he'd despised any Soviet provincial backwater he'd ever visited. The village straggled along a single, rutted lane that ran parallel to the railway yards. A long, barnlike building housed the local LesSovKhoz sawmill, whose machinery shrieked and whined at all hours. The only hot food available was boiled sausages at the sawmill's miserable cafeteria or the revolting boiled buckwheat and cabbage soup at the lopsided village house where they'd rented a room. Their landlady, a slobbering drunk who called herself Babka Simka, muttered in the night as she banged about her cockroach-infested kitchen.

Kirillovka was the first stop west of Kirov, forty-two minutes out of town. Six westbound trains stopped there each day to take on fresh water for the engine and the carriages' washing and toilet tanks, each with a scheduled eighteen- to twenty-five-minute stop. Going down every train was a rush, just a few minutes to barge through every compartment, unceremoniously peer into every male passenger's face, pursued, more often than not, by an indignant conductress. Worst of all, two of the trains arrived in the middle of the night, forcing Vasin and Kuznetsov to haul themselves out of their warm beds and trudge through the freezing night to the station to perform their ritual search.

The strain was beginning to tell on Kuznetsov, too. By dawn on the third day, as the pair stood shivering on the cold platform waiting, Vasin's brilliant plan for intercepting Berezovsky began to seem threadbare to the point of craziness. Neither man had been able to face the moldy squalor of the sawmill bathhouse, so both were starting to look and smell like tramps. Little wonder that the up-and-down glances of each train captain had become more and more suspicious every time an increasingly disheveled Kuznetsov demanded to search the train, flashing his *kontora* identity card.

The Irkutsk–Leningrad express pulled in exactly on time at

10:04. Wearily, Kuznetsov clambered aboard, followed by Vasin, and they began their now-familiar drill of sliding open door after door. Every compartment had its own smell, funky humanity flavored with pickled garlic, roast chicken, mold, feet, and occasionally sex. In almost every one, Vasin found himself grumpily sworn at as he shook sleepers awake.

Nothing in first class. Nothing in second. And then, halfway down the final hard-class *platskart* compartment Vasin froze. Even without seeing the face of the sleeping man wrapped in an Army blanket and wearing a greasy farmworker's cap, Vasin knew. He leaned closer, gingerly, and peered into Berezovsky's face. Silently, careful not to wake the sleeper, Vasin drew the conductress aside and sent her to summon the train captain from the intercom in her cubbyhole.

"Keep an eye on him," he hissed to Kuznetsov. "I'm going to fetch our stuff."

By the time Vasin returned with Kuznetsov's grip and his own rucksack slung over his back, a small crowd had gathered in *platzkart* carriage number 4. Berezovsky sat bleary and alone in the now-vacated open-sided compartment, watched over by Kuznetsov and three conductors. When he saw Vasin, Berezovsky's tense face relaxed. He knew he'd been caught. But not, until the moment the familiar face of Vasin appeared, by whom.

"Look how pleased he is to see you!" said Kuznetsov to Vasin deadpan, before turning to the fugitive. "Congratulations, Comrade. Time for more civilized accommodation. And a half-decent dinner."

Berezovsky registered surprise for only a split second before acquiescing. As the train jolted into motion, he pulled on a patched workers' coat, grabbed a filthy rucksack from under his bunk, and allowed Vasin and Kuznetsov to lead him to the restaurant car.

# 12

Sitting in silence in the crowded buffet wagon, the three men wolfed down everything the kitchen could provide: sour cabbage, pork chops, mash, tinned peaches. Their hunger and weariness made for something like camaraderie. But Berezovsky answered only in monosyllabic grunts, stealing wary glances at Kuznetsov as he ate. When they'd finished, the harassed waitress shooed them from their places to make way for other diners. No chance of playing the big shots in their reduced, scruffy state.

They settled down in a four-person compartment that the train captain had found for them. All three were anxious, each in his own way. It was Berezovsky who did the best imitation of calm, though he was the one facing the greatest jeopardy. The train was due to arrive in Leningrad in less than seven hours.

Vasin broke the silence.

"We're going to help you, Berezovsky."

The man raised an eyebrow, but said nothing.

"Kuznetsov knows about Kennedy, so we are in the same boat now. You need to get out of the USSR. We need your information to save our backsides from the men who were hunting you. Tell us what you know and you'll be safe. I promise."

Berezovsky's face remained blank.

It's a tactic, Vasin thought. This man had been trained in counterinterrogation by the best in the business. They could threaten him. They could try to kindle his sympathy. Or appeal to his sense of self-preservation. Vasin made a quick calculation, leaned close, and hissed low but very clearly in Berezovsky's ear.

"Let me put this another way. Kuznetsov and I work for General Orlov, your old friend. You're out of the loop, but a major political change is coming and Orlov is tottering. You could put all of us on the winning side."

Vasin shot a glance at Kuznetsov, who looked on in unfeigned dismay at his unexpected gambit of complete honesty. He noticed Berezovsky register the look.

"And there's another side to the story," continued Vasin, implacably. "Your information is valuable only as long as the assholes who ordered the assassination are still in power. If they fall, you've got nothing in your hand. You're trading a currency everyone wants right now. Political wheels are turning. Sell now, and you'll get whatever you want. Or you could wait till the Party pig has flopped over onto its other flank. It will settle that way for another generation. And good luck finding anyone who would trade that file of yours for anything other than a bullet."

Vasin leaned back, exhausted. Abruptly, Berezovsky raised his head and almost smiled as he addressed his captors.

"It's just the two of you, right? On your own, against the system. You've got wind of some office gossip about changes at the top. You've got me and you've inserted yourselves into some grand political scheme you guys cooked up between you. My information, your triumph. Am I right?"

The man's mind was like a razor. Vasin looked across at Kuznetsov and saw the bolt strike home. Kuznetsov inhaled noisily, his gaze fixed malevolently on Berezovsky's.

"You boys have gone rogue," continued Berezovsky, pitiless.

Abruptly, Kuznetsov stood. He put an emphatic hand on Berezovsky's chest, pushing him against the padded seat back with his full weight. His voice came from a dark and violent place Vasin had never witnessed before.

"Listen to me, jailbird. All that matters now is that we have *you*. Vasin? Go get some cuffs from the train captain."

Vasin hesitated, then obeyed.

Vasin returned with a pair of old-fashioned police handcuffs and a meter-long chain with a steel plate marked DANGER: HIGH VOLTAGE attached to it with rings. Kuznetsov ran the chain through the radiator pipe and locked Berezovsky to it by one ankle. His face was dark with anger, and once he'd finished Kuznetsov gestured Vasin into the corridor with a tilt of the head.

Kuznetsov slammed the compartment door closed, leaving Berezovsky alone. He and Vasin leaned on the window side of the train corridor.

"You think this treatment is going to encourage him to cooperate?" Vasin's voice was high and tense.

Kuznetsov took his time before replying, his breathing heavy.

"He was never going to cooperate. Or did you think he was going to be swayed by good fellowship?"

"No, by self-interest."

"You're kidding yourself. We can't do anything for him without help from the top. You think he ever really believed that Orlov would arrange a red carpet for him to defect to the West? Come on, Vasin. That so-called deal he wanted was just a ploy to get you out of the room so that he could do a runner. He's not an idiot. Very far from it. The only way this fucker gets out of the USSR alive is to sell his information to some foreign espionage service. *That's* his escape plan. Don't tell me that thought had never entered your mind."

Vasin looked away. It hadn't.

"Now you want to force him to give up what he knows, Kuznetsov?"

Kuznetsov studied the closed compartment door in front of them, brooding.

"If necessary. Who do you have in Leningrad, Vasin? Anyone official?"

A blank. Then, a memory.

"There is an Estonian I used to work with at Homicide in Moscow. Detective Arvo Laar. He was transferred to some police district in Leningrad last year. Vice squad."

"Good. When we arrive, you're going to call him."

Vasin felt a rising unease in his belly. Berezovsky's words had gotten to him. They *were* rogue. On their own. He felt events skittering out of his control.

"You want me to ask Arvo for a secure and private place where we could keep a totally illegal private prisoner while we interrogate him? You think he's not going to ask any questions?"

As Vasin panicked, Kuznetsov went very calm. He drummed his finger against the train wall.

"Yes, Vasin. You'll ask him to find us somewhere to stay in Leningrad. A discreet place, where the police and *kontora* won't bother us."

"Why the hell would he do that?"

"He thinks you're still KGB, right?"

"Arvo knew that I left Homicide for the *kontora*. No way he could know any more."

"Perfect. Call him as soon as we arrive."

Kuznetsov checked his watch.

"Four hours till Leningrad. I suggest we get some shut-eye in shifts while the other guards our prisoner. I'll take the first watch."

Vasin held his old friend's eye for a long moment.

"This is crazy."

"Risky, maybe. But think of the payoff."

"Fifteen years in jail for kidnapping. Or a bullet in the head from the First Chief Directorate."

"This is *your* fucking play, Vasin. You got me into this. If Berezovsky doesn't come through with the goods, he disappears. We walk out blinking into the sun, hands clean and held wide. We tell Orlov we did what we could—the rest is his problem. Either way, you're clear. Again. Now, pull yourself together."

# PART SIX

# 14–17 DECEMBER 1963

If only there were evil people somewhere insidiously committing evil deeds, and it were necessary only to separate them from the rest of us and destroy them. But the line dividing good and evil cuts through the heart of every human being. And who is willing to destroy a piece of his own heart?

—ALEKSANDR SOLZHENITSYN,
*The Gulag Archipelago*

# 1

*Leningrad, USSR*

At Leningrad's Moskovsky Station, Vasin and Kuznetsov manhandled Berezovsky onto the platform. His right wrist was handcuffed to the handles of both his captors' bags. Less conspicuous than handcuffing his hands together, argued Kuznetsov, and more likely to slow him down in case he tried to bolt. Keeping close to their prisoner on both sides, they shuffled to the taxi rank, squeezing Kuznetsov, the bags, and Berezovsky in the back while Vasin rode shotgun in the front.

"To the Central Telegraph," said Vasin.

The driver, professionally determined not to raise an eyebrow at the sight of a passenger handcuffed to his luggage, ground the heavy Volga into gear and moved off.

Leningrad's main post and telephone office was just as crowded as Vasin had hoped. In his Army-green uniform greatcoat he blended effortlessly into the milling crowds. After a ten-minute wait he reached the window marked DIRECTORY INQUIRIES. He handed over a request slip with the name of his old colleague, and the clerk consulted the alphabetical bank of phone books in front of her. In the USSR, such a sensitive thing as a telephone directory was restricted information. With a slap, the clerk laid the slip with the number Vasin was looking for on the zinc counter—but kept her hand over it until he'd paid the twelve-kopeck fee.

"Arvo Janovich Laar. Lieutenant-Colonel, Leningrad Police. Office: 242 2988."

Vasin joined another queue for the public pay phones. He dialed, and by a miracle it connected immediately. By another, his old friend was in his office and answered on the third ring.

# 2

The 62nd Leningrad Police Precinct headquarters occupied a scruffy prewar brick building stained with urban grime and still pockmarked by wartime shrapnel. It was located behind the sprawl of the Kirov steel works, which belched black smoke from a forest of chimneys.

Laar looked much older than Vasin remembered. His long, melancholic face had sagged into middle-aged jowls and his gray police uniform was tight around the midriff.

"Arvo! You're looking great. It's been what, five years?"

"I thought you secret policemen were supposed to be good at telling lies, Sasha." Laar's voice was as heavily accented as ever, a singsong Scandinavian lilt. "But . . . you are in Interior Ministry uniform, I see. One of us again, Sasha? Had enough of *kontora* work?"

"Ah, Arvo, I wish I could talk about it."

"Above my pay grade?"

"Speaking of pay grades—are those lieutenant-colonel's stars I see there?"

"You are correct. Very obser-vant as ever." Laar's voice carried a blast of nostalgia. He sounded so much like a cartoon Estonian that Vasin had to struggle to suppress a smile.

"Vice squad, I hear?"

"Old news. Now, I am in charge of Unsupervised Children."

"You mean homeless?"

"There are no homeless children in the USSR, Sasha. And there is no unemployment. You know that." Laar's upper lip tightened a little, to signal he was trying to crack a dry joke.

"Of course. Listen, I want to sit down and have a proper catch-up. Next few days. But right now, we need your help."

"We?"

"I am on *kontora* business and have a witness. Very sensitive. Internal KGB affair. We need somewhere to hole up for the next few nights. We . . ." Vasin hesitated before coming out with his request. Laar was so utterly inscrutable that Vasin had no idea how he would react. "We need somewhere to stay where the neighbors won't ask too many questions about comings and goings. Or the local cops."

Laar's eyebrow crept up a fraction of an inch.

"Yes. I know a place. A Finnish comrade runs it. She is discreet. If you have money, of course, to compensate her."

"*Runs* it? Like a private hotel?"

"Sasha, this place is a brothel." This time Laar actually smiled. "Though of course there are no prostitutes in the Soviet Union, either. But if you promise me my friend will not get into trouble, I will telephone her."

A *brothel*? Actually—not the worst place to hide. Secure. Under police protection. Bedding and catering provided, presumably. Vasin grabbed his old colleague in a rough bear hug, kissing him on the cheek for good measure.

# 3

The Petrovsky Embankment overlooked the broad expanse of the Neva River, half a kilometer wide and covered in broken ice. On the opposite bank stood the baroque splendor of the Winter Palace. The address Laar had given Vasin was a soaring Stalin-era apartment complex that took up an entire city block. Leaving Kuznetsov and Berezovsky sitting in tense silence in the taxi once more, Vasin made his way through a high arch. A long building with a continuous row of unusually high windows on the second floor stood in the center of the courtyard, screened by bushes and birch trees. A sign in ministerial yellow on red by the second entranceway read, "USSR ALL-UNION MINISTRY OF CULTURE—LENINGRAD ACADEMY OF ARTS."

Of course. Artists' studios. Discreet, as Laar had said. And no nighttime residents.

A husky female voice answered the intercom and instructed Vasin to come up to studio 9. A tall woman in her fifties stood at the top of the stairs, her frizzled hair and silk kimono backlit by low, pink lamplight streaming from the open front door. She smoked a cigarette in a long holder, and her raddled drinker's face was heavily made up.

"Comrade Rosa Mäkinen?"

The woman gave Vasin a long, appraising look and gestured him inside, double-locking the heavy door behind them. Rosa led him through a short vestibule into a large double-height studio. One wall was made up entirely of large plate-glass windows, and the space was dotted with armchairs, sofas, and tables. Canvases were stacked all around, and the walls were filled with a motley collection of oil paintings. The place stank of perfume, spilled wine, and cigarette smoke.

"Arvo said there were three of you." Rosa's voice was smoke cured. She did not invite Vasin to sit.

"Yes, there are three of us. But one is someone we need to keep . . . secure."

"There'll be no trouble for my girls? Or the clients?"

"No trouble. But Arvo said you could keep this secret."

Rosa shook another cigarette from a pack on the table. Imported North State reds, a luxury Finnish brand, Vasin noticed.

"We can keep secrets, Colonel. How many rooms you need?"

"Just one room. And meals. At least two of us will be here around the clock."

The madam lit up with a gold Ronson lighter, took a deep lungful of smoke, and exhaled slowly.

"Fine. It'll be a hundred."

A hundred rubles was half a policeman's monthly salary.

"A hundred rubles a week?"

"A *night*. A hundred a night. Lost earnings. Overheads to pay. Charitable contributions to the police. If you can't afford it . . ."

"We can." Vasin knew he was in no position to bargain.

"Fine. I'll need a week's rent in advance. And, no uniforms around here. Makes the clients nervous."

# 4

"Let me get this straight."

Berezovsky was perched on the edge of an enormous double bed that was covered in a garish satin drape. He was dressed in an ill-fitting shirt, too-tight trousers, and a brightly patterned synthetic sweater—the best that Vasin had been able to find at the DLT, Leningrad's central department store, in a rushed half hour before closing time.

"You claim there's this great political game afoot." Berezovsky leaned toward Vasin and Kuznetsov, who sat in a pair of pink armchairs at the foot of the bed. "And you plan to take my dossier, hawk it about to the Politburo players you think are going to win. And if one of them bites, you produce me to corroborate my story. Then, in time, the grateful victors reward me with a new identity and a one-way ticket to a new life in the West. Is that the deal you want to offer me?"

Vasin, dressed in equally motley new civilian clothes, looked across at Kuznetsov. Their prisoner had an unsettling way of cutting straight to the heart of the matter.

"And in the meantime," continued Berezovsky, clearly making an effort to keep his voice even, "I am a prisoner here in a Leningrad whorehouse. While you two shop my story around Moscow to powerful men you've never met. We'll all be dead by the end of the week."

Kuznetsov, unlike Vasin, showed no sign of nerves or agitation.

"The two of us are the only members of our team you'll see for the time being."

"Bullshit, Kuznetsov. There's no *team*. Just a pair of crazy *kontora* also-rans, far out of their depth. Are you forgetting I'm *kontora*, too? A renegade. It takes one to know one."

Vasin leaned back in his chair. The room was decorated with wall-to-wall canvases, all unframed nudes. From the studio space below came the chatter of gossiping female voices.

"What's *your* plan, Berezovsky?"

"You need to trust me. You need my dossier to topple your boss. And you'll get it, you have my word. But first you need to allow me to do what I need to do."

"Which is what?" Kuznetsov's voice was cold.

"See some people."

"The *kontora*?"

"Obviously not the *kontora*. Like I told Vasin here—there's no one I trust anymore at the Lubyanka."

Kuznetsov was about to respond, but Vasin stilled him with a hand.

"You want to get in touch with your daughter in Moscow. Tell her you're not dead. That the *kontora* set you up. That you'll get her out, somehow. That's it, isn't it?"

The light from a single, red-shaded lamp on a side table was dim. Vasin couldn't make out any obvious tell on Berezovsky's face.

"Believe what you want to, Sasha." An ironic tone was creeping into Berezovsky's voice.

"Come on. You don't have *anyone*? I can't believe that."

"It's none of your business, for the moment. You'll only get your hands on the dossier if you let me go. Or maybe you're planning to torture it out of me? Hang me up by the thumbs? Have the girls downstairs flog me black and blue? Looks like they have the equipment for it."

His sarcastic tone provoked Kuznetsov into a rising anger. Vasin had seen it before, the color boiling up from his colleague's collar like paint spreading in water. Kuznetsov spoke with barely controlled fury.

"You know what, Berezovsky, or whatever the hell your name is? We might just do that. Not us, personally, if you were counting on our decency. And not the fucking *girls,* either. We have professionals who can get men to talk."

"Fine. You'd get me to talk. But how would you know I wasn't sending you into a trap, Kuznetsov? The wrong code word would result in the documents being immediately destroyed. Come on, you know that's not going to work."

Infuriated, Kuznetsov stomped from the room, slamming the door behind him, leaving Vasin and Berezovsky alone together for the first time since Vorkuta.

"Hot-tempered, your comrade." Berezovsky rose from the bed, stretched, and peered out of the narrow, horizontal window that ran along the upper edge of one wall. Too small for a man to squeeze through—which was why Vasin had chosen this room. A light snowfall was dusting the courtyard.

Vasin remained seated, twisting his hands as he forced his brain to think.

"I can't keep calling you Berezovsky. What's your real name? Kozlov called you Andrei, back when he captured you."

"You think that's important?"

"Fine. Have it your way."

"Yes. It's Andrei. If you must know."

His prisoner was a tough, consummately trained officer. But he was not made of steel. Vasin caught something human in Berezovsky's tone. A normal, human longing for companionship. God knows, this man's secret had made him the loneliest man in the Soviet Union—as well as the most wanted.

"Good to meet you, Andrei."

A silence gathered between them.

"We're on the same side, you know," Vasin continued.

"So you keep telling me."

"I want you to be safe. Your loved ones, too, though you say they're none of my business. You saved my life, up north. I owe you. And for what it's worth, I saved yours, too."

The man said nothing, staring silently into the falling snow.

"Andrei, who are you going to go to, if not us? You need protection. A new life. And who in the West could protect you? The CIA and MI6 are full of moles. How many of our defectors have been murdered abroad by *kontora* death squads? Your secret is dangerous for all of us. If it gets out that the KGB assassinated the President of the United States, it will make the Cuban crisis last year look like a game of dominoes. It will be war. You know that, right? Or stand the situation on its head. Let's say you go to the CIA. Maybe they don't want to know your damn secret. Could be they're as keen as the *kontora* to keep the information buried. Literally."

"Are you trying to scare me into cooperating now, Sasha?"

"You must have thought this through. I just don't see a way out of this for you if you try to go it alone. For us."

"For *us*?"

"It's my head on the block, too. And Kuznetsov's, now. You came into my fucking world unbidden. Now, thanks to you, I could lose everything. My family. My life. All because you needed someone to help get your backside out of Vorkuta. You used me, Andrei."

The man returned to his brooding silence for a long moment.

"You're right, Sasha. But maybe you and I are more alike than you think. We both have had our families taken away. We both have injustices to fight."

"What? Andrei—I might have been posted to a hellhole. But I wasn't desperate. I wasn't fleeing for my life . . ."

"Sasha, I'm sorry."

"Don't be fucking *sorry*. Just make it right. Work with us. Trust us."

"I can't do that."

"Because you have some scheme to get yourself out of this with a whole skin? Give us the slip and leave the two of us to swing?"

Delicately, Andrei pressed his fingertips to his eyes.

"I won't leave you to swing, Sasha. You have my word on that. I'm a decent man."

Vasin breathed through his frustration, suppressing an angry retort. A savory smell of boiling soup drifted up from the studio.

"Enough. I'll go find you some food."

# 5

"Tell me, Vasin, when did you become such a coward?" Kuznetsov slurped his cabbage soup and took a long pull from a glass of Crimean red wine. "When we met, back at Arzamas, it was you who were the hard ass. Bullying me into doing all kinds of egregious and illegal shit. And now you just want to let Berezovsky walk? Take his word as a Soviet officer and a Communist that he'll come back and just hand over the goods?"

Kuznetsov and Vasin sat at a table at the end of the long studio, speaking in low voices. The main studio was finally empty after a busy night's business. A radio played in the corner, and two female voices, bickering, came from the kitchen.

"No. Obviously we're not going to let him *walk*. I fell for that once already. I'm saying he's not going to crack. He's stubborn as a mule. So we have to trick him into leading us to where the file is. We have to let him think he's given us the slip."

"Ha. Well, *that's* the Sasha Vasin we need to see more of. Devious Sasha."

A tall, heavily built young woman with a pile of bottle-blond hair appeared from the kitchen bearing plates of greasy cutlets and boiled rice. She had a cheerful, doll-like face and wore a nylon kimono over elaborate pink underwear.

"All done, boys? Madam Rosa said you have to hurry up. Girls need to get to bed. I mean, to sleep." The girl gathered up the soup plates, smiling cheekily at Vasin as she bent low.

"We'll need an extra bed in our room. I told Rosa already."

"On its way, darling. Yura's bringing it up now."

On cue, a stocky teenage boy with a tangle of dark hair appeared in the hall, banging a heavy burden as he came. Rosa followed him in. The boy's face was strangely unexpressive, his eyes small slits as he stared childishly at the strangers.

"Yura. These are friends of ours. *Friends*."

Rosa smoothed the boy's greasy hair in an unmistakably maternal gesture.

"Let me help you with that." Vasin stood and took one end of the folding camp bed that the boy Yury was clutching. Together they maneuvered it up the steep steps to the mezzanine floor, where the three men were staying. Vasin unlocked the door and watched as Berezovsky helped the boy set up the bed.

"Yura. I'm Sasha." Vasin pointed to himself. "Sasha, understand? We need bedding."

*"Sash,"* the kid blurted.

Returning to his now-cold dinner, Vasin leaned close to Kuznetsov. Rosa had begun ostentatiously plumping cushions and laying out clean ashtrays, a clear signal for them to finish up.

"You'll have to babysit our guest on your own tomorrow," Vasin told Kuznetsov. "I'll go see my police contact. I have an idea."

"Always had you down as an ideas man, Vasin. Just let me take a bath now that the post-fuck rush is over."

# 6

Colonel Arvo Laar was waiting impatiently at the Ladoga Station as a crowd of commuters streamed past him. He wore a heavy Army camouflage coat and carried a short fishing rod, a rucksack, and a large ice drill over his shoulder.

"Sasha, over here! Hurry. If we miss this train there's not another for an hour."

The two men hopped on the suburban *elektrichka* train with seconds to spare. The carriage was empty except for a handful of elderly country people and a scattering of solitary ice fishermen. Vasin and Laar took a bench seat as far from the other passengers as possible.

"Going fishing on a Sunday morning, Arvo? You don't prefer to sleep in?"

"I worked yesterday. Now I need to get out on the ice, breathe some fresh air. Is everything at Rosa's satisfactory?"

"It's exactly what we need. Thank you."

"So tell me, how are Vera and Nikita? The boy must be, what, fifteen now?"

A smile of pain flickered across Vasin's face. A realization that he'd barely thought of his son since Berezovsky's arrival in Vorkuta three weeks before. Vera—his wife, in name only—even longer.

"To be honest with you, I haven't seen either of them in nearly a year."

Speaking to Laar felt like turning back the clock to an earlier life. Vasin remembered himself as the eager young homicide cop that Laar had known and befriended. He could pretend, for the forty minutes of the train journey to the shore of Lake Ladoga at least, that Special Cases hadn't happened. That Orlov hadn't happened.

The train trundled through spindly pinewoods dotted with modest wooden dachas, most of them closed up for the winter. With one stop to go before Laar's favored fishing place, Vasin reluctantly returned to business.

"There's another favor I need from you, Arvo."

"I expected this. Go on, my friend."

"You said you worked with street kids."

"This is correct."

"Pickpockets? Petty thieves?"

"Indeed. Both those things. Many of our younger comrades have come under criminal influences."

"Do these kids have bosses? I mean—men, older men who give them orders? Protection? Fence the stuff they steal?"

"Yes. It is as you remember from Moscow. Such corrupters of Soviet youth still exist."

"And could you put me in touch?"

Laar's face clouded with concern.

"Sasha. I am not corrupt. If you think that I, or people in my department, have some kind of understanding . . ."

"God no, Arvo. I didn't mean, are these scum your *friends*. I just mean, do you know where I could find them?"

"Yes, but I don't understand why."

"You don't need to know why, Arvo. I promise you."

The train slowed as it approached Laar's station. Vasin helped his friend gather his fishing gear and they descended onto the narrow platform. Through the trees the white, frozen expanse of Lake Ladoga was visible, dotted with solitary fishermen sitting hunched over their ice holes.

"Sure you won't come and fish with me today, Sasha? Marta made enough sandwiches for two. I have vodka."

"Another time, Arvo. I need to get the first train back into town."

The older cop, with that unnervingly direct look of his, scanned Vasin's face.

"Sasha. You haven't got yourself involved with *bad people,* have you?"

"Oh, Arvo, I did that the moment I joined the *kontora.*"

# 7

It was a raw day of splintering sunlight and scudding clouds. As Vasin mounted the stairs to the studio on the Petrovsky Embankment he felt a stab of envy for his friend Arvo's simple pleasures. Winter silence on the lake, sandwiches made by a plump wife who waited at home for his return, nothing to do all day but wait for the tug on a line from the black depths.

The radio droned in a corner of the studio. In the tiny kitchen a pair of girls he hadn't seen before—a slim, dark-skinned waif from the Caucasus and a frizzy redhead who looked like a young version of Rosa—murmured confidences. Beyond the picture windows the upper branches of a bare linden tree fanned across the sky like a web. Vasin remembered something Orlov had once told him. Some men see the net, others see the spaces between.

Kuznetsov was slumped in an armchair in the corner, his nose buried in a novel and a glass of brandy by his side.

"Hello, darling. I'm home."

Kuznetsov lowered the book and pursed his lips in irritation.

"Had a lovely day in town, did you, *darling*?"

"I have to go out again this evening. Where's our guest?"

Kuznetsov gestured upstairs with a single finger and returned his attention to the novel.

"He's doing just fine. I think he likes it here."

In the room that the three of them shared, Vasin found Berezovsky sitting on the bed with the boy Yury. Each held a hand of children's animal playing cards, which they laid down one by one with slow deliberation. The boy broke into a furious oinking noise as two pig cards appeared.

"Animal snap?" asked Vasin.

"Shhh," slurred Yury, turning indignantly to the interruption.

"Yes, Colonel. This young man is teaching me a fun new game. Please leave us in peace." Berezovsky had shaved and brushed his hair—unlike the disheveled Kuznetsov. His demeanor was cold and composed.

As Vasin closed the door he understood just how formidable his prisoner truly was. A man who knew how to wait. And how to make friends.

# 8

The dim archway stank of rotting rubbish and urine. The night was damp and warm for the time of year. Underfoot, the dirty snow had turned into gray slush, like wet cardboard.

"Doesn't look like these Leningrad gangs of yours are too successful at what they do, if they live like this."

The officer from Laar's department turned to Vasin with a cheerful, almost childish grin. God, thought Vasin, policemen really *were* looking younger every year.

"You'll see. This way."

Officer Tretyak led Vasin on through a grimy courtyard and under another arch illuminated by a single, dirt-encrusted municipal bulb. Ahead, a ground-floor curtain flickered and a light went out. An upper window opened, a figure appeared briefly and whistled. An answering whistle came from the opposite side of the courtyard.

"Don't worry, they know me."

The young cop marched up to a heavy door and pushed it open. The hallway was littered and dim, the once-grand tiles on the floor cracked and the ornate plasterwork peeling. A teenage boy sauntered onto the first-floor landing that overlooked the entrance and leaned on the banister.

*"Cho' nado, a?"* The kid's accent was pure guttersnipe. "Waddya want?"

"Uncle Borya."

"Who wants him?"

"You know who wants him."

"Wait."

The lookout disappeared for several minutes. Only the drip of melting ice and the scurry of rats disturbed the silence of the stairwell. When he reappeared, it was just to give a contemptuous flick of two fingers to summon Vasin and Tretyak upstairs.

The first-floor apartment must once have been grand. A pair of oak double doors, now slathered in brown municipal paint, opened onto a broad, high-ceilinged corridor. Both walls were stacked with piles of every conceivable kind of junk—shoes, ice skates, children's sleds, old radios, and desk lamps. There was an overpowering reek of humanity and boiled cabbage. The lookout led the visitors down a long corridor. From behind closed doors on both sides came the sounds of laughter and guttural, youthful chatter in several languages.

Another pair of double doors opened onto a spacious room lined with shelves and cupboards. Bizarrely, the ceiling was crowded with dozens of antique chandeliers made of brass and crystal. None of them was lit. Ragged gashes in the plasterwork of the walls and ceiling showed where the room had once been divided into smaller cubbyholes, the partitions now demolished to restore the open space.

One wall was filled with records and portable gramophones. A massive armoire stuffed with leather-bound books occupied another corner. And behind an ornate, pre-Revolutionary desk sat an obese, dark-skinned man who eyed Vasin and Tretyak with irritation.

"It's not your day for collection, Comrade Officer," the man snarled in an accented voice, addressing the young cop in the familiar form used for inferiors and children. "What you doing here?"

Tretyak darted a sheepish look at Vasin.

"Uncle Borya, I've brought someone to see you. Friend of Colonel Laar's. He has . . ."

"I am Colonel Vasin. Alexander Ilyich. Interior Ministry. And you are Boris . . . ?"

Vasin waited for the man to introduce himself, at least with his patronymic. But Uncle Boris merely folded his arms and snorted.

"Just Uncle Boris. What do you want, Colonel Vasin of the Interior Ministry?"

Vasin turned to his young companion.

"Officer Tretyak, could you . . ."

Taking the hint, the kid saluted.

"I'll wait for you on the corner, sir."

The door closed behind Tretyak, shutting out the cacophony of voices and music from the rest of the apartment. Vasin noticed that bedrolls were stowed around the corners of the room, alongside piles of underclothes and scattered footwear. A large ancient steel safe stood open behind Uncle Boris's desk.

"How many people live in this place?"

Boris did not answer or invite Vasin to sit down. But Vasin sat anyway, settling himself squarely in front of the man and putting his elbows on the broad desk. Boris's face and head were covered with an even layer of centimeter-long bristle, and he wore a fine woolen dressing gown over an expensive-looking silk shirt. Around his neck was a heavy gold chain thick with charms.

"So, *Boris*. My friend Arvo Laar said you were a friend to many kids."

"We're good-hearted people. Strangers might be angels in disguise, so my mother says."

"You're a gypsy."

"Yup."

"The kids you put up here work for you?"

"We help them. Clothes. Food. And they bring us things that they find. In rubbish bins and the like. You'd be amazed, the things people throw away."

"Laar told me what you are, Boris. I'm not here to question you. I'm here to ask your help. To propose a business deal, if you prefer."

"Huh." Boris's eyes narrowed. "Who did you say you were again?"

Vasin fished his battered Interior Ministry ID from inside his cheap polyester jacket and handed it across the expanse of the desk. The gypsy gave a low, ironic whistle.

"Not often we have the pleasure of such distinguished guests, Comrade Colonel."

"Pleasure's all mine. Here's why I came: I need eyes. Lots of them. Sharp eyes. All around the city. We need to watch one man. His every move. And not lose him. Could your kids help?"

Boris grunted noncommittally.

"Maybe. How many?"

"Ten. Perhaps a dozen. And I'll pay."

"How much?"

"Ten rubles a head. Per day. But they have to be good. I need pickpockets and their lookouts. Petty thieves. Kids who know their way about town. Who can watch and not be seen."

"Ha. Don't know any thieves and pickpockets, Colonel."

"Of course you don't."

"I may know some kids who could do that job for you, though. I'll ask."

"You're not the boss around here?"

For the first time, Boris's blubbery face creased into a toad-like smile.

"We're gypsies. It's my mother who's the boss."

# 9

Vasin waited in the corridor as Boris locked the door of his study behind him, pocketed the key, and disappeared into another of the rooms. Vasin himself had grown up in a communal apartment in Moscow, four families with a room each, sharing a kitchen and bathroom. But he'd never seen a *kommunalka* on this scale before. The place could house a dozen families. From the kitchen came a clattering of pans and a babel of shrill female chatter.

Boris reappeared.

"Come. She wants to speak to you. Take your shoes off."

The air in the dim room was hot and cloyingly perfumed. Every inch of the floor was covered in carpets several layers deep that yielded under Vasin's stocking feet. From behind a large old-fashioned folding screen that obscured half the room came a deep, querulous voice.

"Close the door, Borya. Such a racket!"

As Boris obeyed, Vasin moved past the screen. A vastly overweight woman sat cross-legged on a deep divan. Her round face was heavily made up, and her hair was covered with a sequined headscarf. She looked surprisingly young to be the mother of a fifty-year-old man like Boris. Her gimlet eyes were black, and she peered at Vasin inquisitively.

"So you are the officer who wishes to hire my children." Her Russian was heavily accented, her voice almost as deep as a man's.

"Yes, Comrade."

"Tell me, what work do you wish them to do?"

"What they are best at, Mother. Working the streets. Watching people. I will train them myself, for a day. Then put them to work. For good money."

"No problems for us? You swear this?"

"I swear it."

The gypsy queen pursed her mouth and swayed slightly from her waist, considering.

"Very well. You will have ten of Boris's best. Enough?"

"Enough. We start tomorrow—if you guarantee their good behavior? No shirking. No wandering off. This must be professional."

The old woman gave a wheezing laugh.

"Boris. You heard the man. He needs the children to obey. They will. Understood?"

"*Va, dia,*" Boris murmured. The gypsies' own language, Vasin guessed.

"And . . ." The gypsy woman held up a hand as Vasin turned to leave. "You pay in advance. In full. Twenty rubles a day. Each."

At that rate the two thousand rubles he and Berezovsky had taken from the safe in Vorkuta would be blown in a few days.

"I offered ten."

The woman frowned.

"Fifteen."

"Ten. It's ten each, Mother. And . . . a hundred for you. As a sign of my respect. And I will pay you for the first day as soon as I've talked to the kids. I need to know who they are. What they can do."

A smile that might have been coquettish creased the gypsy queen's face. She tipped her head back in assent and dismissed them both with a gesture of the wrist.

"My blessing."

Vasin made a grave half bow. Out in the corridor, Boris slapped a meaty hand flat on various doors as he passed, calling out nicknames. "Tickler! Left-Foot! Ginger! Spotty! Short-Arse! Dinamo! Come, now! Mama got a good fat job for youse."

# 10

Back at the Petrovsky Embankment, Vasin pressed the bell repeatedly but got no answer. Eventually Rosa's voice, peremptory, crackled on the intercom.

"That you, Vasin? I'll meet you at the top of the stairs."

Vasin trudged up. A square of light opened to the right of the upper landing, a side door at the top of a steep flight of steel steps to the left of the studio's main entrance that accessed the mezzanine floor directly.

"Be quiet, for God's sake. Go straight to your room. We're very busy tonight. Important clients."

Vasin mounted the slippery steel stairs and entered the upper corridor, where the bedrooms were arranged along an open gallery overlooking the studio. Rosa made a shushing gesture with her fingers and bolted the side door behind him. From the studio below came the sound of laughter and drunken voices, male and female.

As he opened the bedroom door Kuznetsov and Berezovsky looked up from their respective reading with identical expressions of irritation.

"Evening, Comrades. Been getting on well, I see."

Neither man smiled.

"Kuznetsov, shall we give our friend some privacy for a while?"

With a flourish, Kuznetsov tossed the novel he'd been reading over his shoulder and rose from his armchair. Berezovsky pretended to be engrossed in a copy of *Krokodil,* the Soviet Union's best-loved comic magazine.

Perching on the steel steps that overlooked the landing, Vasin and Kuznetsov lit up cigarettes.

"The man's fucking infuriating." Kuznetsov inhaled as though he was competing in an all-Union smoking olympiad.

"You reckoned a day of the famous Kuznetsov charm would have him rolling over and agreeing to everything we asked?"

"I thought I could talk some sense into him. Help him see where his true interests lay. Who his friends were."

"Did he tell you his real name, at least?"

"No chance. But yes, he did talk. Silence would have been confrontational. Instead, he chatted about nothing. Promised he'd think about what I was saying. Comrade Fucking Affability. Mister Bloody Nice Guy. Nothing to latch onto. Like boxing cotton candy."

"He's wearing you out, you know that, right? Trying to lull you into a false sense of security."

"Well, he's succeeding. Another day locked up with that man and I swear I'll smack him over the head with that iron frying pan of Rosa's. You're on duty tomorrow. I have to get out of this place."

"Sorry, Comrade. You're babysitting tomorrow, too. I need to spend some time with our new team."

"Team?"

"The best watchers in Leningrad. Let Berezovsky—or whatever his name is—think that he's winning. What we need is for him to run."

"Berezovsky will lose street police in five minutes flat."

"Precisely. But I hired some eyes that Berezovsky will never spot. The minute he's out of here he'll make a beeline for his documents. He's got no choice. We're after him, the First Chief Directorate is after him, and he's got no time or resources. And once he's got his papers he'll make his move. To Finland, maybe. Maybe he has a contact. Whatever he does, we'll be watching."

"Who did you hire, Sasha? Pigeons?"

"Street kids. Gypsies."

"*Pickpockets?* Tell me you're joking."

"I'm not. The only person who can lead us to where Berezovsky hid his papers is Berezovsky himself. Tomorrow, leave him alone with Yura. Let him make better friends with the boy. It's obvious he's cultivating him. So let's allow him to do it. By this time tomorrow, I promise, he'll have persuaded the half-wit to unlock the room and let him out. Your job is to let him think he's getting away with it. Take an afternoon nap, down in the studio. Get lax with the security. But not so lax that he suspects we're setting a trap. And then, the morning of the day after tomorrow, we let Berezovsky give us the slip. My guys will be waiting."

"And what if he gives your kids the slip? He's a professional."

"That's his weak spot. He'll be looking out for *kontora* watchers. For you and me and people like us. Street kids are as invisible to him as they are to everyone else."

"And if he doesn't run? He could just choose to sit tight, right here."

"In that case I'll have to let you hang him up by his arms and you can light pages from *Krokodil* between his toes until he talks. How's that sound?"

# 11

Vasin had not expected gypsies to be punctual. But on the stroke of nine in the morning the entire gang was assembled in the little square outside the Evropeiskaya Hotel. They were a motley crew, not just in age and appearance but also in respectability. A couple could have passed for slightly scruffy Young Pioneers. Others were filthy-faced and ragged as illustrations from a book about the iniquities of Tsarist Russia. But mostly, Vasin's team simply looked drab. Ordinary, gray-faced Soviet kids in standard-issue working-class clothes.

Ginger was the leader. He was maybe sixteen, going by his stubbly, acne-spotted face. He was scrawny, and by no means the biggest of the bunch. But he had a natural, cheeky authority.

"Morning, boss!" he chirped as Vasin approached. The rest skulked at a distance, loitering on park benches and wandering in slow circles kicking up snow. Excellent instincts for not drawing attention to themselves, Vasin noted approvingly.

"Right, boys." For today Vasin had put on his uniform once more—not least because an Army-green overcoat was one of the most common forms of male winter wear in this, and every other, Soviet city. "Gather round. I'm gonna teach you a game. It's called: if you lose sight of your mark, Uncle Borya's gonna skin you all fucking alive. Today, the mark is me. Got it?"

Ginger nodded gravely, looking left and right to check that all his associates had gotten the message.

"Listen carefully, as I will explain this only once." Vasin was channeling the pedantic emphasis of his old teacher at the KGB school, Boris Ignatyevich Schultz. He picked up a stick and began to trace x-marks on a clean snowbank. "The first lesson is how to box your target—here. One group keeps ahead—here, here, here. The second group follows behind . . ."

# 12

Vasin emerged for the second time from the side door of the Leningrad Central Telegraph office to find one of his street kids moping by a lamppost, insouciantly waiting for him. He hopped on a departing trolleybus, only to have a boy squeeze his way in through the back doors at the first traffic-light stop. These kids were good. Vasin had issued each of them a pocketful of the two-kopeck pieces necessary to operate Soviet pay phones, and made them all memorize Rosa's number. That meant they would be able to communicate with Vasin—but not with each other. He made a rule: Call in if you haven't seen the mark for sixty minutes.

Except they didn't know what their mark looked like. Vasin needed a photo of him. That meant camera and film. Did Ginger have any idea where to get one?

Stupid question. Naturally Uncle Borya had quite a collection. Ginger deputized one of his sidekicks to fetch the best military-issue Zenit and bring it to the Petrovsky Embankment. As the winter day turned from clear to overcast and damp, Vasin led his little group back and forth along the tram stops, metro stops, and courtyards around Rosa's, staking out routes where Berezovsky might run.

*If* he ran. If Berezovsky chose to stay put at Rosa's, the whole operation would be for nothing.

The pudgy kid they called Tickler trotted down the embankment, a satchel over his shoulder containing the camera. It was a gorgeous instrument, worth a month of a colonel's salary. Tickler produced a handful of brand-new color-film rolls from his pocket, expertly loaded the camera, and handed it to Vasin.

"Wait down here, shall we, while you take snaps? Bring you back the developed prints in the morning, one for each of us, right? And a couple for you?"

These kids were bloody naturals.

# 13

Vasin found Kuznetsov lounging in the studio. After just three days at Rosa's he had his favorite armchair and his favorite lamp, and the girls were busy making him coffee just the way he liked it.

"Making yourself at home, I see. Any news?"

Kuznetsov gave a weary grin.

"Lots of animal snap going on. Meowing and oinking. I think the kid's getting the hang of it. Last few minutes they've gone quiet. What's that?"

Vasin flourished the camera and mounted the stairs. The bedroom door was unlocked, and Berezovsky and Yura had moved on to rock-paper-scissors.

"Time for your mug shot."

"You're making me new identity papers?"

A gleam of hope appeared in Berezovsky's eye. Shit. The last thing that Vasin needed was for the man to hang about waiting in the hope of a new passport and identity. He racked his brains for a moment thinking what story could be likely to make Berezovsky flee—and lead them to his secret document cache—faster.

"We figured we might need a photo of you for all-points bulletins for police, airports, and train stations, just in case something goes wrong. So it really is a mug shot. Stand over there, Andrei. Back to the door, we need a plain background. Don't smile."

"Not much for me to smile about, Sasha." Berezovsky's voice had gone flat. "Not much at all."

# 14

As he clattered back down the stairs into the main studio space, Vasin gestured to Kuznetsov to follow him out. The courtyard seemed to be deserted, but Ginger appeared from behind a bush and held out his hand for the camera.

"Be outside the Petrovsky Domik Cafe tomorrow at nine with the whole team and a dozen prints. Wrap up warm."

"Sure thing, boss."

Ginger and Tickler disappeared at a trot through the archway toward the trolleybus stop. Vasin turned and saw Kuznetsov eyeing him gloomily.

"You really think a bunch of untrained children can track a professional First Directorate spy with twenty years' field experience who's on the run and desperate?"

"Like I said—he's not looking out for a bunch of kids. And yes, they *are* trained. Trained by their life of dodging cops and angry victims they've pickpocketed. And by me, today. They're good."

"And if they lose Berezovsky?"

"Then we're on our own. We're running through the Vorkuta money fast. We need Berezovsky to break cover and lead us to his file. And soon. Or do you have a better idea?"

Kuznetsov considered for a long moment before flinging away his cigarette.

"Not for the moment."

"So listen. Tomorrow morning, I'll go out again at eight, leaving you two alone. At nine, after breakfast, you lock Berezovsky in his room and go out yourself. Take Rosa with you. Tell Yury you'll be back after lunch. Then we leave the two of them alone, and wait. Bet you Berezovsky talks his simple little friend into letting him escape within an hour."

"You seem very sure."

"I *am* very sure. The guy's like bloody mercury. He'll slip through any crack, given half a chance. Trust me, Kuznetsov."

"Why was I afraid you'd say that?"

# 15

The morning was clear and cold. Stars were still bright in the black sky when Vasin pushed open the front door of the studio. Dawn, in midwinter Leningrad, would not come until past ten. Vasin walked briskly down the embankment toward the golden spire of the Peter and Paul Fortress, his breath steaming. The river had frozen solid overnight, even the central channel. At the cafe by the Gorkovskaya metro station he bought himself a coffee, as well as the cafe's entire supply of sweet buns for his crew. He knew the gypsies wouldn't be welcome in the Petrovsky Domik, or any other cafe or restaurant in the city. Waiters knew thieves when they saw them.

Right on time, Ginger sauntered down the embankment with three others. Six more kids materialized around Vasin in the small park that lay under the fortress walls of the Military Museum. Vasin poured hot coffee from a thermos he'd borrowed from Rosa as his team wolfed down the buns.

"Remember, stick close to the mark. Work in pairs. Don't be afraid if he notices you. There are ten on the team, so it doesn't matter if he spots a few of you. And most important: report. Any time he enters a building, call the number I gave you immediately. Box the premises, like we practiced. Cover all the entrances. If it's a public building, someone go in there after him. Wait in the lobby if you can't get past the doorman. Are we clear?"

"Clear." Most of the voices were gruff teenage growls, with a couple of boyish falsettos.

"Okay." Vasin glanced at his watch. "We have twenty minutes to get into position."

# 16

At ten past nine, Kuznetsov walked into the bread shop on the corner of the Petrovsky Embankment where Vasin waited. Rosa was with him, casting a disapproving look at Vasin as she joined the line for the morning's batch of sweetly aromatic Borodinsky bread.

"All well?" asked Vasin.

"Saw a bunch of your kids messing around on the swing in the courtyard as we left."

"And Berezovsky?"

"His usual charming self."

"You didn't tell him you were going out? Didn't make it too obvious?"

"What do you take me for? I told Yura not to tell him that me and his mum were going out. Which means he'll tell his new mate everything, when he asks."

Rosa approached, a string bag with three fresh loaves on her arm.

"Go do your shopping, as we agreed," Vasin told her. "Look in at this shop before you go home. If we're not here, it's safe to go back. Otherwise, we wait."

"Yura is a good boy. Very trusting. I'm afraid he'll . . ."

"Don't worry, Rosa. Our friend is not a monster. Yura will be safe."

An hour passed. The bread shop manager darted suspicious glances at Vasin and Kuznetsov as they took turns loitering at the edge of the big plate-glass window that overlooked the embankment.

Another half hour, and Vasin's nerves began to fray. He clutched and unclutched his hands, pacing between the cash registers and the window.

"He's broken cover." Kuznetsov's voice was low and urgent. Vasin joined him at the window. On the opposite side of the road a bizarre figure with cropped, dark red hair hurried toward the trolleybus stop. In his wake trailed a pair of Vasin's gypsy boys.

Berezovsky was unmistakable, despite the hastily cropped wig he wore—evidently stolen from Rosa's boudoir. Ginger appeared, breathless, at the door of the bread shop.

"Your man's bolted. We're on him."

# PART SEVEN

# 17–19 DECEMBER 1963

Men in power are so anxious to establish the myth of infallibility that they do their utmost to ignore truth.

—BORIS PASTERNAK,
*Doctor Zhivago*

# 1

*Leningrad, USSR*

The studio at the brothel reeked, as usual, of stale cigarette smoke, perfume, and coffee despite the cold air streaming in through the open windows. Yury sat on the floor, playing with a napkin folded into the shape of a swan. He looked up in alarm as Vasin and Kuznetsov hurried inside, and as he did so the swan unfolded and collapsed.

"Bird!" Yury was indignant. "Bird's gone!"

Vasin crouched by the boy.

"Yura, where did your friend Andrei go?"

"Children's World. Gonna buy me a wind-up bird with flappy wings! Very clever thing. Expensive thing. Present for Yura."

Vasin exchanged a worried glance with Kuznetsov.

"*Expensive?* Did Uncle Andrei ask you for money?"

The kid's face creased in a guilty frown.

"No." Yury looked down and chewed his lip.

"Yura, it's all right. Did you give your friend any money?"

Sheepishly, the boy nodded.

"How much money, Yura? Where did you take it from?"

Rosa blustered in, carrying two heavy bags of groceries. She saw Vasin's concern.

"What's happened?"

"Where do you keep your cash?"

Rosa muttered a curse, dropped her bags, and rushed to the kitchen. She reached up for a coffee tin on a high shelf and tipped it upside down.

"Yuraaaa!" Her voice was a furious shriek. "You stupid little *shit!*"

The boy hid his face in his hands and began to weep.

"How much?"

Rosa raised her hands, exasperated.

"A week's takings. Maybe eight hundred. A thousand."

*Damn.* Vasin hadn't thought of that. That much cash would make Berezovsky significantly more mobile. He could take taxis instead of trolleybuses. Buy a plane ticket. Hole up in some babushka's private apartment, just as they had done in Rosa's studio.

"Don't worry, Rosa, we'll make it up to you," said Vasin reassuringly, though he knew they couldn't.

The phone rang. Kuznetsov snatched it up and held it out to Vasin. It was Ginger.

"Boss? The mark went into the office of *Vecherny Leningrad.* The newspaper. It's on Vasiliyevsky Island, Second Line. It's been ten minutes."

"I'm coming."

Vasin put down the receiver and made a quick calculation. He'd need Kuznetsov's help to pin Berezovsky down. That meant that he would have to rely on Rosa to monitor the phone and keep tabs on his scattered team. He'd need to find a taxi, too, and fast. With Kuznetsov and Rosa staring at him anxiously, Vasin had to try to project a calm that he did not feel. Did he really imagine he could keep a ruthless pro like Berezovsky in a surveillance box with just one man and a bunch of kids? They were about to find out.

"Rosa, we need you to stay here by the phone. Take any messages for us. Write them down, exactly, and I'll call in myself, every hour."

# 2

The offices of *Vercherny Leningrad* occupied a dilapidated neoclassical building on a dreary side street. As Kuznetsov waited in the backseat of their taxi, Vasin sprinted up and down the pavement searching for Ginger. He found the kid loitering on the street corner, hopping from foot to foot with the excitement of the chase.

"You just missed him. He came out five minutes ago and headed toward the Admiralty on foot. But don't worry, six of us are on him. Boxing him, like you showed us. Kipper even stole a kid's bicycle. He and Fingers are riding it together."

Two kids on a single stolen bike, skidding along icy Leningrad pavements? Nothing could be more conspicuous. But Vasin had more urgent problems to deal with.

"Was he carrying anything? Documents?"

"Can't say, boss. He was in a hurry."

Vasin clapped a hand to his face, torn between the urge to stay close to Berezovsky and the desire to find out what the hell he had been doing at the newspaper office.

"Ginger, get in the taxi and wait."

Vasin summoned Kuznetsov to follow him into the building with an urgent wave. On the second floor they pressed a buzzer and were admitted to what must once have been a spacious private apartment. The receptionist was a middle-aged woman with makeup thick as war paint and fashionably tapered cat's-eye glasses.

"Comrade. Have you seen this man?" Vasin flourished one of the mug shots of Berezovsky as Kuznetsov, panting from the run up the stairs, flipped his KGB identity card in the startled woman's face.

"He was just here. He wanted to see Ksenia Pravdeva."

"Who's that? She here?"

"She does the obituaries. Upstairs. Office 302. But . . ."

The two men were already halfway to the landing before the office door closed behind them. The upstairs floor of *Vecherny Leningrad* was identical to the first—grubby plasterwork, piles of unsold back numbers stacked in the hallway. Somewhere a typewriter clacked hesitantly, and a raised voice struggled with a bad phone connection. The door to office 302 was ajar. Inside a tall, handsome woman in her thirties with bobbed hair and an old-fashioned knitted shawl over her shoulders looked up, startled. Vasin flourished the mug shot of Berezovsky.

"Comrade Pravdeva. You know this man. Don't deny it."

The woman was shocked into silence. She stood and backed

toward the row of tall filing cabinets that lined one wall of her cluttered office. Her big gray eyes stared, terrified, into Vasin's.

"Who are you?"

"State Security. Did this man come to see you?"

"Y-yes. He did."

"His name?"

"I don't . . ."

Vasin slammed both hands hard on the desk, spilling a cup full of pencils onto the floor.

"Why are you *lying*?"

"You already know his name."

"What's his *name*?"

"Fyodorov. Andrei Fyodorov."

Vasin turned the name over in his mind. Just a name. But it felt like a mask had fallen away.

"What did Andrei Fyodorov want?"

"Officer, what's this about? Because . . ."

"Because, nothing. Did he take any papers? Ten seconds, and you're in cuffs. Nine. Eight. Seven . . ."

Vasin felt the old thrill from his cop days. The vehemence of his passion to get an answer, coupled with the might of the state that he personally wielded, crushing a lonely individual will. Power: an ugly feeling. But it felt good to be in charge again. And destroying Ksenia Pravdeva's self-possession and elegant beauty felt both disgusting and darkly thrilling at the same time.

"He wanted our obituary file on Comrade Anastas Mikoyan."

"He wanted *what*?"

"Our obituary file. We keep files on all prominent Soviet and world leaders. Press clippings, drafts of obituaries—I keep them up to date. And when one of them passes away, we just take the file . . ."

Her husky voice trailed away as she watched Vasin turn to his companion, the back of his hand to his forehead. Vasin swore, breathily.

"*Fuck.* Cunning *bastard*. He said the information would come out, sooner or later."

Mikoyan was a living relic of Stalin's Kremlin court, a Politburo dinosaur who'd somehow survived purges and political upheavals and was currently a member of the Presidium of the Supreme Soviet. A great Soviet hero whose bulging personal file would easily conceal an additional sheaf of papers. Presumably with an urgent note on the cover with instructions about who to pass it on to. A file that would inevitably be consulted when the great man was summoned to the Central Committee in the sky.

"Show me the file."

Hurriedly, Ksenia opened the M filing cabinet and extracted a thick stack of paper, retreating to a defensive corner by the window as Vasin leafed through it cursorily. But there was no sign of Berezovsky's—Vasin corrected himself—*Fyodorov's* papers.

"Damn the man to hell." He turned angrily to Ksenia. Her face had gone very pale, but her arms were folded defiantly across her chest. "Did you know he'd hidden some papers in there?"

"Officer, I have no idea what you are talking about."

"But you were here when he put them there. Earlier this summer."

"Comrade Fyodorov came to see me. He asked me for the file, and I asked him no questions. I know he is a colleague of yours."

"You are friends?"

"From university." A tell passed across the woman's face that hinted at a deeper relationship. "He asked me for tea, so I left him alone in the office for a while. He drank the tea, then he left. And you arrived. That's all I have to tell you, Comrade Officer."

A steely self-possession had come into Ksenia's eyes that reminded Vasin of Fyodorov's own. Vasin's cop instinct told him that she'd said all she was going to. To get more—to cross-examine her properly—would take time that he didn't have. He ordered Ksenia to show him her passport and hurriedly copied her address and work phone into his notebook. He also scribbled Rosa's number on a piece of paper, which he handed to Ksenia.

"My name is Colonel Vasin, Alexander Ilyich. If you hear from Fyodorov, call this number immediately. Understood?"

Ksenia nodded quickly with minute movements of her head.

Of course she would not do any such thing.

"And pass me that phone. Please."

Vasin dialed Rosa's number.

# 3

Vasin's taxi skidded to a halt on the cobbles of Sennaya Square. On the second turn around the square Vasin had spotted one of his gang, a pale-faced kid straddling a bicycle by a row of newly installed phone boxes marked MEZHGOROD. Intercity calls, from a public pay phone, for just fifteen kopecks. Amazing, the conveniences of modern Soviet life.

"Fingers, where is he?"

"Hi, boss. He used one of the new phone boxes. Spent about fifteen minutes in there. Made a bunch of calls. Then he got a taxi from that taxi stand over there and drove off south. But it's okay. One of the drivers at the stand turned out to be a friend of Uncle Borya's. Kipper and Skinny told him what was up, jumped in, and followed. Even got his taxi's license plate number."

Vasin offered up a private prayer for the resourcefulness of the kids he'd recruited. They'd definitely earned a fat bonus.

"How long ago?"

"Four minutes. Five."

Vasin felt a familiar, icy swell of anxiety. His entire plan, and maybe his life, depended on a pair of teenagers riding in a taxi they couldn't pay for. How long before the driver decided it was a wild-goose chase and kicked them out? How much did friendship with the notorious gypsy thief Uncle Borya count for? Fingers, uncannily reading Vasin's thoughts, piped up.

"Don't worry. We know the driver and he knows us. He'll want to do Uncle Borya a favor. And he values his tires. And his bodywork. Knows better than to piss off Borya's crew. We are famous."

"In certain circles," Kuznetsov muttered under his breath. "So what now?"

Vasin willed his racing brain to slow down. Why had Fyodorov chosen these public phones, well south of Vasiliyevsky Island? There were others much closer to the newspaper offices. Probably he came here because he was heading south. Sennaya Square was the terminus of the main A1 highway from Leningrad to Moscow. Was he planning to run to Moscow in a taxi? Absurd. It was a ten-hour drive. To a suburban railway station? That was a possibility. But he hadn't had time to effect his usual trick of stealing a passport, so a long-distance train was out of the question. An *elektrichka* commuter train? Also possible. If that was the case, they'd lost him—unless the kids jumped on the train along with him. But that would be pushing their devotion a step too far. Vasin's knuckles were white as he tensed his fists. Think. Think, man.

Pursuit was useless. His only choice was to wait for the kids to call in. From wherever they were.

Vasin stationed Kuznetsov fifty yards distant, by a phone box, jealously guarding it against all comers. Rosa had the phone's number. Vasin and Fingers stood by the highway, scanning for Volga taxis returning to the city. Fingers's head whipped back and forth as he tried to get a look at every driver's face while Vasin attempted to read the passing license plates.

Half an hour passed. Forty-five minutes. The taciturn driver Vasin had recruited to wait and chase if necessary chain-smoked Belomorkanal workers' cigarettes as the meter ticked up. It was already at thirty-six rubles. Vasin felt himself going numb. The thrill of the chase was cloying into a chilly presentiment of failure.

From the corner of his eye, he saw Kuznetsov gesticulating and hurrying toward them.

"Russko-Vysotskoe! That's where he is. Village called Russko-Vysotskoe. Past Krasnoe Selo. Got that, driver?"

"Keep yer pants on." The taxi driver tossed his cigarette and started up the engine as Kuznetsov and Fingers climbed in. "Twenty-five clicks from here. Hope you big spenders can afford it."

# 4

The outskirts of Leningrad seemed to be one giant building site. Rows of gray concrete apartment blocks and larger buildings had sprouted like mushrooms. Beyond the city limits, the scenery became grimmer. By the roadside stood half-ruined buildings wrecked in the titanic battles of World War II that nobody had gotten around to demolishing. A few straggling villages, rebuilt in cinder block and corrugated iron, lined the A180 highway. They took a sharp westward turn off the ring road—neither the airport nor the Moscow road, but the highway to Tallinn.

The day was freezing, the sky washed with a hard blue light. A stinging wind blew in off the nearby Baltic. The only vehicles on the road were a handful of farm trucks and a couple of beaten-up prewar M1 Emka sedans.

At the turnoff to the village of Russko-Vysotskoe, a taxi stood parked by a bus stop, next to a solitary phone box. Two of Uncle Borya's boys waited in the back of the cab, both lolling like pashas and insouciantly smoking the driver's cigarettes.

"Kips! Skinny!"

Fingers hopped out of the taxi and his mates did the same. The three street kids began talking at once.

"Everyone shut the fuck up. One at a time." Vasin stilled them with a pointing finger. "You. Kipper. Go."

"Well, he went to Sennaya Square, spent a while on the phone, then he went to get a taxi, an' we thought, shit, we thought, we better follow him."

"You did well. But where is he *now*?"

"Some shithole of a dacha. Two streets in. Marx Street, 6."

"You're sure?"

"Sure we're sure."

"No stops? Anyone in there with him?"

"He stopped for groceries at Krasnoe Selo. An' the house is empty, boss."

Vasin breathed a deep sigh of relief and looked up at the baby-blue winter sky. Thank God. The fucker had gone to ground. When he looked down Vasin realized that a small circle of people stood staring at him—the two drivers, three street kids, Kuznetsov—all waiting for his orders.

"You three, go back to Uncle Borya. Fingers, you tell Borya that I might need you guys on short notice. Tell him I'll pay. Then you go back to Rosa's, collect our bags. Send 'em back here with Ginger in two hours. Here's fifty rubles for your trouble. And, guys—thanks. You all did great. Really fucking great."

# 5

The two taxis rumbled off back toward the city, leaving Vasin and Kuznetsov standing in the wind. The landscape was flat and featureless, punctuated only by an occasional stand of birches. Half of Russko-Vysotskoe was a communal farm—chickens, to judge by the alkaline reek carried on the breeze. The other half, a collection of humble dachas. The country houses, little more than homemade shacks, really, of very modest people.

"What a dump," Kuznetsov snarled.

"He's housed. That's the main thing." Housed—the term of art at the KGB academy for seeing a target bedded down for the night.

"So where do *we* stay?"

Vasin shrugged.

"Next door to our friend, I guess. Look. These are summer dachas. There's no smoke rising. Nobody at home. Except our man Fyodorov."

The fugitive's traces were ludicrously easy to follow. A fresh set of tire tracks led down a lane lined with single-story wooden houses, each set twenty meters from the next in a small garden surrounded by picket fences. A line of footsteps led from where the taxi had pulled up to one of the houses, evidently built fairly recently but already dilapidated, with peeling paint and a sagging deck. Watching from the nearest clump of bushes, Vasin and Kuznetsov observed a figure moving around inside. A puff of white smoke emerged from a steel stovepipe in a corner of the roof.

The house directly opposite had the clearest view. Working their way around the rear of the building to avoid leaving telltale footprints in the undisturbed snow of the village street, Vasin and Kuznetsov stumbled onto the back porch. Both were panting after wading through thigh-deep powder. Vasin picked up an upturned flowerpot, then a glass jam jar, then shook a metal coffee tin.

"Here." Kuznetsov had been feeling along the upper edge of the beam that formed one edge of the porch. He produced a key that Vasin turned in the lock.

The interior of the house felt even colder than the garden. They were in the kitchen. A doorway led to a corridor and a steep staircase to the attic. Two small ground-floor bedrooms overlooked the street, and Fyodorov's house on the other side of the road. Unlike a real Russian peasant house, the dacha had no brick-built stove at its heart. The only heating was a wood-fired steel kitchen range and a portable kerosene heating stove—a prewar model a meter high fueled by a giant circular wick. Vasin found a can of kerosene, filled the contraption, and lit it. An acrid stink filled the room.

"Very cozy." Kuznetsov was rummaging through the cupboards, all empty. Rats, cockroaches, frost, and thieves would get any food left over the winter, so the owners had taken everything. Apart from a tin of tea, a tin of sugar, and a couple of tins of ancient corned beef, the place was devoid of anything to eat. The two men dragged the heater into the closer of the front rooms and huddled in blankets as they waited for the feeble heat to spread. Lights flicked on in the house opposite. Fyodorov had drawn the curtains before switching them on. Smoke was rising in a thick column from his chimney.

"That bastard's got a proper stove. And food."

"Lucky him. Sit tight, Kuznetsov. Ginger should be back with our stuff in an hour. I'll take the taxi and find us some provisions."

"And transportation. Or are we planning to follow this Fyodorov on skis when he makes his next move?"

"Sure, transportation. How much cash do we have left?"

Kuznetsov rummaged in his satchel and retrieved the last of the Vorkuta payroll money.

"Scarcely four hundred rubles."

"Shit."

"It's time to move in on him. Grab him now, while he's got the documents on him. Before he pulls some other move. We've been lucky, so far, but a couple of lucky guesses don't make you clairvoyant, Vasin."

"Go in and grab him, just you and me?"

"Yes. Then I need to head to Moscow. Get to the director of the *kontora*. Speak to Semichastny in person. Immediately."

Vasin pondered for a moment.

"You're sure that Semichastny had no knowledge? That he wasn't one of the conspirators?"

"Berezovsky—I mean, Fyodorov—didn't mention him."

"He wasn't in the room, if that's what you mean. But if Semichastny did know about the plot, and you walk into his office announcing that you and I know all about it, and we could lead him to Fyodorov—where does that leave us? Dead. At minimum."

"You're paranoid, Vasin."

"Just cautious. To be safe we need someone who definitely wasn't in on the Kennedy plot."

"Such as?"

"You said it yourself. Leonid Brezhnev. He's not a *kontora* player. And like you said, I have a way to get to his daughter—through Katya Orlova."

Kuznetsov knitted his brow and peered out of the window. The sunset illuminated the snowfields with a slanting, golden light.

"Maybe you're right. So *you* go to Moscow tomorrow?"

"Not tomorrow. We need to find out what Fyodorov's plan is."

"We don't grab him?"

"We *watch* him. He made a call from Leningrad. He's waiting for an answer from someone. Let's give it one more day."

"And follow him on foot?"

"Leave that to me."

# 6

After Ginger had returned from Leningrad with their things, Vasin rode back toward Leningrad with him. They passed through Krasnoe Selo, a depressing collection of sagging peasant houses clustered around newly built apartment blocks and a complex that contained a post office, a food store, and a handful of shops. The biggest building in the village center was the breeze-block local traffic-police station.

"Stop here."

The night was hard-cold and blustery. The citizens of Krasnoe Selo were sensibly huddled at home. Vasin bought up everything the meager store could provide—muddy potatoes, carrots, onions, and cabbage, some ancient-looking smoked pork, Zhigulevskoe beer, tins of sprats and processed cheese, a jar of marinated tomatoes, a couple of batons of rock-hard bread, a kilo of red beans. No coffee available, only some Georgian tea in a dented tin. No sugar either. No sweets. Or salami. At least they had cigarettes—the cheapest sort, Kazbegi—and matches. It would have to do. Vasin lugged the box of groceries back to the taxi.

A chundering motorcycle with a sidecar passed, driven by an elderly man with his face wrapped in rags against the wind. The heavy machine turned in to the village, fishtailing on the ruts before the driver regained control and irritably gunned the engine as he accelerated away. Vasin tossed the box onto the backseat of the taxi and jumped in.

"Follow that bike!"

There was no other traffic in the village, so it was easy to track the receding red taillight along the main road and off down a smaller lane. Vasin ordered the driver to kill his engine and headlights as he watched the bike's owner dismount, leaving the engine running while he fumbled to open a small jerry-built garage. Opening the double doors against the piles of snow with a struggle, he remounted and drove the machine in before noisily bolting the doors from inside. After a moment the bike's owner emerged from the garage's back door, made his way into his lopsided prewar house, and slammed the door.

"Ginger?"

"You thinkin' what I think you're thinkin', boss?"

"I am. Urgent needs of the state. I'll return it. Driver, wait for us here."

Vasin and Ginger walked down the lane along the fresh tire marks to the garage. Lights were on in the house. A dog barked, but inside. Vasin guessed it was being fed. They had a few minutes before the owner might let the dog out. The gate in the picket fence was open, and Vasin and Ginger crept through the snowbound garden to the garage door. Padlocked. But a small window, evidently salvaged from another house, had been crookedly nailed into one wall.

"Leg up, boss?"

Vasin knelt, his shoulder against the garage wall, as Ginger stepped up and fiddled with the window latch. In a moment the window was open and the kid was scrambling through. A minute later, he'd opened the double front doors from inside. The darkness smelled of low-octane gasoline, engine oil, and animal shit. A frenzied scrambling and bumping came from one corner.

"Fuck's that?"

"Rabbits, city kid. Now help me push this thing out. Be quiet."

It took a few moments of fiddling with his right foot for Vasin to find neutral on the unfamiliar machine, burning his calf on the still-hot exhaust pipe in the process. With a couple of heaves they got the motorbike rolling, Vasin pushing on the handlebars and Ginger hauling on the sidecar. At the doorway the machine was faintly illuminated by the lights from the owner's windows. Vasin rummaged in the sidecar and produced a bag full of what looked like plumber's tools. Carefully, he set them down inside the garage.

"Worth a pretty penny, them tools," whispered Ginger. "Let me have 'em?"

"We're not bloody *thieves*, boy."

"Course not. Forgot."

They got the garage doors closed and struggled, slipping on the icy track, to get the bike rolling up the slight incline to the paved road where the taxi waited. The machine was fiendishly heavy.

"Why not just start it up, boss? We could jump in and make a quick getaway, like in the gangster movies."

"This bike makes a racket to wake the dead. The owner will be out here with a pitchfork in seconds. No. Get the taxi to reverse down here. And get out his towrope."

# 7

Three streets away, Vasin braked the motorbike he'd been riding in tow. The bike was so heavy that with its wheels locked it slowed the trundling Volga to a halt, its tires spinning on the snow. Ginger loaded the groceries into the sidecar as the taxi driver hurriedly gathered up his towrope. Even Vasin's Interior Ministry ID wasn't enough to assuage his nervousness at being roped in—literally—to a serious crime.

Vasin handed the driver fifty rubles and gave Ginger twenty-five more for the taxi fare out to Russko-Vysotskoe if and when he would next be needed.

"Good luck, Ginger. Remember, today's activities are not to be seen as an endorsement of theft or criminal activity of any kind."

The kid's smile shone as Vasin flicked on the motorcycle's headlight.

"Course not, boss."

"Right. Get out of here."

It had been close to fifteen years since Vasin was last on a motorbike, back in his military service days. He found the starting pedal, jumped on it with his full weight, and skinned his ankle as his boot slipped off the icy metal. At least the engine was still warm, despite having been dragged through the snow. That was important for easy starting, Vasin remembered. He also knew not to flood the carburetor. On the sixth attempt the engine stuttered to life, deafeningly loud. Vasin jammed it into gear. Close up, the unmuffled exhaust roared like a helicopter. The bike leapt forward twenty yards, skidded into a snowbank, and stalled. It took Vasin three false starts to get as far as the main road. The enormous bass roar of the old man's motorbike must have been a local nuisance, known and hated by every villager. It was not till he was finally running steadily westward on the highway that Vasin breathed more easily.

Transportation set.

# 8

By the time he'd hidden the bike in a stand of trees and lugged the heavy box of groceries through moonlit snowdrifts, Vasin was half-frozen. He found Kuznetsov slumped in darkness in the bedroom, the only light coming from the glowing blue flame in the paraffin heater. The tiny room reeked of kerosene and cigarette smoke. But it was at least half-warm.

"Took your time."

"Fuck you, too. Move over. I'm freezing."

"There's no water in this house."

"Course there isn't. It's in the well."

"The *well*? Are we in a Pushkin story?"

"You've never drawn water from a well?"

"Have you?"

"Sure. At my in-laws' dacha at Vnukovo."

"Never had you down as a son of the soil, Vasin."

"We could use snow for tonight. Get the cooking stove lit. I saw some dry wood out back. Boil some water for tea. I'll make soup. We have potatoes. Cabbage. Pork."

Grumbling, Kuznetsov heaved himself to his feet.

"You never said we were going to have to get bloody *domestic*, Vasin."

# 9

By dawn the kitchen was an almost cozy temperature. Vasin and Kuznetsov had slept in shifts, keeping watch on the house opposite and stoking the cooking stove in turns. They spotted Fyodorov only once, when he emerged to bring in wood from a shed.

"Well, this is very charming, Vasin. A month in the country, is it? This soup gets better with age, by the way."

Vasin ignored Kuznetsov's wisecracking and slurped the cabbage soup he'd made. Both men were wearing moth-eaten felt boots they'd found in a wardrobe, and Kuznetsov had squeezed on a rabbit-fur hat that was missing one earflap. Vasin checked his watch.

"In two hours it'll be twenty-four hours since he made those calls from Sennaya Square. Maybe he'll try to call back."

"Where from? The pay phone here is just local. He found an intercity booth for a reason."

"Right. My guess is he'll try the post office in the next village."

"Would that be the village where you stole your famous motor-cycle? The owner will be delighted to see it again."

Shit. Vasin frowned. Kuznetsov was right.

"That's why you're going to do the talking, Kuznetsov. And the walking. I'll be on the bike. If he makes a move."

"And if he doesn't?"

"I'll have time to teach you to split logs. And to make a decent cabbage soup."

# 10

It was early afternoon when Fyodorov appeared once more. He was wearing a bulky sheepskin Army-issue greatcoat that was much too big for him, as well as felt boots and a shapeless padded cotton hat. He waded through the snowdrifts on the village main street and tramped off toward the highway.

Cursing the lack of cover in these windblown flatlands, Vasin kept watch from the stand of trees where he'd hidden the bike. Fyodorov waited patiently by the roadside, his thumb out for a lift. By daylight Vasin saw that the machine he had stolen was an Army-green Harley-Davidson, one of thousands shipped over as aid by the USA during the war. A faint white square with the remains of a red cross painted on the sidecar showed that it was once a field medic's bike. It was similar enough to the Dnieprs he'd trained on, copies of German wartime BMWs. The Harley was twenty years old, but it had been lovingly looked after. Vasin just prayed that it was a good cold starter.

It took twenty freezing minutes before a farm truck stopped. After a hurried conversation Fyodorov hopped into the cab and the truck rumbled off. Vasin furiously began to turn over the frozen motorcycle engine, which to his relief started almost as quickly as it had when it was running hot. He found reverse—these sidecar bikes were so heavy they had a reverse gear—and maneuvered it, spitting huge arcs of snow, out onto the road. Kuznetsov, spattered with snow from head to foot from pushing the wheel-spinning bike through the ruts, jumped into the sidecar, and the pair roared off in pursuit.

# 11

"You'll never believe this."

Vasin straightened stiffly. He'd been keeping warm by using a carburetor brush to scrape the white and red paint off the sidecar and make the bike a bit less recognizable. It had been an hour and a half since Fyodorov hopped off his truck on the edge of Krasnoe Selo, with Kuznetsov following on foot at a cautious distance while Vasin hid off-road.

"Where's Fyodorov?"

"He got on the bus toward the shithole we all call home, carrying a bag of shopping, about forty minutes ago. So I talked to the village postmaster. And yes, he did make a call. Moscow number. Then I made a call of my own to a friend of mine at the Lubyanka. Not from Special Cases, before you shit yourself. A guy from my old Cuban team. Asked him to look up the number in the reverse directory. And guess who our sneaky, cunning little shit was speaking to."

"Kuznetsov. I'm freezing. Spit it out."

"The Embassy of the People's fucking Republic of China."

# 12

Vasin huddled a mug of tea in his cupped hands, leaning as close to the cooking stove as he could without singeing his coat.

"Makes sense, of course," said Kuznetsov, sipping tea. "To sell himself to the *Chinese*? The man has no shame."

"Maybe. But the Chinese could certainly put the information to use."

"You mean, to blackmail the USSR?"

"I read the papers, even up in Vorkuta. We're enemies of the Chinese now. And both of us are enemies of the USA. The Sino-Soviet rift, they call it. The Chinese would love to know what Fyodorov knows. And as you say, blackmail. That's why he went to them. Smart."

"You seem very calm about the prospect, Vasin. I thought you were a Soviet State Security officer."

"It's logical to sell himself to the Chinese and not to the CIA or MI6. I'd do the same, in his shoes."

Kuznetsov looked at his partner askance.

"Anything else you two have got in common, apart from a casual attitude to betraying your country?"

"Screw you, Kuznetsov. But since you ask—yes. We both think for ourselves. Take responsibility for the consequences of our actions."

"Ah. Two fellow sufferers of chronic morality. You know that can be a fatal disease, right?"

"So can cynicism."

"I'm the careerist cynic, you're the moral crusader. Do I have it right, Vasin?"

"I'm just trying to save my skin. Get myself out of the mess that Orlov dumped on my head. No more. No less."

"Whatever you say. But we have our cue, I guess. We know the fucker's plan. Time for you to hightail it to Moscow, to your Katya and Galina Brezhneva. But we need to get this guy in a bottle before the Chinese come and pick him up. You'll be taking the night train? Plane?"

"Not tonight."

"*Why?*"

"We need to be sure."

"What the hell are you talking about? He called the Chinese Embassy."

"What if they put the phone down? Dismissed it as a *kontora* provocation?"

"What does it matter?"

"We need to go to Brezhnev with something more concrete than a single phone call."

"You want to wait for Fyodorov to spill all the beans to the Chinese."

"He won't spill everything at once. He'll be coy. He'll wait for guarantees. An exfiltration plan in place. That will take time. Authorization from Peking, logistics. *Then* he'll run. We have time, Vadim. Days."

"Vasin, you're crazy. He's *right there*. A hundred meters across the street. In a house, undefended, with his precious papers hidden somewhere very close. We need to move, now."

"We give him another day and see if the Chinese bite. *Then* I go find Galina Brezhneva. Deal?"

# 13

It was well before dawn when the lights in the house opposite flicked on, then, after ten minutes, off. Fyodorov appeared, a black shape against the white, starlit snow. Vasin kicked Kuznetsov awake.

"Get dressed. He's on the move again."

"Hell."

They didn't dare kindle a light for fear of alerting their neighbor to their presence, so Kuznetsov blundered about in the dark pulling on his boots and trousers. Wallowing through snowdrifts and back gardens, they followed Fyodorov to the deserted bus stop. Once he had boarded the first local bus of the day, the two scrambled to fire up the frozen Harley and get it on the road. As the engine caught, Vasin silently blessed Yankee engineering.

This time Fyodorov rode the bus past Krasnoe Selo to the next village, Novogorelovo. The predawn darkness made it easier for Kuznetsov to linger unseen as Fyodorov consulted the bus time-tables, bought a snack at a kiosk, and boarded another bus, heading to the seaside town of Pushkin.

The Catherine Palace was where he alighted. Vasin had visited, dutifully, on a boyhood trip to Leningrad with his mother and her work colleagues. The place had been built as some Tsarina's Russian version of Versailles, he remembered. There was a seaside tang in the wind that swept off the Baltic. Crawling along in first gear, Vasin followed Fyodorov's shadowy figure to a gatehouse that marked the entrance of the palace's park. It was still well before opening time, and Fyodorov settled down on a bench to wait for the ticket office to open. Shivering in the winter chill, Vasin ached for the black sky in the east to pale into dawn.

A municipal bus drew up, disgorging museum workers, then another bearing a party of tourists. Groundsmen appeared and hauled open the grand wrought-iron gates. With a clack, the small ticket office window snapped open. Fyodorov was first in line.

A broad graveled avenue that led from the palace gates was flanked by mature trees, their bare branches deep black in the milky morning light. Beyond was a grand series of terraced lawns and flower beds, each level decorated with a crowd of baroque statues covered in gold leaf that shone with a dull glow. Some were boxed up in rough pinewood to protect the delicate stonework from splitting in the frost. Fyodorov made his way up the series of wide steps and sloped terraces that ascended to the palace itself. At the top of the rise he stopped and turned, both surveying the view and likely checking for tails. Vasin and Kuznetsov, though they were well hidden in the foliage, froze.

The palace was an imposing cliff of stucco, glass, and columns that stretched across the crest of the rise. An ongoing restoration had made the place look as though it had been built yesterday, the fresh white and blue paint and gold leaf immaculate. One end of the imposing building was still covered in knocked-together wooden scaffolding and surrounded by a construction fence.

Fyodorov perched on a bench in the center of the palace's facade. A group of foreign tourists appeared at the foot of the grand avenue, led by a guide in a plain blue woolen overcoat and knitted beret.

". . . during their retreat before the victorious armies of the Motherland, the barbarous Fascist occupiers attempted to destroy the Catherine Palace in a cowardly act of vengeance against the heritage and inheritance of the Great Soviet People." The woman's voice was like a foghorn. She paused for a mousy companion who stood at her side to translate into English before moving up the slope to the terrace near where Vasin and Kuznetsov were hiding. "The famous Amber Room, a salon decorated entirely in panels of solid Baltic amber, was dismantled, packed, and removed. It has never been seen again. They blew up part of the Northern Wing and set the building on fire. After the comprehensive defeat of Fascism by the heroic peoples of the USSR, a battalion of female sappers was detailed to de-mine the palace. They discovered a total of 3,024 kilos of high-explosive German booby traps. I was one of those sappers, Comrades. Even a year after the Fascist aggression, my life and the lives of other young Soviets could have been ended by the malice of the Hitlerites."

A murmur of appreciation passed through the group of foreign tourists when this information was translated. They were a miserable-looking bunch, mostly skinny with unhealthy, spotty complexions. Their coats were far too thin for midwinter in Leningrad. Evidently, this was a party of British Communists come to see the glories of the workers' paradise.

"The full restoration of the interiors of the palace will be complete by the summer of next year, Comrades," continued the guide. "A party of Soviet artists was even dispatched to Venice, Italy, at the invitation of the Italian Communist Party to study the surviving work of the painters who originally created the ceilings . . ."

The guide's booming voice trailed off as she led the party over the brow of the hill, out of earshot. Fyodorov sat on, motionless.

Another pair of foreign tourists, unaccompanied, began the long walk up the avenue. Fyodorov had chosen a perfect vantage point for observing anyone who approached. The two men wore heavy, boxy greatcoats and rabbit-fur hats. Both were unmistakably Chinese. They passed the bush behind which Vasin and Kuznetsov were hiding without glancing in their direction. Fyodorov stood, hesitated, and raised a hand. The older of the two Chinese men sat beside him while the other waited at a discreet distance.

Kuznetsov gave Vasin a meaningful glance and made to stand from his crouch. But Vasin stilled him with a hand.

"Look. Over there."

On the opposite side of the avenue a man was making his way furtively through the bushes to the side of the gravel path. He disappeared into the foliage for a while, as Vasin and Kuznetsov crept closer to the uppermost terrace, shadowing his movements. The figure reappeared, making a quick dash from the undergrowth to the foot of a monumental classical statue. Unseen by Fyodorov or the Chinese but in plain view of Vasin, the man produced a camera with a long bulky lens from a rucksack. Balancing the lens on a stone ledge, he began to snap off pictures.

"KGB?" Vasin retreated deeper into the foliage, sitting down on the snowy ground. "How the fuck did they find us?"

Kuznetsov joined Vasin, sinking back into an uncomfortable crouch.

"They would have followed the Chinese, I guess. We must be listening in on the Embassy's phone lines. Fyodorov had no choice but to give a rendezvous location on an open line when he called yesterday. And I assume those guys are diplomats. Standard operating procedure for the *kontora* to follow them here."

"Damn. And I bet that guy's not alone. You stay here and keep an eye on Fyodorov. I'll head down to the parking lot. See how many of them there are. Maybe it's just routine surveillance. Maybe they have no idea who Fyodorov is."

"And the parking lot will tell you that how, Sasha?"

"Number of cars. Level of excitement. Local *kontora* goons or out-of-towners. See if anyone we know is around. Like Kozlov. Or his attack dog."

# 14

A single Volga-21 was parked alongside the tourist buses in front of the palace. It bore distinctive red diplomatic license plates. Another Volga with Leningrad plates waited a hundred meters down the road—its whippy aerial giving it away as a classic KGB radio car. Neither the *kontora* nor the Chinese had exactly been subtle about this operation. Vasin casually sauntered past both vehicles, his hands cupped in front of his face in an apparent attempt to light a cigarette. The Russian driver of the Embassy Volga sat in a dull trance, his chin resting on his hands, which lay folded on top of the wheel.

The driver of the *kontora* car was leaning down, his ear pressed to a radio telephone and acknowledging a stream of instructions. Vasin walked quickly on, following signs to a cafe. He bought two paper cups of coffee and a bag full of sweet rolls and walked back to the palace, his hands full with his tangible alibi. The first KGB Volga had been joined by another car, this one containing four youngish men with the distinctive look of *kontora* muscle.

Vasin sat on the bench by the ticket office, sipping one coffee and then—mentally apologizing to Kuznetsov, freezing up there in the park—the other. The driver of the first *kontora* car joined the men in the second, conferring. Vasin made himself breathe slow and think, logically, step by step, just like his old mentor Weiss had taught him. Put yourself in the mind of the opponent.

The Moscow KGB had picked up the suspicious communication with the Chinese Embassy through routine phone surveillance. Check.

The local Leningrad *kontora* followed up, tracking the Chinese diplomatic car to the Catherine Palace. Check.

What were the chances that word had leaked out to Kozlov and his gang at the First Chief Directorate? In a single day? Slim to none. The *kontora*'s diplomatic surveillance department almost certainly had no idea who had made the call.

Why were the KGB here in force? They couldn't touch the Chinese diplomats. So they were here for Fyodorov. A clandestine meeting with a foreign diplomat was cause enough to haul any Soviet citizen in for questioning. If they took him in for interrogation, what were the chances that Kozlov would find out?

In time, pretty much a hundred percent.

Conclusion: Vasin had to get Fyodorov out of there, fast. Or he was a dead man.

# 15

Making an effort to move casually, Vasin dutifully tossed the empty coffee cups in the rubbish can and walked back to the entrance gate before being turned around and forced to buy a new ticket by the dragon lady at the booth. The about-face gave Vasin an opportunity to sneak another look at the parked Volgas. The *kontora* goons were still sitting in the car, except for one, who stood by the curb, talking into a portable military radio. Bad news. Whoever had eyes on Fyodorov in the park was connected to his colleagues by walkie-talkie.

At the foot of the avenue Vasin slid under the cover of the bordering trees and broke into a run. Breathless, he reached Kuznetsov's hiding place.

"What's up?"

"There's a *kontora* snatch squad down there, and I need to warn Fyodorov. You go and get the bike. There are two *kontora* cars parked a hundred meters from the entrance. Drive to the far east end of the park fence. Wait for us there." A worrying thought crossed Vasin's mind. "Have you ever driven a motorcycle?"

"Couple of times."

"Go easy on the throttle when you're starting her. Don't flood the engine. Use the choke. You know where that is, right? And . . ."

"Shut the fuck up, Vasin. I'm on it."

Kuznetsov disappeared into the bushes.

# 16

Behind a corner of the palace, keeping well out of sight of Fyodorov, Vasin found a knocked-together row of workers' barracks. He tried the door—locked. Next to it was a larger barnlike structure in which rough-cut pine planks were stacked to the roof. The place was deserted. By a pile of rakes and hoes Vasin found a padded gray cotton worker's jacket, identical except for its color to the black uniforms worn by the prisoners at Vorkuta. He shrugged it on and grabbed a long-handled shovel.

On the broad terrace in front of the palace, Fyodorov and his Chinese companion were still locked in conversation. It had been nearly forty minutes since they met. Vasin pulled his hat over his eyes, shuffled toward a flower bed, and began shoveling snow.

The Chinese man stood, followed by Fyodorov. They shook hands. The diplomat and his companion began to walk away, leaving Fyodorov standing by the bench, alone. Vasin approached him slowly, praying that the man would control himself as he recognized him. Twenty meters. Ten. Fyodorov began to light a cigarette as Vasin drew level.

"Andrei!" Vasin hissed from the corner of his mouth as he passed, two meters away. "Follow me. *Kontora* is watching."

Vasin didn't dare look back to see if Fyodorov had heard, or recognized him. He kept his eyes forward as he marched doggedly across the terrace, shouldering his shovel and hunching his shoulders. There was no sound of movement from behind. Vasin reached the beginning of the scaffolding and deliberately dropped his tool, giving him an opportunity to glance back. Cool as ice, Fyodorov stood motionless smoking his cigarette, gazing out at the view.

Then he turned and followed.

Vasin's heart raced. The word would be going out on the radio: target on the move. Vasin's guess was that the watchers would prefer to have the Chinese diplomats on their way before moving in for the snatch, which gave them a few minutes. But the *kontora* watchers would be closing in now to keep their target in view. Vasin picked up his shovel and continued to the end of the fencing that surrounded the far side of the palace. Just around the corner was a makeshift door in the fence. It opened to a light heave of Vasin's shoulder. He waited, half-hidden, until Fyodorov appeared around the corner.

"Here!" Vasin's voice was urgent.

Fyodorov, facing the surrounding park with his back to Vasin, made no sign of acknowledgment.

"The *kontora* followed your fucking Chinese contacts. Let's *go*."

With impressive self-control, Fyodorov casually turned the corner and strolled toward Vasin. The moment he was out of sight of the terrace he darted for the open door. When they were safely inside, Fyodorov's and Vasin's eyes met. Fyodorov snatched the shovel that Vasin was uselessly still holding and dug it into the gravel to wedge the door shut.

"Now what?"

A low door led through the palace's three-meter-thick wall to a dark passageway that smelled of damp plaster. The two men blundered down it, kicking over buckets and half-tripping on construction lumber in their hurry. The corridor opened out into a broad stone-flagged semibasement space lit by high windows. A stone staircase led up into the palace itself.

"What you lookin' for?"

The gruff voice belonged to a burly older workman. He'd appeared from the opposite passage, leading two younger men, who carried the top of a stone fireplace between them. The man looked suspiciously from Vasin in his dirty worker's coat to Fyodorov, who was wearing the ordinary civilian clothes Vasin had bought him in Leningrad.

"This is one of the . . . museum people." Vasin made his voice hoarse to disguise his Moscow accent. "He's here to check on the paintings. The Venetian ones. On the ceiling. How they're . . . drying. And all."

The foreman gave a dismissive proletarian grunt and passed on.

"Well, you won't find 'em down here, that's for sure."

# 17

On a darkened landing the two men paused to listen for pursuit. Silence.

"How the hell did you find me?"

"How do you think, Andrei? We followed you to Russko-Vysotskoe. Traced your call to the Chinese Embassy. You're not the only professional around here."

A silence in the darkness.

"Good work, Sasha."

"Thanks."

"Who's out there?"

"Local Leningrad *kontora* is my guess."

"They don't know . . . ?"

"Unless you introduced yourself on the phone they should have no idea who you are or why you are here. But it's protocol to follow up on suspicious contacts. They had your meeting under surveillance. And I assume they're interested in hearing what you were chatting about with your new Chinese friends."

Urgent voices drifted up from the chamber below them, sending Vasin and Fyodorov sprinting up the stairs. They emerged into a grand mirrored hallway that smelled strongly of varnish and fresh-planed wood. A pair of workers perched on a high scaffold ignored them. Fyodorov snatched a roll of plans, a clipboard, and a pencil from a trestle table and marched forward with a confident stride. They passed through an outsize pair of double doors into a dazzlingly vast ballroom, the brand-new parquet covered in cotton sheets. Fyodorov strode on through with the air of a man who knew exactly where he was going. They had now reached the palace's central staircase. A group of men and women, some in overalls and some in civilian clothes, looked up as they appeared. Fyodorov smiled and nodded at the oldest of the men, who gave a hesitant nod of apparent recognition in return. Fyodorov continued past, Vasin in tow, without slowing.

At the next hallway, out of sight of the group at the bottom of the stairwell, Fyodorov made a beeline for the first door. It was locked. He tried another, which opened. He bundled Vasin through and closed it behind them. They found themselves in a large chamber half-full of wooden scaffolding that obscured much of the daylight. The walls were covered in dark, mottled brown paneling, and the air was perfumed with a strong, indefinable musk. His eyes adjusting to the dim light, Vasin made out a stack of broad wooden packing cases, each containing more wall panels. He peered closer and sniffed.

"It's pure amber. This is the new Amber Room!"

Fyodorov was by the door, listening at the keyhole.

"Focus. They're here. They're got the museum staff looking for us. Check the window."

The windows were five meters high and brand-new, beautifully crafted from carved wood and beveled glass. Vasin tried the handle on one and, with a hard tug, pulled open the inner window. But the outer window would not budge. A door in the adjacent room opened, bringing the echo of voices. Fyodorov picked up a chisel and pushed Vasin aside, slapping the tool into the molding of the window with the flat of his hand before giving it a hard push. A long splinter of wood split off.

"Andrei! Careful."

Without pausing, Fyodorov dug the chisel into the window frame again, more savagely this time. The ornate door to the Amber Room opened, but whoever was about to come in was checked by a calling voice.

With a creak, the outer window finally gave way, swinging open. The frame couldn't open more than partway because of the scaffolding on the outside of the building. But the gap was just enough for both men to squeeze through onto the pine scaffolding that ran along the facade. Two stories below, two of the *kontora* men Vasin recognized from the car stood guard on the terrace. The scaffolding was a naked frame, with nothing to conceal the two fugitives from sight if the goons chanced to look up.

The boards underfoot were flimsy and covered with a thick layer of snow, which Vasin and Fyodorov could not help but dislodge as they crept on all fours underneath the long row of windows. The scaffolding extended to the corner of the building. But the ladder down to the next level had been removed, leaving just an opening over the five-meter drop to the lower tier.

Behind them, a window banged open.

Vasin felt himself being propelled bodily over the end of the parapet. Fyodorov's strong hands gripped his shoulders.

"Crossbeam, right under your feet. Now grab that vertical. Go."

In a few seconds they were down one level, Vasin's hands torn and filled with splinters. Mercifully, there was a ladder on this level. In seconds they were on the ground.

"This way!"

Fyodorov sprinted along the inside of the fencing, away from the door where they had entered. The fence was too high to easily climb. Around the corner of the palace, the fence stretched unbroken down the rear of the building. No door.

"Here."

With a mighty kick, Fyodorov sprang the bottom of one of the fence planks from its horizontal support. A few more kicks, and enough planks were free for them to scramble through. Vasin felt the crooked nails scoring his back and buttocks as he wriggled free. The two men sprinted across a wide parterre to the safety of a clump of bushes.

"Which way now?"

Panting, Vasin pointed to the corner of the park closest to the city.

A face appeared at the base of the fence, followed by a shout. Rolling over in the snow, Fyodorov wriggled deeper into the undergrowth.

It took them nearly an hour to work their way through the park to the perimeter fence. Vasin's face was ragged with scratches from flicking branches, and his feet and hands were frozen. The park's fence was wrought iron, four meters high and topped with spikes. Beyond, Vasin could see the huddled figure of Kuznetsov on the green Harley, parked by a bus stop fifty meters away.

"*That's* your transport?"

"Don't insult the workers of Milwaukee. It's a great bike."

Crouching close to the ground, Fyodorov scrambled to a young beech tree that overhung the fence, then shimmied up and over. On the far side he braced his feet and hands on the sides of the iron railings and slid down smoothly. Damn man's as nimble as a commando, thought Vasin. With an exhausted sigh, grunting as he went, Vasin effortfully followed.

Fyodorov and Vasin waited, crouching, for a bus to pass before making their final dash. Vasin bundled Kuznetsov into the sidecar and mounted the bike himself, Fyodorov perching on the rear. Two kicks of the starter and they were off in a cloud of exhaust. As the overloaded bike accelerated on the icy road they almost swerved into the path of a pair of police cars coming in the other direction, sirens blaring.

# PART EIGHT

# 19–20 DECEMBER 1963

The truth shall set you free.

—JOHN 8:32

# 1

Fyodorov's dacha was larger and cozier than the one where Vasin and Kuznetsov had been squatting. The walls were made of solid logs, not planks, and the place was decorated with pieces of painted wooden folk art. A knitted tablecloth covered the table with a red spotted tea service laid out on it. Every object communicated style and bohemian elegance.

"Let me guess. This place belongs to your girlfriend from *Vecherny Leningrad*. Ksenia."

"Let's keep her out of this, Vasin." Fyodorov's tone was hostile.

"You should have thought of that," interjected Kuznetsov, "before you got her involved in your treachery."

Vasin glared at Kuznetsov. It was clear that there was no love lost between them.

"Enough. Can someone help get me patched up, please? Antiseptic? Bandages? I'm bleeding everywhere."

"There's a medical kit in the bathroom." Fyodorov took a step toward the kitchen door to fetch it, but Kuznetsov moved quickly to block his exit.

"Not so fast."

"You think I'm going to dive out of the window?"

"That's exactly what I think, you treacherous bastard. Soon as you've patched up Vasin, we're tying you up. I'm heading to the village to make some calls, and we're taking you into custody. Immediately."

"No need to tie him up, Kuznetsov," breathed Vasin.

"I've had enough of following your lead, Sasha. From now on we do this *my* way. No more running off to the Chinese or whoever the fuck. Everyone okay with that? *I'll* get the damn first-aid box."

Vasin gasped as Fyodorov dabbed iodine solution onto his scratched face.

"When did you last have a tetanus shot?" Fyodorov asked, his voice calm and low, ignoring Kuznetsov's anger.

"No idea. Kuznetsov, who are you going to call?"

"Someone *I* trust."

With a snort, Kuznetsov gathered his bag and slammed the door, turning the key and brandishing it as he tramped past the kitchen window to the deep snow of the front yard. After a few moments the sound of a coughing motorcycle echoed from the road. The engine revved, then died.

"Flooded it."

"Dangerous guy, your friend. Emotional."

The Harley's engine finally spluttered into life, then receded into the distance. Fyodorov carefully packed away the iodine and gauze in the tin first-aid box.

"Fuck you, Fyodorov. Yes—your friend Ksenia told us your name. But really—*fuck* you. We risked our backsides to get you out of that damn palace in one piece. A meeting where you were in the process of betraying your country—*our* country—to an enemy power. Without us you'd be sitting in a KGB cell and you'd stay there for the rest of your very short life."

Fyodorov merely turned to fill a kettle from a bucket of well water that stood by the stove.

"You must know who he's going to call."

"Andrei, I really have no idea. But we need to get you under lock and key."

"My 'very short life,' you said? Remind me why I should be grateful to you for rescuing me from the official KGB only to have me imprisoned by your own little gang?"

"We're not a gang, Andrei. We only want justice."

"Ah yes. Justice. Punish the men who cooked up the Kennedy assassination, is it? Punish Orlov, for his silence? Sounds good—

especially if some careers could be made on the way. But there's no justice for *me*."

"I understand why you hate the *kontora*."

"Vasin, I don't *hate* the *kontora*. I just *know* the *kontora*. How they think. How they operate. And in every possible combination involving the KGB, I die. My colleagues from the First Chief Directorate want to kill me because I know too much about them. Orlov, too. The guys you talk about, these imaginary avengers who are going to roll up evil and bring Soviet justice to all wrongdoers? They'll use me for as long as it takes to bring down their enemies then, oops, I'm dead again. Don't try to tell me I'm wrong."

Vasin held Fyodorov's gaze.

"And what do you think the Chinese will do with your information?"

"China is weak. Poor. We could thrash them in a second, militarily. Not that it'll ever come to that. They need all the leverage they can get against the USSR. Maybe this information will even help *avert* war. Strengthen the Chinese hand against Soviet aggression."

"Listen, Andrei. I'm not a strategic expert and neither are you. But for the record, that sounds like bullshit to me. All you want is to get out of the USSR with your skin intact, and you'll sell your country out to do it."

"You're forgetting one thing, Vasin. I chose *not* to participate in the Kennedy assassination. I went up the ladder to General Orlov like an honest Soviet citizen, and look what I got. So yes, I'll take a whole skin from whoever's offering."

"That's what *we're* offering. I'm offering."

"We both know you can't make that promise. There *is* life outside the USSR, I promise you. Not so bad, either. We're not the only workers' paradise in this wide world."

"Why wouldn't the Chinese just kill you?"

"Because unlike the *kontora*, they need me as living proof."

"They've already agreed to exfiltrate you? They gave you a local Leningrad number as a contact?"

Fyodorov's smile was almost friendly.

"Sasha, you never give up, do you? It's too late for all that now. You got me. I'm your prisoner. End of the road for me. I'm starving, by the way. Want some porridge? There's a pot in the pantry."

"Sure, Andrei. Get some porridge on."

Vasin felt suddenly chilly. Maybe it was blood loss. As Fyodorov ducked out of the room Vasin extended his stocking foot to the hot stove and luxuriated in the warmth.

An oily, metallic click-clack brought him out of his reverie.

Fyodorov stood in the kitchen doorway. In his hands was a shiny black submachine gun Vasin recognized from war films.

"German MP-40." Fyodorov spoke quietly and steadily as he pointed the gun squarely at Vasin's chest. "Designed by Hugo Schmeisser. Who also created our famous Kalashnikov after he was taken prisoner. Not that he got any credit. Did you know that? This was still in its original packing grease when I got it down from the rafters. Ksenia's father found a box of them dumped by the road after the war, stowed it in case the Fascists ever came back this way."

"Aggravated illegal possession of an automatic firearm. Criminal Code article 447. Five to ten years." Vasin's voice, as he stared down the barrel of the gun, was hollow. "Fine. Run, Andrei. But please, give me the file. Your account of your meetings with Oswald. The times and dates. The personnel. The *kontora* officer who organized the job in your place. The names of the people at that meeting. It's enough for me. We'll bring them all in. They'll crack under inter-rogation once we have them in custody. I don't need you. But I need those papers. I beg you. I'm a good guy, too. Remember?"

Fyodorov stared down at Vasin. His face creased in a quick smile, bright and fleeting as a flint strike.

"If it was just you, Sasha. If it was just you, I'd take you with me. But . . ."

"I don't want to bloody escape with you to China. I want Orlov. And I need to get Kozlov off my back."

"That's enough. I can shoot you in the leg or tie you up. You choose, Sasha."

Lowering his eyes, Vasin knelt painfully on the floor and shuffled around, crossing his hands behind his back. As Fyodorov skillfully whipped a length of electrical cord around his wrists, Vasin closed his eyes. The knots finished, Fyodorov pushed Vasin gently in the small of the back and he toppled facefirst onto the floor.

He watched Fyodorov's boots march out of the kitchen and into the hallway. A sudden burst of gunfire, deafening in the small house, was followed by a tinny shower of metal as the door lock fell shattered to the floor.

"Just in case they didn't believe I have a gun," called Fyodorov. He paused in the open door, cold streaming in. "Good luck, Vasin. I mean it."

# 2

"You must be fucking *joking.*" Kuznetsov stood in the open door surveying the wood chips and bullet casings—and Vasin, sprawled uncomfortably on the floorboards with his hands bound behind his back. "How long's he been gone?"

"About half an hour. Forty minutes, maybe. You took your time."

*"Fuck!"*

"I'm freezing here."

Kuznetsov took a step toward the door before turning back to untie Vasin. Unsteadily, Vasin picked himself up, massaging the blood into his hands and wrists as he watched his colleague hurrying toward a local police jeep. Logical enough. Kuznetsov had summoned the village cops—the closest guys available with badges and guns. Kicking one of the two officers out of the passenger seat, Kuznetsov snatched their radio and began barking orders into the receiver. Vasin emerged unsteadily, his legs cramped, onto the dacha's porch, which was littered with pieces of the smashed front door.

". . . repeat armed and dangerous, over. Yes. General alert for all patrols in the district. Got that? Over." Kuznetsov flung down the radio and turned to shout across to Vasin. "What the hell are you waiting for?"

Vasin waded through the deep snow and climbed into the back of the jeep. Both local cops had the stolid, ruddy look of country boys, and they were wide-eyed at the two older officers who had just crashed into their unexciting world.

"Back to Krasnoe Selo," ordered Kuznetsov. "The post office. Fast!"

# 3

—

The village post office and telephone exchange was a flimsy one-story building with barred windows and a corrugated iron roof. Kuznetsov barged in and banged on the door that separated the public area and the back offices with the flat of his hand. He brandished his KGB ID at the startled postmistress as he pushed past her.

"Where are the local switchboards? Quick!"

A back room was filled with ancient-looking racks of telephone equipment—banks of green steel boxes that whirred and snapped as callers from the district dialed numbers.

"We need the switching box for the village of Russko-Vysotskoe. All calls dialed from the public phone box."

A young engineer was hastily summoned and identified the exchange box that handled all telephone communications to and from the village. On Kuznetsov's orders he unscrewed the steel casing. Inside, a row of mechanical dials displayed the last twenty-four digits originating from that line. As Kuznetsov scribbled down the numbers, a light flicked on and the dials began to spin again, one after another, erasing the oldest settings.

"Disconnect it! Disconnect that call right now."

Reaching across Kuznetsov, the kid yanked a cable and the machine went dead, allowing him to finish copying the string of numbers. With the engineer's help they deciphered the numerals into groups of seven figures—the length of a Leningrad local phone number, the first three numbers indicating the exchange and the last four the local number.

"These all local numbers?"

"Nope. Not the last two. 614—that's Leningrad city center. Vasiliyevsky Exchange, I'm pretty sure. 871 is northern Leningrad. Proletarsky Exchange, maybe. I could look it up."

"You do that, kid. And we need a local and intercity phone connection. Now."

The young engineer led them to his own cubbyhole, a tiny office scattered with disassembled radio and telephone parts and piled with amateur radio magazines. As soon as they were alone Kuznetsov picked up the phone and carefully dialed the Vasiliyevsky number, gesturing to Vasin to move close, holding the receiver up so that both could hear.

"Let us pray," whispered Kuznetsov as the number connected and began to ring. Three rings, four. Then a crackle as a woman's voice answered.

"Hello? I am listening."

With a shake of his head Vasin confirmed that he didn't recognize the voice.

"Tell me please, is that the office of *Vecherny Leningrad*?"

"Yes, this is *Vecherny Leningrad*. Who did you wish to speak to? Hello . . . hello?"

Kuznetsov pressed a finger on the cradle.

"Got the bastard. That's Ksenia's work phone."

"What about the other number?"

"We'll find out soon enough."

Kuznetsov picked up the phone again and dialed an 8 for intercity, then a nine-digit number.

"Who are you calling?"

"Friends. Shhh." Kuznetsov raised a finger to silence Vasin as the line connected. "Misha? We need you to find out everything you can about this number, and get an immediate tap up on it. Leningrad 871 9891 . . . Correct . . . Yes . . . Good."

"Who the hell was that? Who knows about this?"

"I called in some people, Vasin. We can't do this on our own."

"What people? *Kontora* people?"

"Yes. They're on a plane to Leningrad and will be here in a couple of hours."

"You realize how . . ."

"Don't say it, Vasin. You have to trust me. Right now we have to see how fast this Ksenia can move. Fyodorov obviously warned her. We still have a chance to catch her. She's a civilian, after all. Not trained like your friend."

"My *friend*?"

"Who you trusted so much you didn't want me to tie him up. *That* friend. Who is now armed and on the run."

"Do you know where Ksenia lives?"

"Like I said, I called in the professionals."


# 4

Kuznetsov hunched over the steering wheel of the commandeered police jeep, careering along the icy road toward Leningrad, tires skidding as he sped around the bends. His driving was so reckless that there was no possibility of conversation. Kuznetsov swung right onto the main Leningrad circular highway, then cut left onto Moskovskoe Shosse and accelerated toward the city center.

No. 16 Varshavskaya Street was a stolid prewar apartment building painted a dull gray. The entrance hall was fogged with the usual domestic winter miasma of tobacco smoke, rotting cardboard, and boiled vegetables. On the third floor, Kuznetsov listened at the door of apartment 33. A tinny radio sounded inside. He banged the door, then pressed the bell, then banged again. A shuffling, a muffled elderly voice, and a clicking of bolts and locks before the wizened face of an old woman peeped out of a crack.

"State Security. Open up!" Vasin had never seen Kuznetsov in all-out secret policeman mode. His shout was convincingly terrifying. "Where is Ksenia Alexeyevna?"

The old woman retreated as Kuznetsov flung open the front door and barged down the corridor. Vasin had seen that terrified look in the eyes of older people before—they'd been through this, back in the '30s, during the Great Terror. A paralyzing fear so deep it had become a reflex.

All the rooms of the communal apartment were locked except one—the old woman's. It contained two single beds, a tumble of clothes on the floor, a strong odor of perfume from a smashed bottle. The walls were decorated with tasteful drawings, and were painted a deep red that reminded Vasin of a museum.

"You shared this room with Ksenia Alexeyevna? She's your daughter?" Kuznetsov began to rummage through a mess of papers on a dressing table. The woman nodded.

"She said she had to go away. Something urgent. She took her jewelry and a small bag. Gave me her savings book. Is she in trouble?"

Ksenia's mother proffered the small cardboard State Sberbank book to Vasin with trembling hands. He leafed through it. The withdrawal sheets at the back had all been freshly signed, but the sums left blank. All Ksenia's meager savings could be cashed by anyone who had the bankbook.

"Look." Vasin proffered the open pages to Kuznetsov. "She's given away all her money. She's not coming back."

The old woman gave a plaintive wail.

"Nothing, Comrade. Nothing to worry about. But if you hear from her, you must call us." Vasin instinctively reached for a pen—but realized that he had no number to give the woman. "I mean—call the police. Tell them she's safe."

"Safe? Safe from what? Officers, please don't leave. Tell me what's happening . . ."

Kuznetsov was already striding away down the corridor. Vasin smiled weakly, shrugged, and followed.

# 5

Kuznetsov parked the police jeep, crookedly, outside the Oktyabr-skaya Hotel. The building was a grim monolith that faced Len-ingrad's Moscow Station across a bleak, snow-swept square. He bounded up the broad stone steps two at a time.

". . . three direct lines should be enough for now," he was telling the reception clerk by the time Vasin had caught up with him. "And internal phones in every room."

"Are you going to tell me what the hell's going on, Kuznetsov?"

"Welcome to our operations center. Better than your brothel, for sure. Come on, let's check out the rooms."

"Who's paying for all this? You said we're nearly out of money."

Kuznetsov ignored Vasin's question and tossed him a room key. "You're right next to me."

# 6

The corner suite was ringed with tall windows. Kuznetsov immedi-ately set to work pushing aside sofas and armchairs and maneuver-ing tables to make a large workspace in the middle of the room. Two hotel bellboys appeared with a trolley full of telephones, which they began to plug into a row of sockets along the baseboard. A waiter wheeled in a second trolley stacked with salami sandwiches, assorted meat pies, and pots of hot coffee.

"Kuznetsov, are you planning to run some kind of military cam-paign out of here? Who's all this food for?"

"The team. *My* team." Kuznetsov spoke with his mouth full of pie. "Eat."

"What fucking *team*?"

The door of the suite banged open. A pudgy, youngish man in

a boxy apparatchik suit staggered in with a heavy suitcase. It was Mikhail Lyubimov, the young officer who was once one of Vasin's most promising watchers, back in the days when Vasin had been a rising star in Special Cases. Could it have been little more than a year since that comfortable, privileged, powerful world had been Vasin's, too? The kid was an apparition from a previous, half-remembered lifetime.

"Afternoon, Alexander Ilyich! Good to see you again, sir!"

Lyubimov was followed by an older, more bookish man with thick-rimmed glasses. "Ears," Vasin's old sound-surveillance man, greeted his former boss equally cheerfully.

Ignoring his young colleagues, Vasin stared at Kuznetsov in disbelief.

"You called *Orlov?*"

Kuznetsov pointedly turned his back to Vasin and raised his arms in an expansive gesture of greeting.

"Comrades! Welcome. There has been a change of plan. This is no longer a debrief operation. It's a manhunt. While you were en route our target escaped, despite Colonel Vasin's, er, valiant efforts to detain him." Kuznetsov threw a contemptuous glance over his shoulder. "Stow your things in your rooms, be back here in five minutes for a full briefing."

The Special Cases men withdrew, meekly poker-faced, leaving Vasin and Kuznetsov alone.

"You asshole, Kuznetsov. Orlov, of all people."

"Who else was there? We had the bastard traitor in our hands. We needed him bottled up before he bolted to the Chinese. We needed help, fast. Help from people who could keep us safe."

"Just like Orlov managed to keep Fyodorov *safe?* What happened to your grand plans? The winds of change? It was all bullshit!"

"We don't have the connections to take this to the very top fast enough. Orlov does."

"You have lost your mind. The only thing that Orlov wants to do with the file is bury it, along with anyone who knows about it. That means you, me, and Fyodorov."

"Orlov appreciates loyalty."

"And Fyodorov?"

"Fyodorov has some catching up to do on that front."

# 7

Within half an hour the Special Cases men had the hotel suite set up as a decent simulacrum of a Lubyanka operations center. The whole team—Vasin, Lyubimov, Ears, plus two young officers that Vasin didn't know—was seated around a long table listening to Kuznetsov make his presentation at a mildewed blackboard that had evidently been brought up from the cellar. Vasin outranked Kuznetsov, but had been unmistakably relegated to a subordinate position. That's how it worked in Special Cases. The man in charge was the man favored by Orlov. And that was clearly no longer Vasin.

"Fyodorov called the Leningrad office of the Xiaowei Sino-Eurasian Shipping Corporation on Kronshtadtskaya Street, number 2, over by the Port of Leningrad. It was registered in the Crown Colony of Hong Kong, therefore notionally a British concern. For obvious reasons we suspect it of being a Chinese Communist Party front. Over the last year, since the breakdown of the USSR's relations with Peking, the company has seen an eightfold increase in its shipping into Leningrad. In 1961, four ships, mostly middle-sized tramp steamers. This year—sixteen, to date. Cargoes are listed as a mix of manufactured goods—thermos flasks and plastic toys, mostly—and raw materials like rabbit fur and tea. That's what the Ministry of Foreign Trade was able to tell us immediately. Lyubimov will be on the case investigating their activities more closely. Grishin . . ." Kuznetsov looked to one of the young Special Cases men. "Grishin, you get up there right now and establish basic street surveillance. We'll send support in a few hours, once we have proper vehicles organized."

Vasin watched his old friend issuing orders with quiet admiration. The diffident, cynical *kontora* officer he'd first met in the secret city of Arzamas, always the ironic observer, the skeptic, had transformed himself into a dynamic field commander.

"We can make a few key assumptions. Fyodorov made two calls from the village pay phone when he fled. One to warn his mistress, Ksenia Alexeyevna Pravdeva, and, we suppose, give her some urgent rendezvous. The other was to Xiaowei, which we presume was the local contact number given to him during his meeting with the Chinese diplomats I observed at the Catherine Palace." Vasin noted that he was already being airbrushed out of Kuznetsov's official account. "We also assume it's the only contact that he has to arrange his exfiltration by the Chinese. He might repeat his earlier tactic of calling the Chinese Embassy in Moscow, but he knows that those telephones are monitored. Ears will be taking over personal audio surveillance of Xiaowei's phone line as soon as a connection to the Avtovo District exchange gets patched through to this operations room."

Ears nodded gravely. The strange indentations on the sides of the lad's head that Vasin remembered, the flesh pinched from thousands of hours wearing headphones, were still there.

"Finally, we have two things against us. First and foremost, Fyodorov is one of us. A highly trained, resourceful, and experienced *kontora* field officer. Two, he is armed after the robbery of a small dacha outside Leningrad"—Kuznetsov shot a withering look at Vasin. "And he has nearly a thousand rubles in cash. However, there are at least five important factors that work against him. One, we know his Chinese handlers have little experience in field work inside the USSR. Two, the decision to exfiltrate him will be politically risky for Peking and will take time to organize, even if they agree. Three, he has no papers, and four, he is carrying an illegal automatic weapon. Finally, and most important: he has a civilian woman with him. You will have Ksenia Alexeyevna's photograph as soon as we recover her personnel file from her employer, the *Vecherny Leningrad* newspaper. Her presence will severely impede Fyodorov's ability to camp out. It will make the pair far more noticeable. Above all, having her to protect will make him vulnerable."

The men began to stand as Kuznetsov busied himself gathering up the scribbled briefing papers he had laid out on the table.

"Hold on," interrupted Vasin. "I have a question."

He waited until every man was settled back in his place before continuing.

"Kuznetsov." Vasin deliberately used his friend's surname only, a form of familiarity used between schoolboys and to address subordinates. "What makes you think he'll wait for the Chinese to save him? Why won't he just make a run for the Finnish border?"

Kuznetsov set down his papers irritably.

"He has already asked for the Chinese to help. Why take that risk if it wasn't his main chance of escape? And as I said, he has this woman Ksenia in tow. We met her. Doesn't strike me as the type who could stand a three-day hike through the winter forests of Karelia. No. He's going to wait for the Chinese to save his treacherous hide."

"How?"

"A shipping company ships goods. They'll be trying to work out a way to smuggle Fyodorov and his girl on board a Chinese ship. What other options do they have? Is that the end of your questions, Alexander Ilyich?" Kuznetsov's formal tone was cold.

"No more questions, Comrade Major. I listen and obey."

# 8

Vasin was asleep in his single room, three doors down from the operations center, when he was woken by a gentle knock, followed by Lyubimov's voice.

"Comrade Colonel? The General wishes to see you."

The luminous green dial of the bedside clock showed two in the morning. The scratches and lacerations on Vasin's face and head stung damnably as he struggled out of bed and tugged on his badly fitting civilian clothes.

The *General*?

Bleary-eyed and still unshaven, Vasin blundered into the operations room. More desks had appeared, and more unknown young faces, in the hours since he went to bed. They ignored him. On a side table, as though in mocking reference to the activities of the Xiaowei Shipping Corporation, a row of garishly decorated metal Chinese thermos flasks stood among a jumble of dirty coffee cups. Lyubimov seemed to have taken over as executive operations officer, occupying the center of the main conference table with papers and telephones spread around him.

"Through there, Alexander Ilyich," said Lyubimov, barely glancing up at his former boss and indicating a communicating door to the next room. "They're waiting for you."

Vasin opened the door without knocking. Kuznetsov and Kozlov sat at a small table. Between them, hunched like an oversize gargoyle, sat General Orlov. The three men, caught midconversation, looked up indignantly at the interruption. Orlov was the first to speak.

"Ah! Sasha! Never one to stand on ceremony, were you? Come in. Shut the door. I think you know Comrade Major Kozlov, from the First Chief Directorate."

"What the hell's *he* doing here?"

"Tssss. What a question! Comrade Kozlov here knows our fugitive friend Fyodorov better than any of us. They are old comrades."

Kozlov shifted in his chair to face Vasin. His square face was a mask of pure hostility.

"That man was sent up to Vorkuta to kill me."

"Goodness, Sasha, did the cold in the north freeze your brain?" Orlov stood. "I remember you were once a clever young fellow. The Comrade Major's mission in Vorkuta concerned our fugitive, not you."

To Vasin's fury, Kuznetsov and Kozlov exchanged a smirk.

"I thought he was on the other side."

"*Side,* Sasha? There is only one side. We are all Soviet officers working for the good of the Motherland." The emphasis on "we" seemed deliberately intended to exclude Vasin.

"So am I." Vasin felt his voice becoming hoarse.

"Naturally, Sasha. Of course."

Orlov caught a look between Vasin and Kuznetsov that crackled with venom.

"I think we should go for a walk, Sasha. Just you and me."

# 9

—

The Leningrad night sky was a deep black and spangled with stars. Orlov buttoned his thick greatcoat to the throat to keep out the wind and set off down Moskovsky Prospekt.

"I'm rarely wrong about people, Sasha."

"You weren't wrong about giving me Kuznetsov, that's for sure. You knew he would come back to you in the end."

"And you chose to try to defy me, again. So predictable."

"That's not what happened."

"Kuznetsov has told me everything about your plan to use Fyodorov's little secret to undermine me."

"Hardly a *little* secret. And how do you know that wasn't Kuznetsov's idea?"

"Shush now. You are being childish. Only a man as naïve as you could come up with such a plan. Tell the truth to the top bosses and expect justice and gratitude in return? 'Ye shall know the truth, and the truth shall set you free,' said the Evangelist. Also the credo of Alexander Vasin, as I have learned, at some cost. Though I have to admit I always had you down as a humble crusader. But to imagine you could bring off the downfall of General Orlov with a little army of whores and gypsies, paid for with a gulag's stolen payroll . . . *that* took me by surprise."

"I'm glad I was able to amuse you."

Vasin and Orlov paused at the corner of the Fontanka Canal as a convoy of bread trucks crossed the intersection. They left a sweet, yeasty breath on the night air as they passed. Orlov turned to face his former favorite.

"Not *amused,* Sasha. I was amazed. You see, when I recruited you I thought . . ."

"Yury. Stop it. You're not a cat, and I'm not a mouse." The General stiffened at the informal use of his first name, but Vasin pressed on, his voice slow and controlled. "Enough philosophical musings about my character and my career. That's all in the past. We both know that. Just tell me this: Why Kozlov? You tried to hide Fyodorov from the First Chief Directorate in Gagry, then in Vorkuta. You deceived them, but they saw through you. They're your enemies."

Impulsively, instead of crossing the now empty street, Orlov veered right down the canal embankment.

"Only a fool has enemies, Sasha. Opponents, yes. And with each round of the tournament the board gets reset. The players change seats."

"Spare me your mystification, Yury. Fyodorov uncovered a conspiracy to kill the President of the United States and came to you. Instead of acting, you waited. If you had taken steps to prevent the killing, John Kennedy would still be in the White House."

"That was always your problem, wasn't it, Sasha? You always believe what you're told. About that bomb up in Arzamas. About those submarines with nuclear torpedoes off Cuba last year."

"I was right about both."

"See what I mean? Right and wrong are just assumptions. And you forgot the first rule—always question your assumptions."

"There were always so many first rules with you, boss. I thought the first rule was never question General Orlov."

"Your anger has taken over your reason, Sasha. That's weakness."

"What was my wrong assumption? There was no *kontora* conspiracy to kill Kennedy? It wasn't the *kontora*'s man Oswald who shot Kennedy?"

"Conspiracy's a childish word. We're not in a fairy tale. Think harder."

Orlov's low, ironic voice, once more chiding him and making Vasin feel like an idiot schoolboy. If the canal hadn't been frozen solid Vasin would have been tempted to grab the infuriating fucker and toss him into the Fontanka. But instead Vasin felt himself irresistibly drawn into Orlov's mind game.

"Not a rogue group but . . . an official *kontora* operation? Sanctioned at the top?"

"The snows of Vorkuta didn't freeze your brain altogether."

"The assassination of Kennedy was sanctioned by the KGB? Or by the Kremlin?"

"Ah! *Now* your brain is finally working as it used to. Excellent question. Indeed, those are two different tops. The Kremlin has many towers."

"So who was it? Semichastny, or Khrushchev? Was this done behind Khrushchev's back to undermine him?"

"You try to jump far above your own head, as usual, Sasha. But I will tell you this—I involved the First Chief Directorate because we are all working to the same end. As for the rest, the Kremlin games . . . who can say?"

"You already have said, Yury. If Khrushchev had sanctioned it you would have told me as much. So killing Kennedy was a *kontora* operation only. But what I don't understand is *why*."

"Why they did it, or why I have spoken to you about these matters? I can answer the latter. It's very obvious, Sasha. We need you to bring in Fyodorov. You two have some kind of bond. That may be useful."

"The man threatened to shoot me and tied me up."

"Yet here you stand. Until we have this man in custody, you are on the team. Cooperating with me, with Kuznetsov, and with Kozlov."

"Because we are the only men here who know *why* we're hunting Fyodorov?"

"Precisely. When we locate him, only the three of you should get close to him."

"In case he starts to talk?"

"The secret of Dallas stays close."

"You're bringing me back to Special Cases, after all that's happened?"

Orlov said nothing. They had reached the end of the Fontanka Canal where it flowed into the broad expanse of the Neva River. In front of them stretched the Trinity Bridge. A set of traffic lights at the foot of the bridge was flashing yellow. A black gap appeared in the snowy asphalt at the bridge's center, and the two sides began to rise slowly to allow shipping to pass down the central channel. Orlov checked his watch.

"Like clockwork, these bridges."

Vasin said nothing as he stared across the bleak, icy water. An icebreaker appeared, busily nosing aside the fresh floes with a steady, rolling creak and thrum of engines.

"Would you like to be back among us, Sasha?"

"Of course." Vasin couldn't keep the dread out of his voice.

"I will give you one last chance, Sasha, to prove your loyalty. But only on condition of your absolute silence. None of your private initiatives. Or you will be dead. And your family will be destroyed. Do I make myself clear?"

It was unlike Orlov to make an explicit threat. His gaze was direct and deadly serious, the usual mocking smirk gone. The man was under pressure. And more dangerous than ever.

"Crystal clear, Comrade General."

# 10

By lunchtime the operations center at the Hotel Oktyabrskaya looked as though it had been up and running for weeks. Full ashtrays and piles of paper littered the desks, and a new, larger bulletin board had replaced the moldy blackboard. On it were detailed lists of all the surveillance teams brought in to catch Fyodorov, every man at Orlov's command, plus dozens more from the First Directorate.

Kuznetsov, looking gray and unshaven, glanced up as Vasin looked into his office and gave him a tired nod.

"Any progress, Vadim?"

"Good afternoon to you, too, *Sasha*." Kuznetsov was clearly needled by Vasin's refusal to treat him as a superior. "The offices of the Xiaowei Sino-Eurasian Shipping Corporation have been surrounded by a full team of Special Cases watchers on four-hour rotation. The home phones of all the employees have been bugged, and the three Hong Kong Chinese nationals who run the office are under close surveillance."

"And Kozlov and his gorilla? Why haven't we seen that pair around here?"

"You are referring to our valued colleague Sergeant Markov, perhaps? Out scouring the countryside. General alert among local cops in the whole Leningrad region now. They're searching the dacha-lands for our fugitive couple. We already ransacked the house, her office and room for clues this morning. Kozlov reckons he can't have gone far. No reports of vehicle thefts. Apart from one Harley-Davidson motorcycle reported stolen in Krasnoe Selo, of course. Now returned to its rightful owner. Perhaps Fyodorov hijacked a car or a truck. Killed the driver and left him in a ditch somewhere."

"He wouldn't do that."

"Why? You don't think he's capable of shooting a man in cold blood?"

"He is desperate. But stealing a vehicle that would be reported missing within a day? Too risky. No. He's back on the trains again. I'd bet he told Ksenia to get on an *elektrichka* suburban train to some provincial town." Vasin stepped over to a large map of the Leningrad region and its environs that had been pinned to the wall and traced a finger along the web of railway lines that radiated from the city all over the northwest of the USSR. "Pskov. Novgorod. Ivangorod. Tallinn. Could be anywhere."

"We sent a team to interrogate Ksenia's mother. And find out about any relatives in the country and so on. And we've got ears on her phone."

"He'll avoid anywhere associated with Ksenia. Fyodorov isn't dumb. We know that much."

"Dumb or not, he needs to make contact with his Chinese friends. And when he does, we have him."

Vasin pondered the map, chewing his lower lip—a childhood habit he hadn't been able to shake whenever he was lost in thought.

"Does he know that we know about his Xiaowei contact?"

"No idea. Probably not."

"He's going to be careful, either way. Or are you expecting him just to pick up a phone and call in?"

Kuznetsov shrugged and stretched. Vasin closed the double doors that linked Kuznetsov's office to the rest of the suite.

"Listen, Kuznetsov. I spoke to Orlov last night. He told me that the Oswald operation was official *kontora* policy. Came from the top. So much for your theory of taking the story to the good guys. Turned out there were no good guys. Not Semichastny. Maybe not even Brezhnev. Not anyone."

Kuznetsov glanced from side to side in alarm.

"God's sake, Vasin. Not here. Not now."

"It's not a long conversation. Just tell me if you believe Orlov or not."

"Why else would our friends from the First Directorate be here if this wasn't an official *kontora* operation?"

"Maybe because Orlov's made a deal with the conspirators to bring in Fyodorov. Get on the winning side. Or in this case, picking the winning side. Orlov's usual game, kingmaking. And for the record, I personally don't believe a word he told me."

Kuznetsov stood, moved toward his old friend, and put a hand on Vasin's shoulder to speak quietly into his ear.

"Vasin—I'm beginning to think that you really don't want to stay alive."

"Do *you* want me to stay alive, Vadim?"

Kuznetsov released his grip and attempted a smile.

"Depends."

"On what?"

"On whether you ever learn to shut the fuck up and do what you're told."

# 11

The Special Cases officer who sat beside Vasin peering through the surveillance van's observation slit swore softly as he lowered his binoculars. Two Chinese men had appeared in the windy, ill-lit courtyard below the Xiaowei Shipping Corporation's offices. Both wore identical green hooded parkas that obscured their faces.

"Not clear who they are, boss. I reckon the big one's the local manager. Sha Hueng-li. Other one, I can't tell."

Vasin waited until the subjects had turned the corner of Kronshtadtskaya Street before flicking on the inside light of the van and opening a folder to the full-page blowups of all the Xiaowei personnel taken from their visa photographs.

"Is it this man, Li Feng Hua? The new guy who showed up yesterday afternoon?"

The Special Cases officer peered at the photos and nodded.

"Looks like him. Think he's the spook who's been sent to run the operation on the ground, boss?"

"Probably. He's on the staff of the Chinese Embassy in Moscow. But leave that end of things to me. Call in the entry team."

At a coded series of beeps on the radio, the doors of half a dozen parked cars opened and shadowy figures emerged—a team of the finest specialists that Orlov and Kozlov had been able to muster on short notice. As Vasin climbed from the utility van he fingered a stiff cardboard identity card in his greatcoat pocket. His newly reissued KGB ID. For all his hatred of Orlov and for the *kontora*, the reassurance of the power he could wield with that little card radiated like heat through Vasin's fingers.

A flick of Vasin's new card got the group past the night watchman, bypassing the visitors' register. The shipping company's offices occupied one floor of a drab five-story building inside the Port of Leningrad complex. At this time of year the icebound harbor was nearly empty of ships and the cranes stood idle, black against the midnight-blue sky. The sea wind carried a tang of rust and rotting seaweed, and the faint sound of metal clanging on metal.

Dangling the watchman's master keys, Vasin strode to the entrance of the block, opened the courtyard door, and skipped up the steps two at a time. The vigorous movement had him panting by the time he reached the fourth floor. But it felt good to be leading a team of his own men. Mentally, Vasin corrected himself. Orlov's men. But at least for the moment, he led them.

Xiaowei's office reeked of some pungent spice that reminded Vasin of a meal he'd once eaten in the Peking restaurant in Moscow. He felt a pang of hunger. But Vasin's men wrinkled their noses. One gingerly picked the lid off a large saucepan in the kitchen to reveal a large pot of chicken feet in a scarlet chili broth.

"Fucking disgusting," muttered the oldest of Vasin's team, a squat, swarthy ape of a man in a workman's padded coat who carried a worn canvas tool bag. Old Levin—Orlov's second-best safecracker, a freelancer who'd stayed out of jail thanks to services rendered to the *kontora*.

An inner office was locked with a key that wasn't on the watchman's ring, but Levin picked it almost casually, with a quick wriggle of a pair of lock picks. Inside, in a corner of the glassed-in room, stood a chest-high steel safe decorated with an impressive brass coat of arms.

"Chubb and Sons Lock end Safe Company Limited, London," pronounced Levin in heavily accented English. "Old but excellent."

"Can you open it?" asked Vasin.

The old rogue raised his eyebrows in an expression of indignation. Instead of answering, he produced a stethoscope from his cloth bag, followed by a thin steel instrument topped with two brass wheels, like a microscope's focus knobs.

"Hold this . . . here," Levin growled, pressing the disk of the stethoscope to an area just below the keyhole and putting the ear tubes into his ears as primly as a doctor. Vasin obeyed. Levin inserted his pick and turned the knob left, then right, then left again. As he worked, the safecracker murmured to the lock as though coaxing a timid animal.

"*Davai, davai, detka,*" he whispered. "Come on, little one. Lever one. There you go. Lever two. Easy does it. Lever three . . . Stop your caprices now, girl. No. I said, stop it."

One by one, the sixteen tumblers all yielded to Old Levin's mumbled entreaties. With an oily click, the pick made a final turn. Levin yanked down the brass handle and hauled open the safe door. Inside were piles of accountant's ledgers, sheaves of invoices . . . and a locked leather briefcase. Giving Vasin a withering look, Levin transferred his pick into his left hand, looked away with a sad sigh, and opened the case's lock with a single twist.

" 'Can you open it?' he asks," muttered the master to himself as he packed his tools away. "Can *Levin* open a Chubb? Huh. Kindergarten work, they give me these days."

Ignoring the old man's grumbling, Vasin rifled through the papers in the briefcase. A sheaf of telegrams and forms with ticker tape from the company's antiquated teletype machine cut and pasted onto the paper. It took Vasin a moment to identify the strings of numbers as coordinates of latitude and longitude. They recorded the positions of various ships strung out from the North Sea to the Mediterranean and the Indian Ocean. Alongside the positions were the ships' names. The *Red East,* a Macau-registered freighter he remembered from the shipping manifests that Lyubimov had dug out of the register, was the closest. The ship's progress was accompanied by a set of dates, charting the freighter's ports of call up the northern coast of France to Germany and the Baltic. Currently, she was lying in Gdansk, Poland. And dates of the final two telegrams, marked "EST"—meaning "estimated," Vasin assumed—lay in the future.

"Port of Tallinn, EST 1100, 22 December."

"Port of Leningrad, EST 2200, 23 December."

Tallinn. The capital of Soviet Estonia. The *Red East* would be steaming into Soviet waters in two days.

Reflexively, Vasin turned from the glass wall that separated the office from the rest of the floor, folded the first of the two telegrams about Tallinn, and pocketed it. The second, concerning Leningrad, he replaced.

"Where's that damned photographer?" Vasin called out as he emerged from the office. "Need to get all these documents snapped, developed, and shown to the team. Double-quick!"

# 12

Vasin rode in a *kontora* Volga to the hotel alone. Back at the Port of Leningrad his team was diligently searching the office for clues. But the main clue, the crucial secret of the *Red East's* first landfall in the USSR, was stuffed into his pocket.

Why had he done it? It would have been so easy to call out for the photographer just half a minute sooner. Instead, he'd chosen to hide the truth from Orlov. From Kozlov. From the KGB.

If Vasin and Kuznetsov's hunch was correct and Fyodorov's plan was to flee on a ship, he and Ksenia would almost certainly board at Tallinn. Then, if the Chinese had an ounce of sense, the boat would immediately steam full ahead into international waters. And then Fyodorov would be free.

Was that what Vasin wanted? Stealing the telegram had been an impulsive gesture—and the impulse, Vasin had to admit to himself, had been to protect Fyodorov. Why? Vasin was in enough trouble already for his rogue attempts at protecting the fugitive. And it wasn't as though Fyodorov had been anything close to grateful. And why would he be? For the hunted man, Vasin represented as grave a danger to his life and liberty as anyone else—regardless of whether Vasin was formally a *kontora* officer or not.

And yet something deep in Vasin resisted the idea of handing the man over to be crushed by Orlov, tortured by the sadistic Macedonian, ending his numbered days in a lonely KGB cell, waiting for his bullet.

Did he really want to save the man's life—or to become keeper of his secret, and the power it would wield? Maybe both.

Vasin's car had pulled up outside the Oktyabrskaya Hotel. The driver peered back quizzically at his lost-in-thought passenger.

"We're here, boss. HQ."

Vasin shook himself free of the looping web of possibility and jeopardy that tangled his brain like knotweed.

"Right."

The pavement was covered in frozen ridges of foot-rutted snow. Vasin hesitated in front of the hotel's portico, turning his back to the wind. Inside, Orlov and Kuznetsov would be awaiting news of what he had found at the Xiaowei Shipping Corporation. Vasin lit a cigarette.

Three days until the ship docked at Leningrad. What they wouldn't know was that a day earlier, the twenty-second, the *Red East* would stop in Tallinn. And that's where Fyodorov and Ksenia would have a chance—a small chance—to run.

Somewhere, in an empty dacha or perhaps an unofficially rented room in a provincial town, Fyodorov and Ksenia would be sitting, waiting. Hoping. Two lives that could be snuffed out with the information on the piece of paper folded inside Vasin's greatcoat pocket.

And Fyodorov, too, had a piece of paper. The details which, according to Orlov, were of interest to nobody—and yet had triggered a manhunt across the USSR by at least two departments of the KGB. The plot to assassinate Kennedy went right to the top, the General had claimed. Did Vasin believe him? Despite his bluster to Kuznetsov, he really had no way of knowing.

There was another thing that Vasin could not quite bring himself to believe—and that was Orlov's assurance that he would be admitted back into the fold of Special Cases after Fyodorov's capture. From what he knew of the old snake, Orlov's forgiveness seemed unlikely. Vasin alive would always be a reminder, to Orlov, of his vulnerability. Kuznetsov was his new golden boy—and Kuznetsov, as Vasin had discovered, had his own ruthless streak of ambition and violence.

Trust Orlov and throw Fyodorov to the wolves. Or . . . find Fyodorov before he fled and get him to tell what he knew.

The wrong choice would land him back in Vorkuta, this time in a prisoner's uniform. Or, more likely, in a fiery car crash. Or hanged in a prison cell.

Vasin flung away his cigarette and swiveled on his heel to enter the hotel.

# PART NINE

# 20–22 DECEMBER 1963

Everything under heaven is in utter chaos; the situation
is excellent.

—MAO TSE-TUNG

# 1

Orlov straightened in his chair at the head of the conference table, winced as he flexed his back, and ran a chubby hand over the back of his neck.

"Adequate, I think. Perfectly adequate."

In front of him lay a scattering of papers covered with circles and scribbles. The plans of the Port of Leningrad's wharves, docks, and access roads, marked with the positions of the snatch squad that would seize Fyodorov as soon as he broke cover.

Vasin and Kuznetsov, to Orlov's left, also sat back from their labors. Only Kozlov remained hunched forward, poring over the plans with the tip of a blue wax pencil.

"I still say we need a full company of Alpha commandos, Comrade General. One hundred and twelve men. At least three times as many as you have planned for."

Orlov waited a long moment, continuing to massage the back of his neck, with closed eyes, before turning his attention to Kozlov.

"Ever commanded men in the field, Comrade Major?"

"No, sir. I have not."

"I have. In Manchuria, 'forty-five. NKVD Motorized Rifles. Know what a company of men *sounds* like, Major?"

"No, sir." Kozlov's voice was weary, resigned to the coming dressing-down.

"They're noisy. Dropped weapons. Muttering. Coughing like a bunch of consumptives. That's if they're not accidentally discharging their weapons. My deputy got shot in the back of the head by some trooper who fumbled loading his rifle." Orlov cracked a grim smile. "That was the official version, anyway."

"With respect, Comrade General—these are Alpha special forces troops we're talking about. The *kontora*'s best. They train for urban operations . . ."

"Our man is wily. He's trained. He's cautious. His Chinese conspirators will mobilize all the men they can, checking for a trap. Therefore we will keep a low profile. Thirty men is more than enough. And we deploy them as we have agreed. On the approaches to the port . . ." Orlov stabbed the plan with a finger, smudging the penciled-in arrows. "And here, in the warehouse. Here, in the diesel depot. Here, on the ends of the wharf. And in a speedboat. In case of mishaps. Any objections?"

It was not, of course, a real question. Dutifully, Kozlov shook his head.

"Very well. Get Lyubimov in here."

Lyubimov, his face gray and eyes red from hours in the smoky operations room, appeared at the door.

"No news of the *Red East,* Comrade General. We have a man stationed at the Soviet Inshore Waters dispatchers' room. The vessel has not radioed in yet, sir. Not here in Leningrad, nor to any other Soviet Baltic port."

"We have no idea where this Chinese junk is?"

"Sir, she's not required to report to anyone as long as she remains in international waters. To enter Soviet waters, the protocol is for her to report her course and destination and receive clearance. Usually, the shipping agent here in the USSR will arrange a berth in port for her in advance, by telegram."

"But?"

"No berths have been booked for the *Red East* in Leningrad yet, sir."

"Which is unusual?"

"Yes, sir. Usually Xiaowei informs the port authorities well in advance of incoming shipping. They have direct contact with their vessels by radio."

Orlov's eyes narrowed.

"Is there any way they could enter Soviet waters without being detected?"

As usual, the old man had honed in on the heart of the matter.

"Don't know, sir. Should I contact the Coast Guard?"

The old general considered for a moment.

"No. A general maritime alert could be picked up by someone at Xiaowei. If we spook Fyodorov now, we could lose him forever. He has to believe that the coast is clear for his escape. Kuznetsov—any word from the listeners?"

Kuznetsov looked as crumpled and exhausted as Lyubimov.

"Nothing unusual from the taps on Xiaowei or from the Chinese Embassy in Moscow. But we have observed the Chinese personnel using various public telephones in central Leningrad. Usually at the top of the hour. Incoming calls."

Vasin, the veteran of a long and fruitless surveillance operation, winced. Random public phones were every professional listener's nightmare. One pay phone could be tapped in advance, maybe two or three. But keeping tabs on all the phones in the city was impossible.

"The wily bastard," breathed Vasin. "Knows his business. Untraceable contacts. I'll bet that system was Fyodorov's idea. He's in control of this operation. Which is bad news—"

"Except that we know where he is going," interrupted Orlov, irritated by Vasin's pessimism. "And he does not know that we know. As soon as this boat comes into the Port of Leningrad, we have him."

Vasin made his face grave, suppressing the knowledge that he possessed information neither Orlov nor anyone in the operations center knew—that the *Red East* was actually due in Tallinn a day earlier. The secret glowed like a coal in his breast.

"You are correct, Comrade General."

# 2

Arvo Laar wore a bow tie, a too-tight sweater, and a boxy new suit that bagged at the knees. Under his arm he carried a bottle of champagne wrapped in shiny paper. Vasin rose from his cafe table and gestured to his old Moscow comrade.

"You're looking very smart, Arvo. Special occasion?"

"My wife's birthday. We go to the puppet theater, every year. Her favorite. Then—dinner. She will pick me up in the car in a few minutes."

Vasin suppressed a smile.

"I love the puppet theater, too. Thanks for seeing me on such short notice. But where's your fishing friend?"

"Sven is usually very punctual, like all military men. I cannot imagine . . . ah! There he is."

An elderly white-bearded man in a worn naval peacoat and woolen watch cap appeared at the door of the Literaturnoye Cafe, peering suspiciously at the luxurious surroundings. He looked like a caricature of an old sea dog, someone Lenfilm would cast in a children's pirate movie. Spotting Laar, he rolled across the room.

"Sven, this is my friend Colonel Alexander Ilyich Vasin. Ex–Moscow Homicide. One of the good ones, grandfather. I vouch for him. Sasha, this is Captain First Class Sven Gustavovich Bechdorff. A countryman of mine. Knows the waters of the Baltic like no man alive."

The old man took Vasin in with a hard little glance, nodded in apparent approval, and unbuttoned his coat. On the breast of his blue cotton jacket was a faded medal ribbon—two vertical yellow stripes on a scarlet ground. The Order of Lenin, the Soviet Union's highest decoration. Vasin saw the Captain notice him notice. A wily old sea dog indeed.

"See you out on the ice as usual, Arvo? This weekend?" Bechdorff's Russian was as heavily accented as Laar's, but he rolled his r's and spoke in a clipped pre-Revolutionary manner. The two old fishing companions shook hands and Laar hurried off to his appointment at the Leningrad Puppet Theater.

"I'm so glad you agreed to meet me, Captain. You see—"

Bechdorff raised a hand to cut Vasin off, pursed his lips, and directed a piercingly loud whistle through his front teeth at the back of a hurrying waiter. The extraordinary sound stopped conversations around them, but the old man was unfazed. The waiter turned, as shocked as if someone had tried to attract his attention by firing a pistol into the ceiling.

"Cognacs. Two. Sugar and lemon!" The old man shouted the order across the room and emphasized it by raising two stubby fingers, to be sure the boy understood what "two" meant. He turned to Vasin. "Right. Colonel. Arvo's friend is my friend. You had a question."

"Yes. He said you know the waters around Estonia."

"Could say that. Commanded four inshore torpedo boats from 'forty-three to 'forty-five, based out of Kronstadt. Had three of 'em shot out from under me. Knocked some merry hell out of the Germans, though. Me and my men sent forty thousand tons of enemy shipping to the bottom of the Baltic. Close to thirty hulls. Better kill record than all but the best Fascist U-boats. So yeah. I know the waters. Shoals. Tides. Minefields. Why, son? You goin' boating?"

"Not exactly. Could a boat come to the Soviet coast without being observed?"

"Depends on the size of the boat. A blacked-out skiff, sure. If the skipper knew the border patrol boats' schedule. And if he had some good strong rowers on board. Not using a motor. They listen, you know, for motors."

The white-coated waiter appeared with two balloon glasses of cognac on a steel tray. Bechdorff had knocked back the first one before the waiter had a chance to offload the second.

"Good. And one more while you're about it." Again the raised finger to indicate one. To the Captain the cafe was clearly foreign territory where he was in danger of being misunderstood. Color rose in his face as he warmed to his theme. "Unobserved, you say. Well, like I said a *skiff* or a *launch* might come in unobserved. But what about the vessel she's coming from? Or returning to? She'd have to heave to offshore. Blacked out, if necessary. But then there's the radar. Anything over a hundred tons will show up on the Coast Guard radar. And heaving-to without riding lights is a damned suspicious way of proceeding. Then there's the ice. Shallow parts of the sea are all icebound this time of year. The mouth of the Neva. The Courland Lagoon. Bothnian Bay. By February your sea ice would be about seventy centimeters thick, if it's land-fast."

"Wait." Vasin struggled to keep up as he scribbled in his notebook. "What about Estonia? Is that coast icebound?"

"Not most of it. Strong currents around the northern coast keep the Port of Tallinn clear most of the winter. Farther west, around the mouths of the Gulf of Riga and Saaremaa Island, you'll find sea ice. But it wouldn't be land-fast ice, this would be *drifting* sea ice we're talking about . . ."

"Forget the blacked-out skiffs and the land-fast ice. What about a *ship*? A freighter. Fifteen hundred tons. Is there anywhere she could put in unobserved?"

Bechdorff, bristling at being interrupted, grumbled into his second glass of cognac before answering.

"Not a chance. She'd be seen on the Coast Guard radar and raised on the radio the minute she entered Soviet waters. If she didn't respond and identify herself, she'd be intercepted. Simple as that."

"Soviet territorial waters, that's twenty kilometers?"

"Twelve nautical miles. Twenty-two kilometers."

"How long would that take to cross in a commercial freighter?"

"Gunning her diesels? Seventy minutes, at a guess."

"So a ship in international waters only has to give the Soviet Coast Guard an hour's warning of their arrival?"

"Only if the skipper's being sneaky. An hour offshore is when you have to report yourself. But you said you're interested in Estonia? There are no international waters off Tallinn."

"What do you mean?"

The captain rolled his eyes, dipped a finger in the dregs of Vasin's coffee, and drew on the glass tabletop.

"Here's us, Leningrad, at the mouth of the Neva River, which flows into the Gulf of Finland. The northern coast of the gulf runs west . . . like that. That's capitalist Finland. The Soviet coast runs roughly parallel . . . there. It makes a narrow funnel. Tallinn and Helsinki face each other right here, close to the mouth of the gulf. There's an Estonian island called Naissaar right here, on the northwest approach to Tallinn. And opposite it there's a Finnish peninsula. Name of Porkkala. Distance between them is forty-two kilometers. That means that Soviet waters and Finnish waters overlap down the middle of the whole gulf. To get to international waters you need to get clear of the Gulf of Finland entirely. Twenty-two kilometers clear, to be precise."

"No ship can get into the Gulf of Finland without reporting itself to the Soviet Coast Guard, do I have it right?"

"Soviet or *Finnish* Coast Guard. The Finns own the northern coast, remember? If she sails through Finnish waters she can get within a hundred and fifty kilometers of Leningrad before reporting in. Anyway, don't know why you're so hung up on the international waters question. A Soviet border patrol boat in hot pursuit of fugitives can run right up to the Finnish coast. Seen it done."

"In pursuit of *Soviet* fugitives, you mean. What about a foreign-flagged ship?"

The Captain shrugged. His third cognac had arrived, and he sniffed it contemplatively.

"Interesting question."

"What Soviet ports could a freighter of that size use?"

"In the eastern Baltic? Just Riga, Tallinn, and Leningrad. Kronstadt Island, of course, headquarters of the Baltic Fleet. But that's just for warships. There are no others." The old man's eye on Vasin's was fierce, his tone hardening. "Now. Are you going to tell me what you need all this nautical general knowledge for, Colonel? And why you couldn't ask anyone inside your own service? Whatever *that* might be. You wanting to catch someone trying to escape? Or helping someone on their way out?"

Vasin ignored the question.

"One more thing. When a commercial vessel enters Soviet waters, it has to declare its course, right?"

"*She*. She needs to declare her course and destination, correct."

"Let's say if . . . *she* . . . declares she's heading to Leningrad. But to get to Leningrad she would have to sail right past Tallinn?"

"Uh-huh."

"So what's to stop her changing course? Turning into Tallinn suddenly, as she passes, on whatever pretext?"

"She'd need the Tallinn harbormaster's permission to enter the port, of course. But the skipper could report engine trouble. Shifting cargo. Sick crewman. Anything, really."

"Does anyone keep track of all these shipping movements? Centrally, I mean?"

"All ships docked in Soviet ports are logged at the Maritime Ministry in Leningrad. Each harbormaster sends a daily report."

"What time would they send this report of the ships that dock?"

"Early morning the following day, usually."

Bechdorff's voice had gone very flat. Slowly, he placed his powerful hands on the tabletop and sat back, contemplating them, as though considering whether to take a grip on the polished glass and snap it in half.

"You know what, young man? I don't think I care for your line of questioning. You know what the penalty is for abetting a breach of the Soviet borders?"

"Article 322 of the Criminal Code of the USSR. Punishable by up to fifteen years of hard labor. So, yes, Captain. I do know. I'm a *cop*, remember?"

# 3

By the time Vasin returned to the Oktyabrskaya Hotel, the operations room looked as though a foreign army had sacked it. Cleaners had been barred. Dirty cups, overflowing ashtrays, piles of paper, and discarded ties were scattered all over. The place reeked of coffee, stale cigarette smoke, and male sweat. The blackboards on which the operational plans were pinned had been draped in hotel sheets to keep them from prying eyes.

The place was empty apart from a trio of junior officers who tapped diligently at typewriters, filling out forms. Of the senior officers only Kuznetsov remained, slumped in an armchair in the private office. He stopped writing in a black notebook and glared at Vasin.

"Good meeting, Sasha?"

There was no point in lying. Vasin could easily have been followed to the Literaturnoye Cafe. He'd made the call to Laar earlier in the afternoon from a hotel phone.

"I met an old sailor who knows Baltic shipping. He filled me in on some details, though I had to drag the information out of the old bugger. He seemed convinced that I was planning to flee our great Soviet Motherland."

"Which you would never contemplate, of course."

Vasin waited a moment before answering. His old friend's tone was not jocular.

"Is that what you think? That I want to defect to the West?"

"Devil knows what's going on in that fevered brain of yours."

"You think I would betray my country?"

"I don't know, Sasha. Perhaps Fyodorov talked up the delights of London. Sold you on the glamour girls of New York. Maybe even the exotic cuisine of Peking. In my long and painful experience, you're easily influenced by the last person you've happened to speak to."

"You're kidding."

Kuznetsov's mouth smiled. His eyes did not.

"So what did your old sea dog tell you?"

Vasin breathed deep. Was Kuznetsov just jealous that Orlov had taken him back into the fold, or did he really have Vasin marked as a potential traitor? There was no way to know for sure.

"The *Red East* will have to radio in her coordinates and course as soon as she enters Soviet waters, which start at the mouth of the Gulf of Finland. That's close to four hundred and fifty kilometers from the Port of Leningrad. Fifty hours' sailing time, so we'll have good warning. If she chooses to come down the northern side of the gulf, in Finnish waters, we'll only have fifteen hours' notice. Either way, we'll be forewarned."

"Huh." Kuznetsov sounded unimpressed by the information.

"Where's Orlov?"

"Having dinner at the Hotel Evropeiskaya. He is waiting for you to join him, in fact."

"That's nice of him, I'm starving. Shall we?"

"I'm not invited. Just you and the boss. And Kozlov. For a cozy little chat. Anyway, I'm on duty here."

Vasin searched his old companion's face for a sign—jealousy, maybe, or pity. But he saw nothing behind Kuznetsov's low stare except smoldering dislike.

# 4

The hulking doorman at the Hotel Evropeiskaya eyed Vasin's cheap civilian overcoat disapprovingly, but Vasin was in no mood to be thwarted. The hotel, once the haunt of the aristocrats of pre-Revolutionary Saint Petersburg, was now the preserve of senior Party officials, visiting foreign dignitaries, and senior spies. He ignored the doorman's challenge and barged straight through to the glass-ceilinged restaurant. A piano tinkled gently over the murmur of polite conversation and clinking glassware.

"I'm looking for General Orlov."

The maître d'hôtel, who wore a firmly unproletarian dinner jacket and bow tie, raised an eyebrow but gestured for Vasin to follow. Maintaining a slow, dignified pace, the elderly man led Vasin up a red-carpeted staircase to the mezzanine, which was lined with velvet-curtained booths.

"Your party is in here, sir." The maître d' pulled back the curtain, revealing a private loggia that opened onto the main restaurant like an opera box. Inside, on plush chairs, sat Orlov and Kozlov. A partly drunk bottle of cognac and another of wine stood between them among a large collection of half-eaten dishes of sturgeon, caviar, pickled tongue, and smoked salmon.

"Ah! Sasha. Good." Orlov drew himself up to his full seated height and spread his hands expansively. "You're just in time. Sergei Yefimovich, would you bring some duck à l'orange for my guest?"

The old man bowed deferentially and pulled the curtain shut behind him.

"Come. Let us break bread together. It's time for you to make peace with Comrade Kozlov. I know you have had your differences, but I need you both harnessed to the same plow."

Kozlov smiled, and Vasin felt himself reflexively forcing the same. He shrugged off his coat and took a seat at the round table. Below, the pianist had been joined by a pretty young female violinist in a white ball gown.

"I hope you're hungry, Sasha."

Vasin smiled tightly and filled his plate as his two companions ate in silence. Orlov was the only one of them who seemed at ease, as though his twisted spirit fed on conflict and distrust. A Tchaikovsky minuet drew to a shaky crescendo as Vasin stuffed a caviar-loaded blin into his mouth, wiped his lips, and took a long pull of wine.

"When are you going to tell me what this is about, Yury?"

Kozlov flinched at Vasin's familiar tone, his eyes flicking from the General to Vasin. But Orlov showed no sign of noticing. Ignoring Vasin, he addressed only Kozlov.

"Sasha's time up in the Arctic has put a hard edge on him. He was always smart, you see. But he didn't know the dirty edges of the world till he went to Vorkuta. Now he's the complete Chekist. Brains *and* toughness. Just the man for the job."

"What job, General?" Vasin knew that gleam in his boss's eye. Whatever fiendish hell-pot the old bastard had cooked up, it was not likely to spell good news for him. Orlov now turned his entire attention to Vasin.

"Fyodorov has gone silent. The Chinese ship has gone silent. We have no idea where either of them are. We only have a radiogram from the ship reporting its intention to dock at Leningrad on

December twenty-third. But that information is now at least a day old. We have no idea what plan Fyodorov has come up with to get on board the freighter. We have no idea what his channels of communication with the Chinese may be. Or even if he intends to get out on the damn boat."

Vasin's mouth had gone dry, despite another deep drink of wine.

"What do you want me to do?"

"We need to shake the tree a little, Sasha. Throw the Chinese something that will make them think. Muddy the waters. Put Fyodorov's credibility, his story, in doubt. And give us something to work with—"

A loud "ahem" from the doorway interrupted Orlov's flow. A pair of waiters edged in. One balanced three platters on his arm as the other cleared the *zakuski* from the table. Steaming plates of duck, beef, and lamb were ceremoniously placed before the diners and the waiters withdrew. The heavy curtain closed with a zip of brass rings on brass rail. Ignoring the aroma of his côte-de-boeuf, Kozlov leaned forward and fixed Vasin with a steady stare.

"Colonel, you must approach the Chinese. You will tell them that you have been part of the hunt for the traitor Fyodorov. You will tell them that you have had a disagreement with your boss, whom you hate, and that you have been fired from the case. You will offer to tell them the truth of the story that Fyodorov has been offering them. Which will of course be a different truth from the one that the traitor is currently trying to sell them."

"You want me to offer to betray my country, Kozlov?"

A heavy rumble which could have been the beginnings of a laugh rose in Orlov's chest.

"Come now. Without going into *details*." Orlov flicked his head in Kozlov's direction. "Without delving into any *ancient history*, you and I both know that offering to betray your country would not be entirely unknown territory for you? No. No, Sasha, don't get angry. You considered your reasons good at the time. But we are not here to discuss the past. Comrade Kozlov has been admirably clear. We have an important mission for you. One that only you can carry out. You know Fyodorov well. You know the details of his recent movements. You know what he wishes to tell them about the events in Dallas."

"Events in Dallas that our comrade here knows much more about than I do. Why not send *him*?"

Kozlov leaned forward aggressively.

"And what if those events are none of your damn business?"

*"Events,"* continued Vasin, "that culminated in the death of the American President. Events that could have led to war. Could still, if certain parties knew the truth of the crazy, reckless, stupid, murderous—"

"Comrades! Comrades, enough!" Orlov's outstretched palm came between the two men's faces like a boxing referee's. "Vasin, you are here to discuss the details of your mission. Nothing else. We face forward, not backward. The past is past. Understood?"

Vasin winced, looked down, and came up again with a twisted smile on his face.

"Yes, General. My apologies, Comrade Major."

"To business. To make your story of a fight with your bosses credible, tonight you will move into a hostel for foreign students out near Pulkovo. It is a shithole, commensurate with your new status as a fired and disgraced ex-member of the team. It is also a place where visiting foreigners—for instance, Chinese diplomats under cover—will not be remarked upon. Tomorrow morning you will telephone the Chinese deputy military attaché at his office in the Embassy in Moscow. You will give him the number of a pay phone near the hostel, and ask him to call you there from a Moscow pay phone an hour later. Major Kozlov has prepared a script for you. It contains important key words you will mention to establish your bona fides with the Chinese. Words that will convince them you know something of interest about Fyodorov and his attempted defection. At that point, they will probably offer a personal meeting. Major Kozlov will be your main point of contact . . ."

"Never. I'm not working with him."

"Vasin!" Orlov's manner had abruptly switched from gently cajoling to cold and commanding. "You forget your position. You will work with whomever I order you to work. Or do I need to remind you of your duty as a Soviet officer?"

"No, sir."

Vasin picked up his knife and fork and began eating the duck breast. It had gone cold. Kozlov poured him more wine and took up Orlov's old ingratiating tone.

"Comrade Vasin. Alexander Ilyich. Sasha, if I may? I understand. It is a shocking thing to approach the enemy, to play the role of a traitor. Any decent Soviet officer would react as you have. But as I know from your distinguished career, you are well aware that to wrestle a pig, you must get down in the mud."

"You can switch off the charm, Kozlov. You're putting me off my food." Vasin turned to Orlov. "Can I get your orders to betray my country in writing, sir? Handwritten will do. Just in case."

"In *writing*, Sasha?"

Orlov and Kozlov exchanged a glance. A suspicion passed across Vasin's mind—this was a private booth. The perfect place to get a good sound recording. The *kontora* had wired such private rooms all across Moscow's top restaurants. Was Orlov weighing his response for the microphones?

"In case of what, Sasha?"

"In case anything happens to either of you. Just so that I don't get left dangling. Holding my balls, if you know what I mean."

Orlov's face softened. He looked at Vasin almost affectionately, as though observing a charmingly wayward child.

"Oh, Sasha. How lost you are. But don't worry. Special Cases will help you find your way back to the real world. What an officer you will be, Sasha, in time. Because we both know where your loyalties lie. In your heart you are a patriot. You are not a man who would ever contemplate abandoning your homeland like the traitor Fyodorov. You have too great a future ahead of you. You have a family. And also—you don't have the balls."

Vasin's mouth went dry. Maybe Orlov was right. For all his wriggling, Orlov's hook was lodged deep in his gullet.

"And my orders, sir?"

"*Those* orders? In *writing*?" Orlov's pudgy face broke into one of his rare grins. "You must be fucking joking."

# 5

The Hotel Yunost was indeed a shithole. The nine-story prefab concrete building was only a few years old, yet the plaster was already cracking and the floor tiles in the shared shower rooms were slick with human slime. Most rooms were shared by two or three screaming, jabbering, drunken foreign students. At least Vasin had a room to himself, a narrow space almost filled with two single beds and a flimsy wardrobe. As the hotel finally went quiet, well after midnight, Vasin sat on his bed, unable to sleep.

He'd allowed Orlov to get him good and drunk. Now the rich food, the wine, and the cognac burned up from his stomach and prevented Vasin from thinking straight.

But he knew three things. One, he had been cut loose from the hunt for Fyodorov. Whether that meant that Orlov trusted him or the opposite, he had no way of knowing. Two, he was now required to play the part of an officer left out in the cold—which meant no contact with Kuznetsov or any of the team except for Kozlov, his handler. Vasin would still be under the *kontora*'s eye, for sure. But he would have at least some degree of liberty. And that led him to his third, most shocking, realization. Orlov's plan made it much easier for him to make a dash to intercept Fyodorov.

To Tallinn.

He could be there in five hours. There and back in a day. And if he was careful about what he told Kozlov, the *kontora* might never notice.

# 6

Breakfast at the Hotel Yunost consisted of sliced brown bread topped with curling salami and dry cheese. The coffee tasted like someone else had drunk it already. Vasin didn't even risk the congealing porridge, which looked like boiled cardboard.

Kozlov appeared on the dot of eight. Sliding a contemptuous glance along the buffet, he nodded to Vasin from across the dining room. Vasin followed Kozlov's gray-coated figure as he walked, absurdly, ten steps ahead of him through the freshly fallen snow. The public intercity phone box was two blocks away, past a noisy kindergarten and public swimming baths. Behind them, Kozlov's *kontora* Volga followed at a steady distance at a crawl. KGB security theater at its most pedantic. Even before Vasin had made his call to the Chinese, Kozlov was putting on an unconvincing show of pretending that Vasin was operating on his own.

As agreed, Kozlov went through the motions of making a call while Vasin waited patiently at a polite distance, the way Soviet citizens did. Then they swapped places—Kozlov standing nearer now, to listen in so he could be sure that Vasin stuck to the script.

It took twenty minutes and three calls to reach Giao Peng at his desk in the military attaché's office at the Chinese Embassy in Moscow. The man's Russian was halting—maybe intentionally worse than it really was—and it took Vasin another fifteen minutes to get Kozlov's message across, with the contact numbers and key words. Finally, the Chinese diplomat said that he'd understood. In an hour, they would speak again.

Christ, thought Vasin, it's amazing any spying gets done in this country. It's impossible to get hold of anyone. And when you do, they have no clue about what you're trying to ask or tell them.

The next phone box, one metro stop away, was guarded against ordinary citizens by an obvious *kontora* watcher. Dutifully, Vasin stood by the apparatus, waiting. Snow flurries had started once more, turning the passing cars of Moskovsky Prospekt into swirling gray ghosts, spewing slush.

The phone rang. On the second ring, Vasin picked it up and hung up. It rang again. Vasin answered on the third ring. He assumed the line was tapped. A heavily accented voice, not Giao Peng's, came on the line.

"How may I help you?"

"Comrade." Vasin took a deep breath and tucked the receiver under his cheek as he unfolded the handwritten script that Kozlov had given him. "I have some information which could greatly contribute to the increase of mutual understanding between our peoples . . ."

# 7

"Happy, Kozlov?"

Kozlov and Vasin sat alone in the back of a *kontora* Volga. The driver stood a few yards away, contemplatively smoking a cigarette with his back discreetly turned toward them.

"Not a bad performance." Kozlov pored over the handwritten script that Vasin had read out to the Chinese diplomat. "Should get them interested."

"So are you going to tell me what this is all about? 'I have specific details of a Soviet special operation in Dallas, Texas.' What the fuck do you want me to tell them next?"

Kozlov lowered the paper and glowered at Vasin.

"More of your games?"

"No games, Kozlov. I really want to know. You're sending me to sell a secret to the Chinese, but I don't know what you want me to tell them. Unless of course it's Fyodorov's big secret. Which I doubt."

Kozlov narrowed his eyes.

"You'll follow the next script I draft for you. To the letter."

"Suit yourself. So the plan is to wait for the Chinese to make contact with me at the hostel. You think no earlier than tomorrow?"

"As discussed. Yes."

"And I am to go with them, wherever they take me, then report back."

"Correct. And I'll have the second part of your script prepared by tomorrow morning. From this moment on we will assume that the Chinese will attempt to put you under some kind of surveillance, so our communication will be only through the reception desk at the Hotel Yunost. Or through your neighbor in the next room."

"The Vietnamese students? You really are an international bunch over at the First Chief Directorate."

Kozlov failed to smile.

"The Vietnamese comrades are gone. One of our men will be checking in today. He will leave written messages under your mattress, or speak to you directly if urgent."

"Fine. So I'll see you when I see you. Write me letters."

Vasin picked up his hat from the seat between them and opened the car door. Kozlov grabbed the hem of Vasin's coat.

"Where are you going?"

"Into town. I need some less awful clothes. Maybe take a sauna. See a film. I'm pretending to be a free man, remember?"

Vasin tugged his coat from Kozlov's grip, slammed the sedan door, and walked quickly to the nearby metro station.

# 8

Vasin rode the metro, checking for tails in the most obvious and effective way he'd been taught by old Boris Schultz at KGB school—ride back and forth between two adjacent stations over and over. No surveillance team in the world would have enough personnel to follow for more than three such switchbacks. Nobody among the late-morning travelers struck Vasin as an obvious goon. Satisfied that he was clean, he stayed on the train to Moskovsky Station and walked five blocks to Uncle Borya's squalid headquarters.

This time Vasin was not greeted by the lookout's strange, hoot-like whistle but with a coarse shout. From an upper window, Fingers waved enthusiastically, struggled with a stiff latch, and leaned out into the courtyard.

"It's Colonel Fancy-Pants! Hey! How are ya, Commander?"

"Fingers, that you? I need a word with Uncle Borya."

"Got another job for us?"

Vasin merely winked and put a finger to his lips—partly to hide his smile at the nickname the gypsies had coined for him. The boy clattered down the stairs, met Vasin in the reeking lobby, and let him into the communal apartment. The place was emptier than the last time Vasin had visited—presumably the gypsy kids were out pursuing their various gainful employments. They found Boris sitting at a large plastic-covered table in the kitchen, slurping soup from a garish Uzbek bowl.

"Friend! Welcome." Boris lumbered to his feet and seized Vasin's hand in his two giant paws. "Food? Asya! Food."

A dark-skinned girl with enormous dark eyes and unruly hair half-pinned under a bright headscarf brought Vasin a steaming bowl of spicy stew.

"Try this. *Kharcho*. Lamb and coriander. We always get the best meat from the market."

Vasin sat, sipped, and winced.

"Not hot enough for you? We have more smoked paprika if you'd like."

"No thanks," Vasin rasped, his face flushing.

Boris ate on, chuckling.

"What's it this time? The kids had quite the outing, last time. They couldn't stop talking about it for days."

"That's nice. Told them to sew their little mouths fucking shut. But fine. No kids this time, Boris. I need a Chinese. And a car."

"A *Chinese car*?"

"No. A civilian car. Respectable and reliable enough for a long drive, and with a well-dressed Chinese man to go in it. Plus a driver. He can be Chinese, too, but he doesn't matter so much."

"You want to rent a Chinese gentleman, plus luxury transport?"

"For one day. Starting tomorrow at five a.m., at the Hotel Yunost. Know anyone?"

Boris pursed his fleshly lips and wiped his mustache with a knuckle.

"Got Koreans, if you like. Will a Korean do?"

"He needs to look like a diplomat. Suit and tie."

"Yeah. Got the guy you need. Deals cards for a living, down at a club I know, dresses nice. And the car's no problem. How much you paying?"

Vasin smiled broadly. The money from the safe at VorkutLag was long gone. The truth was that Vasin had just fifty-five rubles in his pocket.

"Well, Uncle Boris. I was hoping that this job you could do out of sheer patriotic devotion." Boris's face clouded as he prepared to curse Vasin for his insolence, but Vasin raised a finger and fished in his pocket. "You see, I have a new job now."

Vasin produced his newly reissued KGB ID card with its gold shield-and-sword emblem on the front and held it up to Boris's face.

"See? This time, Boris, it's official. And the *kontora* will owe you."

# 9

Vasin was already awake when the impatient tap came on the door just before five. He opened it a crack and the middle-aged gorgon who manned the desk in front of the elevators on his floor scowled at him.

"Some kind of foreigner for you, down at reception." The woman hugged her shawl around her shoulders and waddled back down the corridor in her slippers.

By the time Vasin followed, the door to the room next to his was open. Inside, standing in boxer shorts and a striped sailor's under-shirt, stood Sergeant Markov—the Macedonian. His bruised eye had gone an alarming shade of blue and yellow, a lasting reminder of their previous encounter in Vorkuta. The giant gave Vasin an appraising, professional look, like a butcher sizing up a carcass that he was about to dismember with a meat ax. Vasin paused, met the man's stare, and smiled crookedly.

"Keep it up, Cossack. One day you'll be an ataman."

In the lobby a team of stork-like Uzbek girls in matching tracksuits—basketball players, presumably—hovered in front of the restaurant waiting for opening time. A slight young East Asian man in a too-big shirt and chunky tie hovered self-consciously by the reception desk.

"Comrade Nikolai?" he said, loudly, within hearing of the desk clerk, as Vasin had stipulated.

"That's me."

Vasin scanned the lobby. A single KGB goon sat in one of the sagging armchairs pretending to be absorbed in a copy of *Izvestia*.

"My name is Kim. Please come with me. My car is outside."

Vasin dropped his key on the desk and followed Uncle Boris's Korean croupier out of the double doors into the still night. On the curb, a bulbous red sedan with futuristic air vents on its sides and an extraordinary triple headlight stood in a freezing cloud of its own exhaust.

"What the hell is *that?*" A flashy car that drew stares was the last thing Vasin needed.

"A Tatra 603. A beautiful Czech machine," replied Kim, defen-sively. "Lovely runner. Imported last year!"

Halfway down the steps, Vasin froze. A pair of local policemen, both swaddled in bulky greatcoats, were walking up to the car. Vasin saw that the driver, too, was Asian. He cursed himself for not thinking. Non-Russian drivers attracted racist Soviet policemen like catnip. And with a gorgeous foreign car, doubly so.

One cop circled the sedan as the other motioned the driver to wind down the window and produce his papers. A common enough procedure, something that most Soviet drivers encountered a couple of times a week. Vasin prayed that the driver's license and insurance were in order. To make their loitering on the stairs more natural he offered his new companion an Orbita and lit one for himself.

Some kind of altercation was taking place. The driver was out of the car now, gesticulating as one of the policemen pointed insistently at the front hood.

"Idiots," whispered Kim. "The engine's in the rear. Trunk's in the front."

Within five minutes both the front and back hatches of the Tatra stood open. One cop inspected the trunk while the other, alongside the driver, examined the engine. Silently Vasin cursed their curiosity. It was a five-hour drive to Tallinn. The *Red East* was due to dock at 1100. And if Vasin's luck really had turned completely to shit, his real Chinese contact could show up at any moment.

But the hatches were eventually slammed; the policemen saluted the driver and walked on. As soon as they had rounded the end of the block, Vasin and Kim piled into the car.

"Hi, Commander! I'm Dong-Hyun Kim. But they call me Petya." The two men could have been brothers. Perhaps they were. He slid the car into gear and they moved off smoothly. "Know what those dumb cops usually say when they see the engine in the back? They say—you've stolen an engine! And recently! It's still running!"

The Koreans laughed uproariously at their inside joke. Only Vasin, sitting in the back, nervously eyed the road behind them. He saw no obvious tails. He pondered ordering some evasive maneuvers, but they had no time for subtlety.

"Take the ring road, northbound. We're heading to Tallinn."

# 10

The E20 highway ran through flat farmland, a blur of dirty white in the darkness beyond the sedan windows. The traffic heading into town was heavy. Their side of the road, westbound toward the Baltic coast, was empty but for a few lumbering buses. Krasnoe Selo, where he'd chased Fyodorov, flashed past like a bad memory, followed by Russko-Vysotskoe. Vasin wondered if the *kontora* had bothered to close up Ksenia's dacha, or whether they'd just left the shattered door open for her cozy little nest to be plundered by the neighbors.

The heavy Czech sedan ran smooth and fast, its triple headlight illuminating kilometer after kilometer of snowy, black-iced highway. After two and a half hours on the road they came to their first police checkpoint, a two-story bunker on the outskirts of Narva, just past a bilingual sign of welcome to the Estonian Soviet Socialist Republic. Traffic had slowed to a crawl as a bored traffic cop nodded the cars through the partial barrier one by one. But inevitably his eyes lit up when he saw the sleek, plum-colored contours of the Tatra 603. With a practiced movement of his black-and-white striped truncheon, he waved them into the holding area. Vasin cursed under his breath.

Petya, who seemed to treat the attentions of traffic cops as a kind of homage to his beloved car, wound down his window and greeted the officer with a friendly grin. Vasin rapped peremptorily on his own back window to summon the policeman. The cop straightened, took in the flashy car with an impatient Party bigwig in the back, and sighed. Without even asking Vasin for ID, he saluted and waved them on with a regretful twirl of his baton.

They stopped for refreshments at Narva's bus station cafe. The night air was damper than Leningrad's, and carried the faintly sweet, decaying smell of floodwater. Petya cajoled three weak coffees from a surly blond waitress who pretended not to understand his Russian.

Twenty minutes beyond Narva, Vasin heard the sound of surf through the darkness and smelled the ozone tang of fresh salt-sea air. The roadside houses looked different, too. Not the tumbledown, slovenly log cabins of the Leningrad region but neat little plank-built dwellings with steeply raked roofs painted in bright primary colors. The place-names, too, were bizarre. Kiiu. Kodasoo. Ruu. Loo. For the first time in his life, Vasin felt like he was in a foreign country.

At Rakvere, with nine a.m. approaching, the first hint of dawn revealed a landscape shrouded in patchy white fog, drifting slowly across the Estonian heathlands like a monster that had crawled from the sea. Nervously checking every few minutes through the rear window, Vasin saw the curls of mist swirling in crazy patterns behind the sedan. More and more often Petya had to brake hard as the rear lights of a truck or a wobbling cyclist appeared from nowhere on the mist-shrouded road. Vasin peered at his watch. He tried to reassure himself that if the *Red East* was still going to make its rendezvous at Tallinn, the skipper would wait for full daylight before risking the approach in the fog.

Or maybe the damn fog would be too thick for shipping. Fyodorov would make some other arrangement. And by that evening Vasin would be back in the Hotel Yunost, watching the scuttling cockroaches and waiting for someone from the actual Chinese Embassy to make contact.

Wooden village houses gave way to handsome stone buildings with stepped roofs that looked like illustrations from a book of German fairy tales Vasin remembered from childhood. They reached the Tallinn city limits a little before eleven, just as full day was breaking. They stopped at an intersection to ask directions—but the blond woman with a baby carriage to whom Vasin called out simply glared at the car and looked away with a haughty turn of her head. Eventually a Russian traffic policeman directed them to the port.

The Tatra pulled up by a long, squat medieval fortress that overlooked the harbor. The flags of the USSR, the Estonian SSR, and the Soviet merchant marine hung limp over the gatehouse, barely visible in the thickening fog. Vasin got out of the car, stretched, breathed deeply the seaside air, and fished in his pocket for his ID card. The young, pale blond man who manned the security gate eyed the KGB logo with frank hostility—something Vasin had never experienced—then reached for the visitors' logbook with deliberate slowness.

"Where's the harbormaster's office? Quick, man."

The gate guard, ignoring Vasin's impatience, continued to write his details with painstaking care in his book. As the man wrote, an uncomfortable thought flashed through Vasin's mind. It takes two people to believe in an identity card's power—the holder and the beholder. Here in Soviet Estonia, that bond felt shaky. What happens when one party ceases to believe? Or to respect?

Vasin dismissed the thought. The guard handed back his papers and offhandedly indicated the office. Vasin sprinted across the courtyard, still in shadow in the slanting morning light.

# 11

The high windows of the harbormaster's radio room looked out onto a wall of pure whiteness. The office was nearly deserted.

"Fog means no shipping," a paunchy, middle-aged Russian merchant marine officer explained to Vasin, as if to a half-wit. But Vasin had insisted on checking the radio log for incoming vessels.

The room was equipped with an antiquated black-cased radio set the size of a small car. The dials were in German, Vasin noticed, and the manufacturer's plate proclaimed SIEMENS-SCHUCKERTWERKE. A relic of the prewar days of independent Estonia. A lanky sailor about Vasin's age, in a striped shirt and cable-knit sweater, sat with his feet up on the control panel reading a soccer magazine.

"Shipping? On a day like this?" The man's Estonian accent was almost incomprehensible. "We got . . ." The operator consulted a clipboard. "Five vessel due overnight. All heaved-to at sea. None come."

"No Hong Kong–registered ship? The *Red East*."

The radioman merely shrugged and proffered the clipboard to Vasin.

"No today."

"And when will the fog lift?"

The two seamen exchanged an amused look.

"You'd have to ask the boss, Comrade," called the Russian. "Only he knows."

"The *boss*?"

The operator pointed to the ceiling.

"Ya know. *That* boss."

Vasin leaned in toward the windows, his face close enough to the glass to feel its radiating cold. A mere shadow marked the outline of a freighter moored just fifty meters away. A gull, drifting in the wind, swung into sight before being swallowed by the fog.

"I'll wait. Back in an hour."

Out in the damp, freezing air, Vasin walked along the waterside. He passed a once-handsome prewar steamer, now streaked with rust, then a large fishing trawler, then a pleasure cruiser. He reached a barbed-wire fence that evidently separated the merchant port from the Coast Guard station, and peered through to make out the outlines of three fast-looking, heavily armed Soviet cutters moored in a row. Apart from an old man on a bosun's chair who was desultorily painting the side of the trawler, Vasin was alone.

No shipping.

So this was it. The end of the road. Or at least the end of the Fyodorov story—for Vasin at least. All that remained was to continue to play his part in whatever pantomime Kozlov had cooked up for him. But it was already clear from the convoluted wording of the script the man had left for Vasin that morning that his role would be as a mere spreader of low-grade disinformation designed to confuse and distract the Chinese and discredit Fyodorov. If that man ever made it out of the USSR alive, he would quickly convince them that he, not Vasin, was telling the truth.

And then what? A warm reception back on the ninth floor of the Lubyanka, if they caught Fyodorov? Somehow, Vasin doubted it. Nobody came back from openly defying Orlov. Definitely not if the General ever got wind of Vasin's Tallinn adventure. Some mediocre provincial posting would be about as good as he could hope for. Not as bad as Vorkuta. But for sure somewhere obscure and shitty. No more commandeering smart Czech sedans, no more racing about the Soviet Union on secret missions. His life would once more become . . . ordinary. A one-room bachelor apartment in some distant city as average as Vasin was. He'd try to get up to Moscow for the holidays to see his son, Nikita. Maybe they could go fishing together in the summer. He'd have to learn to fish, though. And learn to like fishing. Perhaps Arvo would teach him.

Vasin looked out over the steel-colored, lapping sea. He picked up a stone and flicked it, underhand, at the water. It did not skip but sank with a disappointing plop. Vasin turned and walked back toward the car.

# 12

*"Hei!"*

Vasin ignored the voice, his eyes on the gravel.

*"Hei, sina!* You! China ship guy!"

Vasin swiveled and saw the radio operator calling from an upper window.

"What?"

"Your ship radioed in."

Vasin was panting hard by the time he'd sprinted up the three flights of stairs to the radio room. The operator, grinning, tapped a pencil on a notepad with a scribbled message.

"*Red East.* Report medical emergency. Psychiatric case. Urgent. Position west of Naissaar Island. They head in. Expected in the Tallinn roadsteads two hours."

"A *psychiatric* case?"

"Crew member. Requests medics from town psychiatric clinic. Give me number, even."

"A Chinese ship knew the phone number of the Tallinn nuthouse?"

The operator shrugged.

"Not my problem. I call number. It the nuthouse all right."

"Two hours before they come in, you say?"

"*They* say. I reckon four. I warn them of the fog in the channel. Once they hit, they come in at crawl. But they have radar. Should make it fine into the roads. But not able to land. They send sick man in tender, I guess."

"A *what?*"

"Tender. Small boat. You no speak Russian? Only way ship to shore. Visibility—shit. Big boat—crash."

Vasin checked his watch. Nearly midday. It would be twilight in two hours. Pitch-dark in four.

"At night? How will they find their way back to the ship in the fog?"

"Nighttime you see lights better. And they have radio. Ship has foghorn. They come here all way from China, no? They will find way."

"Do you have to report the arrival of the ship to anyone?"

"What? Report to medical authorities—yes. Ambulance on way."

"Anyone else? The Marine Ministry in Leningrad?"

"No ship dock, no report."

Vasin felt his heart beat faster. He could feel Fyodorov's mind casting its webs all around him. The man was somewhere close, checking the variables, just like Vasin was doing. Adjusting his plan according to contingencies. And right now, the night and fog would be Fyodorov's allies. The man had the devil's own luck.

"I'll be back. And one last thing. The most important thing. If anyone comes by asking if someone has been around here asking questions, keep your mouth shut."

The radio operator picked up his soccer magazine without answering.

# 13

Vasin ordered his driver to head to the center of town. The red Tatra was far too conspicuous to leave parked near the docks. The main square of Tallinn rose in the fog like a dream of foreignness, all peaked Gothic church gables and gingerbread houses. But Vasin's mind was racing too fast to absorb its strangeness. The sausages and coffee they ate at a cafe tasted of nothing. The rudeness of the Estonian taxi driver who brought Vasin back to the port an hour later also made no impression. His thoughts were too tightly focused on what he would say to Fyodorov when he appeared. *If* he appeared. How to stop him from running. How to get him to talk. Where the hell he'd be if he didn't.

"Any news of *Red East*?"

The radio operator finished the salami sandwich he had been eating before replying.

"Heaved to. In the roads."

"The *roads*?"

"Harbor approach. Your Russian really not so good, boss. She sends in her tender. Ambulance already here. Arrived twenty minutes more-less."

Vasin struggled to control his breathing.

"Who's in it?"

"Dunno. Nurse, looking like. And a doc in white coat. They're down there, dockside."

Vasin rushed to the panoramic window that overlooked the waterside. Parked in the lee of the fortress wall was a white Volga station wagon with a red cross on its side and an emergency light on its roof. The windows were shrouded by white curtains. Vasin sprinted from the room, toppling a chair with a clatter as he ran.

The ambulance driver's window was open a crack, and a wisp of cigarette smoke drifted out to join the fog. Vasin slowed as he approached, pulling up his collar to hide his face. The last thing he needed was for Fyodorov to panic and bolt as soon as he set eyes on Vasin. If it *was* Fyodorov. If this whole scenario wasn't just a figment of his imagination.

It was Ksenia who recognized him first. She glanced right, did a double take, and her mouth fell open in panic. No wonder. The last time she'd seen him, Vasin had banged the desk at the newspaper office and threatened her with arrest. Vasin quickly moved in front of the car, his hands raised in a gesture of surrender, then placed them on the hood, leaning forward. Fyodorov sat in the driver's seat, wearing a white lab coat and doctor's cap tied with strings behind his head. His eyes met Vasin's, then closed. Vasin walked over to the driver's side window.

"Hi, Andrei."

"Sasha!"

"Yes. Me. But it's okay. I'm alone. Nobody knows I'm here. Can I get in?"

Without waiting for an answer Vasin climbed into the back of the ambulance, squeezing in alongside an aluminum gurney that filled the space. Ksenia, her face pale with fear, glared at him.

"You're a fool, Vasin." Fyodorov's voice was flat and hostile. "You've fucked everything."

"I wasn't followed."

"So what was a *kontora* pelengator car doing cruising around central Tallinn? We passed it forty minutes ago."

"A *what* car?"

"Pelengator. Mobile radio-direction-finding station. A little truck with a rotating antenna on the roof. Designed to locate radio signals. Like, from a radio tracker."

Vasin had seen such devices in films, but never in real life. A chill ran down his body. He remembered the policemen outside the Yunost. The open trunks. One man keeping the driver chatting while the other pretended to admire the engine. Could they have planted a *tracker* in the car? And if they had, was Kozlov's whole cock-and-bull story about sending Vasin on a distraction mission just an excuse to encourage him to make contact with Fyodorov?

*Orlov had set him up.*

"Talk to me, Vasin. Are you sure they didn't track your car?"

"I'm . . . I'm not sure. Possibly."

"Fuck. Where is it now?"

"Parked in town."

"Anyone in it?"

"My . . . driver. And another guy."

"*Kontora?*"

"No. Couple of Uncle Borya's guys. A . . . friend of mine. One's a Korean croupier pretending to be a Chinese diplomat. The other's a driver for some Leningrad bigwig. I hired them."

"Talk fucking sense, man. Do these guys know you're at the port?"

Vasin nodded.

"Are they loyal? Will they keep their mouths shut for you?"

Slowly but emphatically, Vasin shook his head. His brain was reeling. How could he not have guessed that Orlov was playing his old game, pay the line out long and slack and allow the fish to think it's free. Allow the fish to lead you to his friends. And then tug on the line. Hard.

"You led them straight to us." Fyodorov's voice was more desolate than angry. "Why the hell did you come, Sasha?"

"To ask you one last time. For the details of what you know. To help me protect myself."

"And what were you planning to do if I said no? Blow the whistle on us? Send us both to the execution chamber?"

"No. I wasn't going to do that." Vasin's voice was so desolate that he barely believed himself. Especially now that everything he had hoped to get from Fyodorov—the names of the Kennedy assassination plotters, the operational details of the killing—was utterly pointless. If Kozlov had followed him to Tallinn, all three of them were doomed. Unless of course Orlov had some final twist up his sleeve. Kill Fyodorov and Ksenia and keep Vasin alive as his eternally obedient dragonfly, trapped forever in glass?

A silence fell in the car. Ksenia began weeping, gently, in tiny ragged sighs. Fyodorov put his hands on the steering wheel and gripped and ungripped the hard plastic, his eyes focused on the wall of fog that veiled the harbor. Vasin could guess what he was thinking. To drive away now, to run, take his chances as a fugitive in the USSR, or to wait for the boat, and risk being pinned down on this dockside by Orlov's men?

"You were just up in the radio room?"

"I was."

"What did they say about the ship?"

"It's just offshore. They launched a boat. A *tender*. It's on its way in."

"How long?"

"I don't know."

Fyodorov flexed his hands on the wheel again and glanced at his watch. Beyond the drifting fog illuminated by the feeble lights of the port, the gathering dark was growing impenetrable. The ambulance in which they sat seemed to be cocooned in a small, private world, supernaturally walled in by cloud and night.

"Right. Vasin, you're going to . . ."

Fyodorov was interrupted by a muffled but distinct mechanical noise, a piercing whoop-whoop-whoop that echoed from the sea and reverberated off the stone fortress walls. A moment later, it came again, the same staccato triple whoop. And then again.

Vasin opened the door and stepped out of the car to listen better. Fyodorov followed. Above, in the harbormaster's command post, figures could be seen moving. With an abrupt clunk, a row of lights snapped on along the quayside, followed by a second set that illuminated one arching arm of the harbor. From somewhere high in the bastion of the fortress, a powerful foghorn emitted a deafening moan. The incoming boat answered. Fyodorov leaned inside the ambulance, grabbed a heavy canvas bag from behind the seat, and hissed urgently to Ksenia.

"It's them. Come on. Put your coat on."

Ksenia emerged in a cheap rabbit-fur coat. She clutched a small tapestry bag to her body as though hugging it.

"Andrei." Vasin took a step toward Fyodorov and put a hand on his arm. "Please. I'm begging you. I need those papers. I'm not going to stop you from going. But you need to help me . . ."

Angrily, Fyodorov jerked his arm away.

"I don't *need* to help you. All I need to do is get out of this fucking country alive. Which right now you're getting in the way of. Clear the fuck out of here. Turn around, right now, and walk . . ."

From behind them came a roar of speeding cars, and gravel crunching under heavy tires. A pair of headlights, followed by two more, swept through the fog. Footsteps, then voices, then raised voices, came from by the harbormaster's office.

*"Goddamn."* Fyodorov dropped the bag to the ground and unzipped it. From inside he produced the oiled black Schmeisser and slapped in the magazine.

More snatches of urgent conversation came from the mist, followed by a shout—heavily accented and familiar.

"Vasin! Fyodorov!" The Macedonian's reedy and shrill voice echoed off the stone bastion of the fortress. "Put the gun down, your hands up, and nobody gets hurt."

# 14

Fyodorov shot Vasin a look of pure animal hatred. He backed around the car to where Ksenia stood, paralyzed with fear, and pulled her down into a crouch beside him. Vasin, too, flattened himself against the side of the Volga. Glancing under the chassis, he could see dim forms moving into position to the left and right of them.

Vasin pressed himself harder against the cold steel of the car. So this was how it would end. During lonely drunken evenings in Vorkuta he'd allowed himself morbid thoughts on how he would die. Now he knew. Shot down like a dog, here on this freezing quayside. Or later, in some execution cellar. Either way, this final betrayal was one with no hope of forgiveness. He and Orlov were through. And Orlov had won.

Was there anything he would miss? Not seeing Nikita grow up. Never playing chess with the boy again. Never going on the rides in Gorky Park with him. Apart from that?

Nothing.

In an urgent whisper, Fyodorov was comforting and cajoling Ksenia. Her breathing came fast and jagged; she was hyperventilating. Vasin edged around so that he sat beside her. He reached a hand to find hers. It was cold and clenched hard. She pulled it away from Vasin's touch.

"Vasin? Fyodorov? Come out." The Macedonian's voice, now distorted through a tinny megaphone, rang through the night. "This is your last warning. Surrender, and you'll all live. Think of the woman, Fyodorov."

Ksenia buried her face in Fyodorov's coat and whispered something to him. He murmured a reply and smoothed her hair.

"It's your last chance, Vasin," hissed Fyodorov. "Get out of here now. Go to your people."

"They're *not* my people."

"Suit yourself." Fyodorov cocked his submachine gun with an oily click-clack. "We're sitting ducks here. Need to get around to the darker side of the rampart before they can outflank us. You go first. Keep low. Ksenia will follow . . ."

From the sea came the sound, faint but distinctive, of a marine engine. Fyodorov froze to listen. It was puttering slowly, but unmistakably approaching. A feeble searchlight swung back and forth along the harbor wall, followed by an indecipherable shout. The engine slowed to a crawl.

"*Ei, Tallinn? Eto Krasny Vostok. Kuda vstat' to nam?*" The voice came faint but clear across the water. "Ahoy, Tallinn? *Red East* here. Where do we tie up?"

The outline of a small boat appeared black against the bright harbor lights, moving dead slow through the fog and the shadows cast by moored ships.

"Here! Here! We're here!" Fyodorov bellowed. "*Red East!* Over here! Help!"

He scrambled to his feet, dropping the gun and cupping his hands to his mouth.

"*White Fox!* Emergency!" shouted Fyodorov. The recognition code he had agreed on with the Chinese? Vasin's guess was confirmed by an answering shout from the water.

"White Fox! White Fox!"

A shot cracked out, shattering the rear window of the ambulance.

Fyodorov ducked, snatched up his gun, and fired two long bursts into the fog. Answering automatic fire erupted all around them, the rounds smacking into the car's chassis and engine block with metallic dings and ricocheting off the concrete around them. Ksenia screamed, a thin and piercing shriek of alarm, as she and Vasin cowered for cover. She gripped Vasin's coat, hard, with trembling hands.

Vasin's ears rang after the intense burst of noise. The *Red East's* tender reappeared momentarily, brightly illuminated, by the quayside, before her hull was swallowed from view by the height of the harbor wall as she came alongside with a soft thud. Only the raised superstructure of the cabin and a short mast with riding lights were visible above the stone quayside. About fifty meters of open ground lay between the boat and the ambulance.

Vasin put an arm around Ksenia, comforting her. They had met only once—when he'd threatened and terrified her. But as he cradled her slender body, he felt an instinct to protect this woman. Save her, even.

It seemed suddenly obvious to Vasin what he had to do. The three of them could die here, or one of them could stay to hold off Kozlov's gunmen while the other ran for the boat. That person could be Vasin, or it could be Fyodorov. But Ksenia would never leave her lover to die. So it had to be Vasin. One life in exchange for two. It would be suicide. But it would make Vasin's death less meaningless.

His life, maybe, too.

And Orlov would know that he had died by his own choice, saving others. That idea pleased him. Unless, of course, Orlov had actually *wanted* Vasin to escape. In which case he would fuck up the old man's final plan for him, too.

"Fyodorov! Give me the gun. Give me the gun, man! I'll cover you. Go. Go, before they get better positions and cut us down. Run for the boat."

Fyodorov, his knees doubled up to his chin as he crouched by the ambulance's shattered headlight, turned his face toward Vasin but said nothing. He smiled, slowly, and shook his head. Fyodorov pulled his right hand from where it had been pressed against his body, and Vasin saw that it was black with blood. A thick pool had formed under his body. Fyodorov's torso began to tremble gently then, within seconds, uncontrollably.

"Oh my God!" Ksenia pushed Vasin aside and went to cradle Fyodorov's head in her hands. "Andrei! What's happened? Where are you hit?"

"Sasha. Gasoline. Canister in the back. Punctured. Careful." Fyodorov's voice came in gulping gasps. It was true. The acrid smell around them was unmistakable. Vasin picked up his hand from the cold concrete and smelled it. It was wet with gasoline. "Gimme. Your. Lighter."

Another rifle round smacked into the car, smashing through the dashboard and radiator and zinging just over their heads. The Macedonian's powerful sniper rifle.

So it would be Vasin who ran with Ksenia. Behind him was encroaching menace, gunfire, certain death. Ahead, blackness. Sea. The bobbing roof of the tender, for as long as they dared to remain moored in the unfolding mayhem. Did such a thing as hallucinatory clarity exist? It did now. Fifty steps across open ground lay between him and life.

Vasin fumbled in his trousers and produced the pressed-steel Wehrmacht lighter his father had once given him.

"Look after Ksenia." Painfully, Fyodorov unfolded his legs and rolled into a crouch. Reaching under the tire he retrieved his canvas bag and tugged it toward Vasin. "And don't forget your papers."

Another round cracked out, shattering the side mirror. Ksenia wrapped her arms around Fyodorov, weeping and whispering desperately in his ear. Vasin pulled her away from him, dragging the woman with a strength he never knew he had. A shot kicked up a spray of concrete just by Ksenia's shoe. The Macedonian was moving around them. Soon he'd have a straight shot.

"Ksenia! Do as I do. We run for the boat. Keep low."

Fyodorov was sitting up on his knees now, his gun cradled in his arms and his chin on his chest, breathing heavily, gathering strength. He was deliberately facing away from Vasin and Ksenia. But his voice, when it came, was loud and steady.

"On my three. One." A round whistled over their heads. "Two. Three! Go! Go! Go!"

Fyodorov hauled himself to his feet, holding on to the antler mascot on the hood of the Volga as he rose. He fired steadily in the direction of the Macedonian, a shattering blaze of muzzle-flash and noise. Vasin launched himself forward, Ksenia's hand in one of his and the canvas bag in the other. He ran blind and at a crouch, aware of a cacophony of gunfire behind him. Ksenia stumbled and fell, forcing him to stop and retreat a step to help her up. As Vasin glanced back, a blinding flash of warm yellow light washed through the cold white fog. A second later, as he hauled her to her feet, the light blossomed into a ball of fire that rolled and spilled across the dock. Vasin sprinted on, his eyes on the roof of the tender's cabin. Stray rounds had shattered one of the cabin windows, and the crew were nowhere to be seen.

"Start the engines! White Fox here! Start the fucking engines! WHITE FOX!"

As they reached the edge of the dock Vasin didn't dare to check his pace. Releasing Ksenia's hand, he leapt into the darkness. He landed hard, with a crunch of cracking wood, on the roof.

Ksenia did not follow. Vasin jumped to his feet, ignoring a shooting pain in his ankle, and looked back. Ksenia stood, silhouetted in firelight, staring back at the flame-engulfed ambulance.

"Jump, girl! *Jump,* for Christ's sake."

Below him on the shadow-darkened deck Vasin saw scurrying figures and felt the roar of the diesel revving up to full power. Water churned at the stern and he felt the boat sway sharply away from the quay.

"Ksenia! He's gone. Fucking *jump!*"

Ksenia's body jerked forward, as though she was about to leap. But instead she spun as though punched from behind. The distinctive crack of the Macedonian's rifle rang out from the night. Her body tumbled off the dock into the blackness.

It took her an endless second to fall.

But instead of a splash, Vasin heard a heavy thump as she hit the wooden deck. The boat gave a final lurch and shot forward, veering hard to avoid the stern of a moored freighter directly ahead of them. Shouts and shots came from the quayside. Figures appeared, framed in firelight, leveling rifles. There was a series of dull clangs as rifle rounds slammed into the freighter's iron hull. Then the tender was behind the ship, sheltered. And a moment later the freighter too disappeared into the night and fog, and they were surrounded only by darkness, and sea.

The roll of the boat knocked Vasin sideways as he crawled to the edge of the cabin roof, but he clung desperately to the fairing to avoid being tipped into the sea.

"The girl?" he called down to the blacked-out deck over the roar of the engine. "Is she alive?"

A murmur of voices conferring. Then a reply, in Chinese-accented Russian.

"*Zhiva, kommandir. Zhiva.* Alive, Commander. Alive."

# AUTHOR'S NOTE

On Saturday, September 28, 1963, Lee Harvey Oswald walked into the Soviet Consulate in Cuauhtémoc, Mexico City. There he met Valeriy Vladimirovich Kostikov, the Soviet consul. What Oswald and Kostikov talked about is unknown. But three days later, on October 1, a Central Intelligence Agency wiretap picked up a call made by Oswald to the switchboard of the Soviet Embassy. "Identifying himself by name and speaking broken Russian," Oswald asked "the guard who answered the phone whether there was 'anything new concerning the telegram to Washington.' The guard checked and then told Oswald that a request had been sent, but nothing had as yet been received" (cable 6453, 9 October 1963).

The CIA's Mexico City station reported Oswald's only known contact with the KGB to the CIA headquarters at Langley, Virginia, on November 23—seven weeks after it had occurred. The previous day, Oswald had shot President John F. Kennedy. The day after, Oswald would himself be shot dead by Jack Ruby in the basement of a Dallas police station.

The title of the CIA's 23 November 1963 memorandum was "Subject: Contact of Lee Oswald with a member of Soviet KGB Assassination Department." For Kostikov was not only "an identified KGB officer" but also an officer of "the KGB's 13th Department (responsible for sabotage and assassination)." The CIA knew this, the memo explained, because Kostikov had been a case officer in an operation "controlled by the FBI under the cryptonym TUMBLEWEED." Kostikov had been the contact for an FBI double agent, "a German national resident of Oklahoma who was recruited in Europe, and met this year with Kostikov in Mexico City and shortly thereafter with a known 13th Department officer, Oleg BRYKIN, in New York." Brykin had been operating under diplomatic cover as a member of the USSR's Trade Mission. Kostikov and Brykin had given TUMBLE-WEED instructions to "pinpoint objectives for sabotage." The behavior of the two Soviets and "the circumstances of their involvement in this case left no doubt that both of them were working for the same KGB component, the 13th," concluded the CIA report.

That Kennedy's killer had met with a Soviet KGB officer from a department specializing in assassination was unwelcome news for US intelligence. Especially as the information appears to have been reported to Langley in the 9 October 1963 cable mentioned in the November 28 report—but not acted upon. The CIA chose not to share the information about Oswald's KGB contact with the Warren Commission on Kennedy's assassination, which concluded that Oswald acted alone. And the memorandum itself—CIA Record number 104-10004-10258/Agency file number 201-289248—was declassified only on December 15, 2021.

Another tantalizing piece of information was disclosed among the same trove of nearly 1,500 documents released by the National Archives and Records Administration. On October 15, 1962, an anonymous tipster warned US Embassy officials in Canberra, Australia, that Kennedy would be assassinated by the Soviet Union for a $100,000 bounty. On November 24, 1963, two days after the Kennedy assassination, another call came through to the US naval attaché in Australia from a man identifying himself as a Polish driver for the Soviet Embassy in Canberra, who claimed that the Soviets were behind the assassination. It's not clear if this was the same caller. Neither tip was considered serious enough to report to CIA headquarters until a year and a half later, when a memorandum was drawn up for acting CIA chief Tennent Bagley on May 22, 1964. "This individual, while discussing several matters of intelligence interest, touched on the possibility that the Soviet Government had financed the assassination of President Kennedy," the memo read. "It should be noted that CIA had not previously known of the 1962 telephone call."

So there we are. Three wisps of information linking the KGB to the Kennedy assassination, none of them remotely conclusive. But intriguing enough to base a fiction upon.

The first two books of the Black Sun trilogy rested foursquare on incredible true stories. *Black Sun* was based on the real-life secret city of Arzamas-16, where Soviet scientists created the most powerful hydrogen bomb ever detonated. *Red Traitor* was woven around two real-life stories—the Soviet military intelligence officer Colonel Oleg Penkovsky, who spied for the CIA during the Cuban Missile Crisis, and Soviet Naval Captain First Class Vasily Arkhipov, whose heroic refusal to fire his submarine's nuclear-armed torpedo saved the world from nuclear war.

*White Fox,* by contrast, is based on a fantasy. I do not believe that the KGB, or rogue elements in the KGB, played a role in Oswald's decision to shoot Kennedy in Dallas on November 22, 1963. But I have, at least, tried to make the fantasy a plausible one.

The idea that the Soviet Politburo or KGB would officially have decided to murder the President of the United States is absurd. But a rogue KGB operation has a more authentic ring to it. All the more so because the world of political intrigue in which the plot of *White Fox* unfolds is accurate. General Secretary Nikita Khrushchev's climbdown during the Cuban Missile Crisis of October 1962 was a profound humiliation, which severely damaged his standing in the upper levels of the Soviet Communist Party. Through 1963 several contenders jockeyed to replace him—and to work out how a living Soviet leader could be removed from office, for the first time in the USSR's history. In the end Leonid Brezhnev, then chairman of the Presidium of the Supreme Soviet, and KGB Chairman Vladimir Semichastny conspired to get the Politburo onside for the palace coup that would depose Khrushchev in 1964.

There are other true elements to the story. Lee Harvey Oswald did indeed defect to the USSR, in October 1959, when he was nineteen years old. Weeks after his discharge from the US Marine Corps, where he had served as a radio operator, Oswald took a ship to Le Havre, France, then on to England and Finland. He crossed the Soviet border on 16 October 1959 by train from Helsinki, traveling on a tourist visa. Almost immediately on arrival in the USSR Oswald announced to his Intourist guide that he wished to become a Soviet citizen. But the Soviets didn't want him. On October 21, the day his visa was due to expire, he was told that his citizenship application had been refused, and that he had to leave the Soviet Union that evening. Distraught, Oswald inflicted a minor but bloody wound to his left wrist in his hotel room bathtub. He was sent to a Moscow psychiatric hospital for observation. On his release, according to his diary, he spoke to "four Soviet officials." It's safe to assume that among them were KGB officers. And it's also safe to assume that they decided this eccentric and unstable young American was of no operational use to them. However, permission was granted for Oswald to remain in the USSR.

Oswald had wanted to attend Moscow State University. Instead, he was sent to Minsk, Belarus—probably because the KGB decided that he might cause embarrassment if left in Moscow—to work as a lathe operator at the Gorizont Electronics Factory. Gorizont produced radios, televisions, and military and space electronics. He was taught Russian by a fellow Gorizont worker named Stanislau Shushkevich, who later became the first head of state of independent Belarus. Oswald lived in a fully furnished studio apartment in a prestigious building in central Minsk and received higher pay than his factory comrades. But he soon became bored. "I am starting to reconsider my desire about staying," Oswald wrote in his diary in January 1961 in his characteristically awkward prose. "The work is drab, the money I get has nowhere to be spent. No nightclubs or bowling alleys, no places of recreation except the trade union dances. I have had enough."

Soon after, Oswald met and married a nineteen-year-old pharmacology student, Marina Prusakova, and they had a daughter together. In June 1961 the family returned to the United States with the help of a $430 US Consular loan. Oswald had been expecting a press fanfare but was disappointed. He and Marina moved to Fort Worth, Texas (Marina Oswald Porter still lives nearby, in Rockwall). Back in his homeland Oswald embarked on a series of dead-end jobs and began to suffer the murderous obsessions that led him eventually to the Texas School Book Depository in Dealey Plaza in Dallas, Texas, with a mail-order sniper rifle.

In truth, if a secret plot among rogue KGB agents to assassinate Kennedy in 1963 had existed, Oswald would have been a very unlikely choice of assassin. His psychological instability, volatile naïveté, and low educational level would have made him a potential liability under questioning. And his time in the USSR made Oswald far too obvious a choice had the KGB indeed been involved.

In the fictional world of *White Fox,* however, reality is tilted a little on its axis. My fictional Fyodorov is a career foreign-service officer loosely based on Valeriy Vladimirovich Kostikov. VorkutLag 51 is based on the ruins of real gulags I visited in late November 2020. The Arctic darkness, the bleak landscapes, the biting cold, and the toughness of the local people are entirely real. The street kids of Leningrad are also based on a real-life community of homeless kids with whom I spent time in Saint Petersburg in 1997. These kids lived not in a palatial communal apartment run by a gypsy king but in a system of underground heating ducts in a grim suburb. But their cheerful camaraderie and resourceful thieving are drawn from life.

Finally, Vasin. The real Alexander Ilyich Vasin was my uncle—the husband of my mother's older sister, Lenina. They got engaged during the war, when he was a young tank captain, after just a couple of meetings. Vasin returned to the front in 1944 and was critically injured when his staff car drove over a mine near Smolensk. His leg had to be amputated with a wood saw, but he survived. He wrote to his fiancée that he had been disfigured and that she should look for someone else. Instead Lenina went to find him in a military hospital in Ivanovo and they married as soon as he was discharged. A lawyer by training, Vasin rose to be the USSR's Deputy Minister of Justice. He served the Soviet system all his life, but was also a highly moral man. Like his fictional counterpart, he was a good, decent, humane person trapped in an inhuman system. And yet, despite all the jeopardies inwardly stalking him, he always retained his moral compass. This trilogy is dedicated to his memory.

# ACKNOWLEDGMENTS

First and foremost I'd like to thank the two people who made this book, and the whole Black Sun Trilogy, possible: my excellent agent Toby Mundy and my incomparable editor Robert Bloom. I've worked with many editors over the years, but Rob's devotion to detail and wonderful feel for the plot and characters was on a wondrous new level of sensitivity and involvement. For any author, the definition of an excellent editor is a person who knows what your book is really about better than you do yourself. At Doubleday I would also like to thank Carolyn Williams, who has brought this final part of the trilogy home and dry despite many Ukraine-war-related delays.

I'd also like to thank my early readers Andrew Meier, Mark Franchetti, and Charles Cumming for crucial early steers and advice on how to keep a complex machine like a thriller running at high speed. My friends Andrew Jeffreys and Orlando Mostyn-Owen offered crucial hospitality and refuge while this was being written and put up with endless evenings of complaint, despair, and occasionally exhilaration on the part of their author guest.

Finally, my long-suffering wife, Ksenia, has borne the brunt of the travails of the writer's life with amazing good grace and good humor (in strong contrast to the moods of the author himself). My sons, Nikita and Theodore, have also been constantly supportive and cheerful over the four years that they lived with the fictional Alexander Vasin and his creator.

# ABOUT THE AUTHOR

Owen Matthews reported on conflicts in Bosnia, Lebanon, Afghanistan, Chechnya, Iraq, and Ukraine, and was *Newsweek*'s bureau chief in Moscow. He is the author of the Black Sun Trilogy: *Black Sun, Red Traitor,* and *White Fox,* as well as several nonfiction books, including *Overreach, Stalin's Children, Glorious Misadventures,* and *An Impeccable Spy.*